THE McCALL INITIATIVE

Episodes 1.1–1.3
Deception, *Revelation*, and *Conspiracy*

Lisa Nowak

Published by Webfoot Publishing
Milwaukie, Oregon

Publishing

The McCall Initiative Episodes 1.1–1.3

The text of this book is set in 11-point Georgia.

Book design by Lisa Nowak

Cover design by Steven Novak

ISBN-13: 978-1-937167-29-5

First Edition

DEDICATION

This series is dedicated to Oregon's finest governor, Tom McCall, who harkened in a wave of environmental awareness in the late '60s and early '70s that transformed the state and influenced the entire nation.

Among many other accomplishments, McCall was responsible for:

- The first Bottle Bill in the nation. Nine other states have since adopted this legislation, and more are currently in the process of doing so.
- The Beach Bill, which gives the public access to all beaches.
- Land use planning, which protects the farm and forest land Oregon's economy relies on and prevents urban sprawl.
- The Bicycle Bill, which dedicates 1% of transportation funds to bike and pedestrian paths
- Vortex 1, the first and only state-sponsored rock concert.

Tom McCall was a creative problem solver who believed in making short-term sacrifices for the long-term greater good. To learn more about this amazing man, visit the Tom McCall Legacy Project's website: http://www.tommccall.org

"Heroes are not giant statues framed against a red sky. They are people who say; This is my community, and it's my responsibility to make it better."

- Governor Tom McCall

CASCADIA 2063

THE
MCCALL
INITIATIVE
EPISODE 1.1: DECEPTION

LISA NOWAK

CHAPTER 1

Piper

Portland, Oregon, Friday, May 18, 2063

My little brother Nick's stories are so far-fetched, there's no way anyone could believe them, but there's something so compelling about the way he tells them, you just can't help wondering.

"You know those rumors about how people are disappearing?" he asks, his black hair hanging in eyes that spark with excitement. "Well, *I* know what's happening to them."

And I'm sure he's going to tell me all about it.

"The crimps—that's what they call the guys who do the shanghaiing—they're like dogcatchers," Nick says, not disappointing. "They round up poor people and put them on big trucks, then they take them to this compound in eastern Oregon. It's really spooky, with machine guns everywhere, and vicious dogs that'll rip your arm right off your body. Everybody stays away because they think it's a high-security prison. They say the U.S. government paid off President Cooper to put it in Cascadia so Americans wouldn't have to deal with all those criminals. But really? It's owned by a drug company. They use the people for drug testing. And sometimes they do other kinds of weird experiments, like seeing if they can transplant brains and stuff."

My nine-year-old brother sits on the closed toilet lid, his mouth going a mile a minute as I get ready for my shift at OHSU.

"Don't you think that's a little over the top?" I touch up my eye shadow, keeping it discreet, the way it should be when you're in the medical field. Some of the girls in the Junior

Student Assistant Program plaster it on like they work in a strip club. Combined with the skintight jeans they wear, it's enough to make the old guys in the cardiac unit go into v-fib.

"The disappearances aren't real," I add. "It's an urban legend."

"Grandpa thinks they're real."

"Oh, there's an endorsement." Much as I love my grandpa, I don't believe half of what comes out of his mouth. He thinks the climate crisis was engineered by big box stores in the early 21st century so they could sell more air conditioners. He's got a stash of cash under the floorboards in his room, along with a collection of hand-written journals, because he's sure an electromagnetic pulse is going to wipe out all the computers any day now.

"If the disappearances aren't real, how come there aren't any homeless people anymore?" Nick asks, tossing his shaggy hair out of his face.

I lean in toward the mirror, sweeping mascara over the lashes of my left eye. "Maybe because the mayor didn't want the capital of Cascadia to look like a giant armpit?"

"Right," Nick says, giving me an eye roll full of pre-pubescent drama. "That's what all you naysayers think."

Naysayers. Now there's a word straight off Grandpa's lips. I'm going to have to talk to Mom about how he's corrupting her only son. Not that there's much she can do about it. Grandpa's been living with us since the accident, and with Mom wrangling two jobs, she counts on him to watch Nick when I'm at work or my volunteer position at the hospital.

"If the disappearances were real, there would be documented accounts instead of just rumors, Nick. You should type up all that fiction and put it on Amazon. I hear there's a high demand for conspiracy stories these days." I drop my makeup into a drawer and push it shut. "Now get lost so I can use that toilet for its intended purpose."

I walk several blocks through the cool May mist and catch the bus to Lloyd Center. Normally, I'd take the 66 straight across the Ross Island Bridge, but Grandpa needs a new journal, and the Nostalgia Store is the only place that still carries the kind of paper notebooks he likes.

That inconvenience is fourth on his list of pet peeves, right after low-flow toilets and the high cost of meat. The number one spot goes to self-driving cars. I guess when Grandpa was a kid, most families had more than one vehicle, and getting your driver's license when you turned sixteen was a rite of passage. Now anyone can drive, but lots of people can't afford to. Cars got crazy expensive to register after the first wave of climate refugees swarmed here in the early '30s, causing major gridlock. We've been lucky to afford a car at all since Dad died and Grandpa moved in with us. But I don't care. Riding public transit gives me a chance to do my homework, and I like watching the colorful people who "keep Portland weird."

When I'm done at the mall, I catch the MAX—Portland's light rail system. The train is crowded with commuters cutting out of work early on Friday, so I have to stand.

"Hey, Piper," a guy calls to me.

"Uh . . . hey," I say. Why's he even talking to me? I recognize him from the Junior Student Assistant Program, but it's not like that means we have to be buddies.

The train swooshes toward the city center, with riders piling on and off at each stop. Just before it goes across the bridge, it pulls into the Rose Quarter. A herd of people spills out, freeing up some seats, and I nab one. I glance out the window at the Rose Garden Arena, where Jefferson Cooper grins back from his re-election billboard. Among all the electronic signs-in-motion that plaster the sides of buildings and vehicles, the stillness of this one stands out. Doesn't hurt that it's four stories tall. Dressed in jeans, an untucked button-down

3

shirt, and a sport coat, Cooper leans against an early Stump-town brick wall. His dark hair is short on the sides and long on top, with that disheveled-on-purpose sort of styling that makes my friend Bailey swoon. His full beard is so closely cropped it almost looks scruffy, and his brown eyes stare out at his con-stituency with a let's-go-have-a-beer kind of friendliness. He's the picture of casual leadership, which is pretty much what you get when you elect a rock star for president.

I turn away from the window. Even though it'll only take ten minutes to get to Oregon Health and Science University up on Pill Hill, I'd like to pull out my laptop and finish the history chapter I'll be quizzed on tomorrow. But I forgot to download it, and I know the craptastic city Net service isn't going to let me access the cloud while I'm on the MAX. Despite the pro-Cascadia hype, not everything's coming up roses in the Rose City. The thing I don't understand is, if Jefferson Cooper's as great as everyone says, why the hell can't he get us some decent NetMax?

I entertain myself by looking out the opposite window at the Willamette River and Waterfront Park, which will be trampled into a muddy wasteland next week by Rose Festival crowds. Nick wants to go this year—he still remembers Dad taking him to the carnival when he was in kindergarten—but we never have the money. We don't have the money for anything, which makes Nick's stories and Grandpa's conspiracy theories just a little bit spooky. If someone really is shanghaiing poor people off the streets of Portland, we'll be the next to go. I want to help, but even if I win one of the twenty-five spots in the Senior Student Assistant program, and the scholarship that comes with it, I'll have four years of college and four more of med school before I start making any money. Nick will be my age by then.

At the hospital, my shift goes smoothly. I don't mind dealing with bedpans and vomit, because at least at OHSU we get to work with patients, even if it's on a limited and closely monitored basis.

High school volunteers at most hospitals are stuck pushing magazine carts and running errands. I could do a lot more than they let me, but I understand why that will never happen. The only official medical training I have is what I got when I joined the program last fall. Watching twenty million surgeries on YouTube and out-scoring most med students at Sim Surgery does not qualify one to be a doctor.

When I'm done at nine, I call to remind Mom I'm stopping by Bailey's and won't be home till late. She doesn't answer. *Huh.* Usually she's off work by now. Maybe she's in the bathroom or got stuck pulling a long shift. I leave a message and, just in case, call Nick's phone to make sure he knows not to expect me. He doesn't pick up either.

Worry wiggles around in my gut. Nick *always* answers. Maybe I should go home to make sure everything's okay. But it's Bailey's seventeenth birthday, and as much as I hate parties, I can't stand her up. Of all my grade school friends, she alone braved the nerd alert issued on me in middle school and remained loyal all these years.

I fit my moldable plastic phone around my wrist and head for the locker room to get my backpack. I don't bother shucking off my scrub shirt—the only part of the uniform they'll let us wear, since they don't want people mistaking us for someone who knows what they're doing. It's not dirty, and anyway, I sort of like being seen in it.

"Piper, can I have a minute?"

Dr. Alvarez stands in the doorway. She's an angel in a lab coat. The one person who sees me as an individual in the mob of first-year JSAs. I hitch my backpack over my shoulder and follow her into the hall.

"I hear you're going to stay with us for the summer," she says as I fall into step beside her. She's petite—a good two inches shorter than me—and she wears her dark hair in a long braid.

"Yeah. I don't want to get rusty." Normally, JSAs don't

work between their junior and senior years, but I managed to snag a shift.

Dr. Alvarez laughs. "I hardly think that's possible. Let's go to my office and have a chat."

My heart races a little. I relish every minute she spares for me. Most Junior Student Assistants aren't lucky enough to have a doctor show interest in them. Dr. Alvarez not only takes me seriously, she also gives me perks, like the access code to the hospital's website, so I can watch training videos. Usually, people don't get that privilege until they're SSAs.

Once we're in her office, Dr. Alvarez takes a seat behind her desk. I drop into the familiar chair across from her, glancing at the diplomas on the wall, the abundance of bonsai plants, and the neatly ordered desktop, with each item meticulously lined up. This is one of my favorite places. Someday, I'll have an office just like it.

"So which medical advances are on the agenda today?" I ask. "The new Swedish drug that's supposed to cure Alzheimer's? That lab-grown kidney they say they've perfected at Oxford?" We've spent a lot of time discussing the latest developments. Before the climate crisis diverted so much funding, OHSU was cutting edge in research, but for the past thirty years, the Europeans and Japanese have been kicking our butts. It's only since Cascadia broke away from the U.S. that we're starting to gain ground. Of course, if President Cooper would dedicate as much money to medicine as he does to green energy, it might speed things up a little.

Dr. Alvarez smiles. "Actually, I've got something for you." She slides a drawer open, pulls out a MedEval device, and places it on the desk. "I upgraded to the G6 model, and I figured you might enjoy having my old one."

She sounds casual, like this is something she'd toss in the trash if I didn't take it, but the fact is, she could've traded it in for credit.

"Thank you," I say, lifting the monitor and finger clip off the desk. The two words aren't anywhere near adequate, but I've always tanked at spilling my feelings. I hope the grin on my face gets the job done.

This is the single most awesome thing anyone has ever given me. I haven't touched one since Dad showed me how to work the G4 model the ambulance service assigned him. This one's smaller. The size of a phone instead of a tablet. I push the power button and slip the clip over my finger. After a few seconds, it wirelessly transmits my heart rate, temperature, blood pressure, and blood oxygen level to the screen. With the use of the two tiny electrodes tucked away in the back compartment, I could also run an EKG on myself. Tapping a button will let me save all the data to a patient's file and add voice notes.

"You might want to be discreet with that," Dr. Alvarez says. "Keep it at home for now."

"Of course." If I pull this thing out in front of the other JSAs, they're going to think I got some special favor. We aren't assigned MedEvals until we're in the SSA program, and even then, they're beat-up loaners.

"I really appreciate this," I say, taking another shot at being human.

Dr. Alvarez smiles. "I know."

I stuff the MedEval into my backpack then look up at her. She's leaning forward, her hands steepled over her desk. The smile has disappeared, quick as spring snow on Mt. Hood.

"There's something else I'd like to talk to you about, Piper."

Uh oh. Dr. Alvarez has never said a harsh word to me, but something in her tone tells me she's about to. How did I mess up?

"I'm glad you're staying for the summer," she says. "I want you to have a strong chance of getting into the SSA program, so I'm assigning you to a group where you'll work closely with others. It'll give you an opportunity to develop your skills as a team player. That's the one area where you fall a little short."

What? My face freezes, my smile going stiff and fake as shock threatens to melt it away. "I do everything anybody asks me to," I say. "No matter who I get stuck working with." The words pour off my tongue without passing through that part of my brain that's supposed to act as a filter. *Ah, crap.*

Dr. Alvarez has the good grace not to mention the size eight sneaker planted firmly in my mouth. "Of course you do. Your reviews are exemplary in that regard. The nurses say you're a joy to work with, and the patients rave about your compassion and willingness to go the extra mile. But your peers say you're cold and wooden with them at best, and treat them like they're beneath you at worst."

The freeze travels down my neck until my whole body is in cryogenic lockdown. I can't argue. It's true. But how am I supposed to feel? While they were playing with Barbie dolls and skateboards, I was suturing pigs' feet and making my paramedic Dad quiz me on the circulatory system.

"You've got a brilliant mind and great instincts, Piper. You're going to make an excellent doctor. But if you can't learn to be a team player, you're going to cheat yourself out of the scholarship you'll need to get there."

I *am* a team player. It's just that my team is my family, not a bunch of kids who want to edge me out of my one chance at getting a medical degree.

"I think you'll like the project I've assigned you to," Dr. Alvarez says, like she's afraid I might implode if she doesn't soften the blow she just delivered. "There's a study over at Doernbecher for Magnusson-Bell Syndrome. That's a—"

"Condition caused by a virus scientists accidentally created while genetically engineering cattle. Most people fight it off easily, but in little kids, the elderly, and anyone with a compromised immune system it leads to heart failure and—"

Dr. Alvarez lifts a hand to shut me up. "All right, you know what it is." She shakes her head, the faint curve of her lips not a smile at all. "You don't have to prove to me how smart you are, Piper."

My face burns like a Colorado wildfire. Why do I have to be such a dork? "I'll work hard on being a team player," I say. If there's one thing I know how to do, it's apply myself.

"I hope so," Dr. Alvarez says. "Because I'd hate to see you sabotage your career before it even begins."

CHAPTER 2

Piper

Half an hour later, I'm standing on the front steps of Bailey's house—one of the bigger ones in Ladd's Addition—dreading what I'm about to do. Parties and I don't get along. It wouldn't be so bad if her parents were here, but they're in Upper Seaside for the weekend.

Music and voices pulse through the door. I have the perfect excuse to go home—I need to find out why Nick didn't answer the phone earlier, or again while I was on the bus—but Bailey's expecting me. Anyway, the lack of response has to be a fluke. If there was an emergency, someone would've called.

I draw cool air deep into my chest, trying to forget Dr. Alvarez's lecture and drum up my courage. The drizzle is still falling—a calm before the perfect storm. Hard to believe most of the U.S. is a sun-baked cinder this time of year. Except for less snow in the mountains, a few more dams on the rivers, and a big dead zone off the coast, the climate crisis hasn't affected the Northwest much.

With my courage as drummed-up as it's likely to get, I open the door and step inside. Half of Cleveland High must be crammed into the living room, dining room, and foyer. A fog of mojo smoke assaults my lungs, and the whole place reeks of pot. The full-wall video screen, streaming a music station, blasts sound and images that make me want to take shelter in the nearest closet. Only for Bailey would I subject myself to this kind of madness.

I spot her on the couch.

"Piper! Come sit." Her voice beams across the room, about three shades more cheerful than normal. The toothy grin she flashes, and the warm Latina complexion that makes her look tan even in winter, came from her dad. She got lucky there. She could've wound up pale like me, with her mom's Irish skin instead of just her auburn highlights and hazel eyes.

I push through the throng and lean down to give her a hug. "Happy birthday."

As I take a seat beside her, I set my backpack on the floor and paw through it. Bailey's dad owns condos and industrial properties all over town, so there's really nothing I can buy that she doesn't already have. All that leaves is picking out the funniest card in existence. It's kind of become a tradition between us, trying to top each other every year.

I hand the envelope to Bailey. She slides a fingernail along the top to slit it, pulls out the card, and starts busting a gut. The guy to my left, Derek or Eric Something-or-other from English, offers me the pipe he's holding. Judging by the look of people, it's already made the rounds a few times.

"No thanks." Mojo—a combination stimulant and hallucinogen—is supposed to be where it's at these days, but why would I subject my brain to that crap?

Derek/Eric passes the pipe—which is appropriately shaped like a skull—to Bailey, who glances at me guiltily before handing it off to the girl beside her. No freakin' way. Bailey Torres is stoned? I should've known something was up from the way she howled at my card, but getting buzzed is totally unlike her. She's an athlete. Not just on a school team, but in club soccer, too. One of those hard-core types who play year-round in any kind of weather. She jokes about partying, but I've never seen her do more than take a few sips of beer. I'd better stick close.

The video wailing from the wall monitor ends, and another starts up—*The Tom McCall Song*. It's an anti-U.S. protest that immortalizes a popular Oregon governor from the 20th century. Jefferson Cooper's band, Frequent Deadly Lightning, released it years ago, before the McCall Initiative, but now that Cooper's running for re-election, it's huge again. Not that it needed the boost. It's practically Cascadia's national anthem.

The familiar lyrics pulse through the room:

> *Way back in the '60s, a hundred years ago,*
> *There was a man, who took a stand,*
> *And made our state the promised land.*
> *He saved our air and rivers,*
> *he made our beaches free.*
> *When others came to stake a claim,*
> *He said, "Just let us be."*
> *What we need now is a hero,*
> *a legend who can save us all.*
> *What we need now is a hero,*
> *a man like Tom McCall.*

The song might be the same, but the video is new. Someone combined original band footage with clips of Cooper's rise to fame, from his early activist days to his election.

> *Who's gonna be our savior,*
> *who's gonna say "enough?"*
> *Who's gonna take our borders,*
> *and close them suckers up?*
> *Superstorms slamming the East Coast,*
> *drought burning up the Midwest,*
> *Wildfires in the Rockies,*
> *crops eaten up by pests.*
> *A feast or famine of flood and drought,*
> *The whole damn country's a mess.*

Popular moments from Cooper's first three years as president flash across the screen: him cutting the ribbon at Coho Dam, breaking ground for a geothermal plant in BC, shaking hands with the project manager of the Moma Wind Farm.

As the chorus gives way to the final verse, the camera zeros in on Cooper jamming on his electric guitar, looking positively pissed off. This is the part that made the song go viral. The part that turned him into a legend.

The Northwest ain't your Band-Aid,
the Northwest ain't your crutch.
It's time to solve these problems
and not just cover 'em up.
Stop leeching off our power supply.
Stop trying to drain our rivers dry.
We can't save you all and we don't wanna try.
Just go away and let us be.
What we need now is a hero,
a legend who can save us all.
What we need now is a hero,
a man like Tom McCall.
Tom McCall, you've gotta save us all.
Tom McCall, you've gotta save us all.
Tom McCall—please come back.
We need a hero who can save us all.

Bailey, eyes glued to the screen, sighs as the song ends. "And six years later, he's still scorching."

I laugh. "He's twice your age. Give it up."

"He's thirty-one. That's only . . ." she stops to count on her fingers, ". . . fourteen years older. We could make it work. I'm open-minded."

"Yeah, but his Secret Service would—" A burst of snickering breaks out on my left, and I turn to see the guy beside Derek/Eric playing with my MedEval. My backpack lies open on the floor. That son of a—

"Dude, check it out!" He holds up the monitor as he tokes off the pipe, which has made its way back around the room to him.

"Hey, give me that!" I reach for the MedEval, but Loser Boy sweeps it away, holding it up out of reach.

"Did you see what happened to my heart rate when I took a hit?"

"No kidding, dimwad. That oughta give you a clue about how stupid it is to smoke that stuff. Now give it back!" I latch onto the MedEval screen, and he releases it.

"Whatever you say, Doc," he grunts, tossing the finger clip at me. I snatch it out of the air as he snickers and Derek/Eric joins in, along with a couple of others.

"Whassamatter?" Loser Boy motions toward my scrub shirt. "All your real clothes in the wash?"

Everyone stares at me, making my face burn. I stuff the MedEval into my backpack and jam it between me and Bailey on the couch.

She hooks an arm around my neck. "Grow up, jerk," she says to Loser Boy. "Just because Piper knows what she wants to do with her life doesn't give you any excuse to rip on her."

"Aw, I was just messing around."

"Well, do it somewhere else. This is an asshole-free zone."

I want to get up and leave, and not just because I'm humiliated. But with Bailey sampling the stratosphere, I can't. Even though she looks okay now, that could change fast if she keeps sucking that stuff down. What if some creeper tries to take advantage of her, or these bozos trash her house?

I stick it out until the end of the party, sitting by Bailey and trying not to think about what a craptastic night this has turned into. Chaos swirls around me, but my guilt-inducing presence keeps her from imbibing more mojo, and by the time everyone leaves, she's border-line sober.

We throw the food scraps into the compost bin, pour the half-empties down the drain, and shove the furniture back into position. The place still looks like a superstorm swept through, but Bailey assures me she can take care of the rest tomorrow.

"Thanks for staying," she says, twisting a long strand of hair around her finger. "I know it had to be your idea of hell."

I shrug as I swing my backpack over my shoulder.

"And the mojo. It was twenty kinds of stupid. I could get kicked off the team for that."

Right. Because nuking half a million brain cells is nothing, so long as you can still kick a soccer ball. "You're not going to do it again, are you?"

She shakes her head.

"Okay. Then we're cool." I give her a hug and head out the door.

As I walk the twelve blocks home, I try not to psych over my conversation with Dr. Alvarez. It's not like she's ditching me from the program. It was just a warning. I've got three months to fix things.

I round the corner to see our house completely dark, and something cold skitters up my spine. Mom always waits up for me. Even if she crashed, the flicker of video should be spilling from the living room window. Grandpa lives for *Midnight with Maddox.*

Spooked, I jog up the driveway and onto the porch. The doorknob won't turn in my hand. My heart thumps. Mom never locks up before I get home. Did something happen to Grandpa? A glance confirms our old beater Mazda's still here. If Mom had to call an ambulance, she would've followed it in her car.

I yank my key out of my pocket, fighting to get it into the lock. When the door finally gives way, dead quiet greets me.

I flip on the light. "Mom? Grandpa?"

Silence.

The pounding of my pulse fills the void. Adrenaline surges through my veins. I hurry across the living room to check the kitchen. If something bad happened, Mom would leave a note where I'd be sure to see it—on the table, or the video screen. I find nothing.

Damn! Why didn't I come home right after work? Why didn't I pay attention to that first prickle of worry?

I head down the hallway, my breath tight in my chest. Nick's door is closed. When I swing it open, I find the bed empty, the tangled blankets trailing to the floor. Fear grips me, an icy hand squeezing my heart.

"Mom?" My voice comes out in a shriek. I rush to her room, the hallway suddenly five miles long. No one here, either.

Shit. Oh shit! What's going on?

I stand with one hand on the wall, trying to get a grip. *Think, Piper. There has to be an explanation.* But not one shred of logic can penetrate my rattled brain.

The slightest creak sounds behind me. I jump and turn. A man steps out of Grandpa's bedroom. He raises his hand, and I don't wait to see what's in it. I just throw myself into Mom's room, slamming the door behind me. My panicked fingers fumble with the lock, and then I'm rushing across the floor as the guy tries to kick his way in.

I slide open the window, rip loose the screen. Behind me, wood splinters and light floods in from the hallway. I scramble over the sill and into the night. There's no time to think, no time to figure things out. I need to run, to hide. Instinct screams not to risk circling around the house, so I cut from our small, unfenced yard into the neighbor's. I sprint down Woodward, up 22nd, along Taggart. If the guy is still on my tail, maybe I'll lose him by changing course. My phone lets out the *beep-beep-beep-squeal* of an incoming emergency alert, but I ignore it. I don't slow down until I'm across Division.

Finally I stop, leaning forward, hands on thighs. My breath rages through my throat. Now what? My family's gone. Some maniac is after me. What am I supposed to do?

Bailey. She'll help. She's a goofball and a flirt—not exactly the type to step up in an emergency—but she'd rip her own kidney out of her body for me. I run to her house and knock on the door. It takes her only a second to answer.

"Piper! Get in here, quick." She drags me inside.

"My family," I gasp, falling back against the closed door. "They're gone, just like in those stories Nick tells. There was a strange man in my house. I think he had a gun."

"That explains the alert they just sent out." Bailey wags her wrist phone in my face.

That was about *me*?

"There's a warrant out for your arrest," Bailey tells me, sounding fully sober now. "They say you held up some doctor at OHSU to get drugs."

"What?"

"We need to go." She pulls off her phone, tossing it on the coffee table. "They'll know you're here now."

Crap. My phone. They can track me through it. I pull it off, dropping it to the table like it's contaminated with flesh-eating bacteria.

Bailey scoops it up and snaps the moldable plastic back around my wrist. "No, we've got to use this to throw them off your trail. Let's go."

My mind is such a scramble, I can't even ask questions. I follow her out the door, down the street, to the bus stop on 12th. The buses only run every fifteen minutes between midnight and 6 a.m., so we have to wait. I pace back and forth, yammering about what just happened. Bailey mutters soothing things. She's freaking amazing. Not once has she stopped to ask questions—to wonder if that broadcast might be true. My eyes prickle, and the babble chokes off in my throat.

"Don't lose it on me, Piper," Bailey says, pulling me into a hug. "We're gonna get rid of your phone, then I'll take you some place safe, and tomorrow morning we'll figure this whole thing out."

Figure it out? How? My family's gone. I'm a fugitive. My life is over.

The bus rolls up before I can put all that in words. I follow Bailey on board and we ride toward the MAX station. Questions keep cycling through my head. Where are Nick, Mom, and Grandpa? Who took them? Are they okay? My thoughts go back to the stuff Nick said about drug testing and weird experiments. I know those things can't be true, but I didn't think the disappearances were real either.

"I should've gone home," I mumble, my head resting against the cool glass of the window.

"What?"

"I called Mom and Nick, but they didn't answer. I should've gone home. Maybe I could've saved them."

"Right. You just would've gotten nabbed, too."

Maybe. Probably. But that doesn't make me feel any less guilty. "This whole thing is whacked. Why would anyone go to so much trouble to set me up?" I keep my voice to a whisper even though there's only a couple other people on the bus.

"They obviously don't want witnesses. I'm guessing when you got away from the guy at your house, they let loose with that emergency alert. Probably had it ready to go, just in case."

Who has that kind of power? Some weird Cascadian mafia? The government? I let out a breath and close my eyes, my head jiggling against the window every few seconds when the bus smacks a pothole.

Bailey's fingers close over mine and squeeze. "Don't worry, Piper. I've got your back."

And she's going to take on people who can control the police and media?

When we reach the transit center by the Rose Garden Arena, Bailey gets up, taking my hand to pull me with her. Like a mother undressing a little kid, she snaps the phone off my wrist. "Wait here."

She jogs across the plaza to the raised platform for Super-MAX, the light rail that runs the heavily populated I-5 corridor between Medford and New Seattle. When a train whooshes to a stop, she slips through the open door and emerges a second later without the phone.

"There," she says. "You're now officially on your way to Medford."

I gawk. I've never seen Bailey take charge like this. She's lucky if she remembers her lunch money. Every thing she's done—leaving her phone at home, taking me on the bus instead of in her car, luring the cops away from Portland—is like a carefully orchestrated surgery. Where did she learn to think on her feet like this?

"Now what?" I ask. Even though I've got a jacket, and the temperature must be in the upper fifties, I'm shivering.

"Now we get you off the streets." Bailey slings an arm over my shoulders and directs me to the MAX yellow line.

We ride to the Albina/Mississippi stop, where she gets up and leads me out into the darkness. The streets are deserted.

"What are we doing here?" I ask.

"You'll see." She walks briskly, leading me up Albina, then down Russell, where she ducks into an empty parking lot that's closed in on three sides.

"This is the White Eagle Saloon, one of Dad's properties," she says, cutting through an overgrown tangle of trees and vines to an outdoor seating area beside the long, narrow brick building. The vegetation is so thick it blots out the streetlights.

"The city wants to build condos here, so they've condemned everything on this block," Bailey adds. "This place has been closed for almost a year, but they aren't going to tear it down until next winter." Her dad pays her a hefty allowance for helping him keep an eye on properties like this, reporting back to him about graffiti and anything that looks suspicious.

I follow her to the side door, where she punches a code into a keypad. Inside, the building is pitch black and smells faintly of stale beer and fry grease. Bailey pulls a light tube out of her purse and clicks it on. The plastic gives off a bright white glow that illuminates a ten foot circle around us and makes the few remaining chairs and tables cast eerie shadows against the walls.

"You can stay here as long as you need to," Bailey says. "I'll bring you some clothes and food tomorrow." She sets her purse down on the bar. "C'mon, let's go upstairs to see if the last owners left behind any mattresses or bedding."

The full extent of what I'm up against only now sinks in. I'm going to have to camp out in this creepy old tavern. For days, maybe. Thank God Bailey seems to know what she's doing. Without her, I would've collapsed in the street by now, a zombified mess.

I follow her outside. She takes me around to the back of the building and up an open metal staircase. The lights of downtown Portland glimmer from just across the river. Even with the darkness hiding me, I feel exposed up here on the landing. I huddle against the wall and dart inside as soon as Bailey opens the door.

"This was the hotel," she says. "It's not accessible from the bar. It'd probably be more comfortable than downstairs, but if you have to get in and out, you'll be too visible coming up the back steps." She leads me along the narrow hallway, opening one door after another to shine her light into the tiny rooms. We find a small closet, but there's nothing inside.

"The front entry's out, too," Bailey says. "It's in plain sight of Widmer Brewery down the street, and their restaurant gets a lot of traffic. Your best bet's coming in and out the way I showed you. Unless we can find the tunnel."

"Tunnel?" It's the first word I've said since we got off the MAX.

"Yeah, there's supposed to be one that leads to the waterfront, but it's been closed off for eons. Rumor has it, guys used to get shanghaied out of the bar in the early twentieth century and dragged through the tunnel to ships waiting on the river, but really it was probably just used to bring in illegal liquor. This place is supposed to be haunted, too, so if someone sees you, maybe you'll get lucky and they'll think you're a ghost."

The way she's talking—like I'm destined to spend the rest of my life camped out in a derelict building—sucks my already-tanked mood into a bottomless pit. Is that all I can expect now? In the course of an hour, I went from being an ambitious, law-abiding high school student to becoming a wanted criminal. A wanted criminal without a family. My mind darts off in twelve directions, all of them sinister. *Shut up!* I scream silently at myself. *You can't think like that. You just can't.*

Bailey opens a door near the front of the building to reveal a bigger room with a bed. "Bonus!"

We lug the mattress down the stairs, through the narrow gap in the vegetation, and into the bar. After we thump it onto the small, wooden stage in the back corner, Bailey flops down on top of it. I wiggle out of my backpack and tuck it into the space between the mattress and wall before collapsing beside my friend, breathing hard. Staring up at the ceiling, I try not to think.

"We can check the basement for bedding," Bailey says after a long silence.

"Don't worry about it." I don't give a rat's right foot about bedding. How can I care about anything like that now?

My eyes tear as the stillness lets all my fears rush me at once. My throat goes tight, but I manage to squeeze a few words past the obstruction. "What if they hurt them, Bailey . . . ? What if they killed them?"

She turns toward me, propping herself on one elbow. "They didn't! You listen to me, Piper. Your family is okay, and we're going to find them. You got that?"

My eyes fill, and I close them, feeling the hot wetness of tears run down my temples and into my hair.

Bailey shakes my shoulder. "You *got* that, Piper?"

"Y-yeah," I gulp.

"Good." She lays back down, her arm draped across my rib cage and her forehead pressed against my cheek as I cry.

I'd like to believe this new take-charge Bailey can fix everything. But deep down, I know I'm screwed.

CHAPTER 3

Logan

Several days prior, Chicago, Illinois

I inch forward, mindful of my footing. Three of my best men are right behind me. We slink along the canyon floor, watching for tripwires and landmines. As dusk settles around us, each step becomes more treacherous. Acrid smoke from a smoldering village burns my throat, and I stifle a cough in the sleeve of my fatigues. The slightest sound could tip off the enemy.

My team is exhausted. They need rest, but I know not one of them will utter a single word of complaint. They are the very definition of courage and loyalty.

A few hundred feet more, and we'll be at the base of the hill. If we can get to the top and plant the bomb, we can neutralize this outpost and gain control of the entire sector.

The hard-packed ground ahead, which should be easy to navigate, is obscured by scattered rock and small rivulets of soil, dislodged from the canyon wall by recent bombings. I step forward tentatively and—

"Logan!"

My attention is diverted for only a split-second, but that's enough. My foot comes down wrong and *bam!* A flash of sound and light knocks me backward, blowing my legs into a million bloody pieces.

"Turn that thing off, Logan. I need to talk to you."

The virtual reality is so lifelike, I feel an electric sting all the way up my thighs. I push a button on the armor at the back of my left wrist and the simulation ends, leaving me staring at the inside of my darkened visor. My back throbs from landing on the game room's floor. I flip up the helmet to see Dad staring down at me. He's five-foot-eight and thirty pounds over-weight—so pale and doughy, you'd swear his skin has never seen sunlight and his only exercise consists of wrestling donuts out of a box. But put his engineer's brain up against my athlete's body in an equalized competition, and he'd kick my butt.

He retracts the rear screen, opening the room to expose the furniture in back, and sits down on the couch. I continue to lie on the floor. Even though I know it wasn't really my flesh scattered all over that canyon, it takes me several moments to recover from the shock.

Dad shakes his head as I finally hoist myself to my feet. "Still playing those shoot 'em up games. I can't for the life of me figure out how I raised a violent kid."

It's got nothing to do with violence. It's about strategy—about taking a team of men on a dangerous mission and keeping the casualties to a minimum, about outwitting an enemy that has you out-powered, outnumbered, and backed into a corner. But it's no use trying to explain this to him. He didn't understand the first two dozen times. He doesn't get why I play football either.

Still feeling a little shaky, I lower myself onto a chair. "What's up, Dad?"

He strong-arms his frown into a smile. "I've got good news. We're moving to Portland."

"Maine?" Inside I'm screaming *what the hell?* But I'd never disrespect him by saying it out loud. "Well," I venture, "it's cooler there at least. That will be good for Zoey." Of course with superstorms hitting the East Coast every couple of years, and the shoreline being swallowed up by the rising sea, Maine's problems are nearly as bad as Illinois'.

"No," Dad says, "the other Portland. Portland, Oregon."

He can't be serious. The border's been closed for four years. "How? Nobody can get into Cascadia."

"There are exceptions."

"What—did you buy our way in?" I grin, meaning it as a joke. Sure, we have that kind of money, but my father is the most honest, ethical man I know.

"Of course not!" His expression crumbles into a scowl. "That kind of thing doesn't really happen. A headhunter from Intel recruited me."

"Really? That's great." It's a monumental honor. Dad's a software engineer, and he's wanted to work at Intel for a long time. They're the largest, most powerful computer component company in North America, and they're very selective about who they hire.

But as happy as I'd like to be for Dad, I'm stunned at the idea of moving. I only have one year of high school left, and I'm captain of our football team. Besides, I don't want to leave my JROTC battalion. I'm sure Cascadia's got a program of their own, but it wouldn't be the same.

Of course, I can't tell him any of this. It'll just lead to another lecture about what I should be doing with my life. And while I'm not willing to sacrifice my identity to win his approval, I can at least earn some respect by not arguing.

"The important thing is, this will mean getting your sister out of Chicago," Dad says. "The climate in Oregon will be much easier on her. And a new study just opened up for Magnusson-Bell at Doernbecher Children's Hospital. One of the treatments is showing real promise."

It's the best news we've had in years. "Can you get her in?"

"Of course. That's one of the agreements."

I'm afraid to let myself have any hope. Zoey's eleven, and no one with Magnusson-Bell Syndrome has lived past the age of nineteen. Usually, they're lucky to make it to seventeen.

"I know this is short notice," Dad says. "But we'll be leaving next Monday."

"*What?*" This time, I can't keep my irritation to myself. "There are only a few weeks left before summer vacation. Why can't we wait until school's out?"

Dad releases a long sigh. "Logan, we've already had three blackouts this spring. The weathermen are saying it's gearing up to be the hottest summer yet."

For people like me, the heat is only an inconvenience, but for the sick and elderly, it's deadly. Still, we're talking about less than a month, and it's not like we don't have ways of coping.

"Zoey does okay in the cool room," I say. The small space at the center of the house is insulated by the rooms around it, so it stays relatively comfortable during our power-outages, which sometimes last for weeks.

"The cool room is a joke. It barely keeps her from getting overheated, and your mother thinks it's unhealthy for her to be hiding in the dark like a mole."

He knows as well as I do, Zoey doesn't care about being stuck in a windowless room. The heart problems caused by her MB have limited her physical world so much she's had to build a virtual one. As long as she has her computer, she's happy.

"I know this will be a big change for you." Dad stands up to signal he's done with the conversation. "But it's the opportunity of a lifetime. Not just anyone gets to immigrate to Cascadia."

That's true. A good majority of Americans would give everything they own for the chance. And I'm not completely opposed to the idea. What Jefferson Cooper did, leading an uprising and peacefully breaking away from the U.S., is nothing short of amazing. I'd love to learn more about it from an insider's perspective. But my goal since junior high has been to go into the Army.

How can I do that if I'm no longer a U.S. citizen?

Over the next few days, I silently stew about the impending move, hunting for alternatives. My friend Paulo's family might let me spend my senior year with them. I doubt Dad would pay my room and board, and it's virtually impossible for anyone under eighteen to find work in Chicago, but Mom might take pity and give me the money.

I ultimately dismiss the plan and the half-dozen others I come up with. It's not that they aren't workable. It's Zoey. I've accepted that joining the military will mean missing out on the last few years of her life. What I haven't planned on is losing the upcoming one. That's too much of a sacrifice. I have no choice but to go to Cascadia.

CHAPTER 4

Piper

The White Eagle Saloon, Saturday, May 19, 2063

All night long, my mind bobs to the surface of consciousness, and I will myself back into oblivion, hoping the next time I wake up, this will all just be a nightmare. Eventually, the trick stops working. A little light seeps through the overgrown bushes around the side door to tell me it's morning. I lie on the bare, funky-smelling mattress, paralyzed by my new reality as I stare at the ceiling and listen to Bailey snore.

The scene from last night keeps replaying in my mind, but no matter how many times I go over it, I can't change it. What if I never see Mom or Nick or Grandpa again? A tightness grips my chest, making it hard to breathe. It's not the first time I've been through this. I guess I should be grateful that at least now there's hope, even if it's slim. Three-and-a-half years ago, I wasn't so lucky.

Memories rush in to ambush me. Rain pounding down outside, the smell of turkey filling the house, Dad telling me he'll be back in an hour, and that I can't go with him to pick up Grandma and Grandpa because I have to help Mom with Thanksgiving dinner.

We didn't really worry when that hour stretched into two, but then there was a knock at the door. The cop standing on our front porch told us there'd been an accident. We forgot the turkey in our hurry to get to the hospital, where we sat up all night. But there's only so much anyone can do when things are that bad. The next day, the father who'd been my whole world—who'd urged me to follow my dream of being a doctor the way he wished he had—died.

For weeks, the rest didn't matter. The only thing I could think about was the chasm of emptiness I was drowning in. And then Grandpa came to live with us because the accident had cost him everything, killing his wife and son and putting him in a wheelchair. That was right after the whole secession thing happened, so medical coverage—shifting from the U.S. National Health Service to the Cascadian version—was a mess. Grandpa was left with huge debts, while Dad's hospital bills sucked up every bit of his life insurance and almost cost us our house.

Beside me, Bailey snorts and rolls over, rubbing a hand across her face.

"Piper, are you awake?"

I scramble to pull myself together, to shove those awful memories back in the vault. "Yeah."

"Are you okay?"

How am I supposed to answer that? I'll be damned if I'm going to cry again, but my throat aches from holding back tears.

Bailey pushes herself up on one elbow and looks at me. "Your family's okay, Piper. I'm sure of it. Whoever's taking these people is probably just dumping them outside the border. We'll get this figured out."

"How?" My voice sounds hollow. "Nobody believes the disappearances are real."

"Right," Bailey says, nodding. "People don't want to think anything bad can happen in Cascadia, so they ignore the rumors. But we know they're true now, right? And that means there must be evidence somewhere. We've just gotta find it."

"Don't you think someone's already tried?"

Bailey runs a hand through her long, tangled mess of hair, sweeping it out of her face. "Maybe. Maybe not. These people are going to an awful lot of trouble to track you down, so my guess is, they don't want to leave stragglers behind. They probably target small families so there won't be anyone left to ask questions."

I go on staring at the ceiling. Bailey's argument doesn't explain why no one's heard back from the people who got abducted. If they're safely outside the border, why haven't they gone online and raised a big stink?

"It's not gonna do you any good to lie here stewing about it," Bailey says, squeezing my arm. "C'mon, get up. You'll feel better with some food in your stomach." She swings her legs over the side of the stage's low platform and reaches for her purse. After digging around in it for a few seconds she says, "Ah, here we go. The breakfast of champions."

She pulls out a bag of peanut M&Ms—Cascadian edition. Even when the secession threatened to take away a good chunk of their electrical supply, the Mars Corporation couldn't resist an opportunity to make a buck.

Bailey pours some green, white, and blue candies into her hand and tries to force them on me.

"Maybe later." What I really want now—what I'd practically kill for—is a good cup of coffee.

I get up and head for the bathroom, which is behind the stage at the very back of the building. After I do my business, I splash water on my face and try to swish my teeth clean. This is even worse than the camping trips Mom and Dad used to drag me on. At least then I had a toothbrush.

Feeling dirty and disgusting, I schlep myself out to the main room. There's not much light coming from the side door, which is right at the end of the bar on the east wall, but more oozes from the windows at the front of the narrow building. Even though we're far enough back from them that there's virtually no risk of somebody accidentally seeing us, I still feel like I'm walking through Waterfront Park in my underwear.

"Wouldn't you know it, not a single drop of booze," complains Bailey, who's rooting around behind the bar. "All the last owner left were a few glasses, half a box of napkins, and these stupid drink umbrellas." She dumps a handful of them on the bar then slips out from behind it. "C'mon, let's go do a little reconnaissance in the basement."

I'm up for anything that'll distract me, so I follow, shivering in the tavern's chill.

To get to the staircase, we have to cut through a tiny kitchen tucked along the center of the wall opposite the bar. Bailey steps inside and flips on the light, stopping a minute to take inventory.

I lean against the doorjamb and wait. There's not much in here but a carton of salt, a couple of beat up pots and pans, and a huge grill and stove assembly that looks like it wasn't worth anyone's time to haul away. Bailey spots one of those little dorm refrigerators under the counter and plugs it in.

"Hey, it works," she says. "Now you'll be able to store some real food."

Shouldn't she sound a little more regretful about the prospect of me being stuck here that long?

"Won't your dad notice the electricity?" I ask.

Bailey shrugs and heads for the staircase. "If he does, it won't be for, like, a month. But probably not, because there's solar panels on the roof."

"How do you know these things?"

"Simple. This was a bar. They needed to keep their beer cold and their music hot, which was kinda hard to do with the power cutting out the way it used to when the U.S. was sucking us dry. Solar kept places like this in business."

I guess she must've learned that kind of thing from her dad, but it's another side of Bailey I've never seen.

She leads me down into a creepy, windowless basement, where the concrete floor is so uneven it looks like it was allowed to set the way it was poured. Pipes and wires, which seem more modern than the rest of the building, hang low over our heads. A brick wall divides the front of the basement east to west, and another separates the north end from the south.

"The entrance to that tunnel I was telling you about is supposed to be under here." Bailey kicks a wooden platform that covers the floor at the foot of the stairs. "C'mon. Help me lift this."

I grab one corner of the structure, which is maybe six inches tall and four by five feet across. We heave, raising the front edge. Underneath, the concrete looks different. Like someone patched it with a porous, substandard material and ran out before they got the job done. The area is wet and cluttered with old drink coasters, scrap lumber, and a single Pabst Blue Ribbon can.

"Well, obviously nobody's cleaned under here in a while," Bailey says, toeing the container. "Didn't the PBR guys bite it, like, twenty years ago?"

I shrug. "Sorry. I don't keep up on the alcoholic beverage culture. Doesn't look like much of a tunnel entrance, though."

"Of course not. They filled it in. But maybe we can bust through."

"Maybe *you* can." There's no way I'm going outside as long as people are chasing me, and if I change my mind, I'll use the door.

"Fine." Bailey lets go of the platform. Gravity rips it from my fingers, and it thumps to the ground.

She turns to explore the basement, which is mostly empty except for a walk-in cooler, a regular-sized freezer, and a set of shelves that holds rejected towels and bedding. A few empty boxes lie around on the floor.

"Can we go back upstairs?" I ask. "It's a little creepy down here."

"You're probably sensing one of the ghosts," Bailey says as she sorts through the linens. "I was kinda hoping we'd have seen one by now."

"Ghosts, hell. It's rats I'm worried about. You don't really believe in that woo woo stuff, do you?"

"Maybe." She leads me back toward the staircase. "There are at least two of them. Rose was a prostitute who lived in the brothel on the second floor. She was supposedly stabbed by a jilted lover. The other ghost is Sam. The owner took him in as a little kid and gave him a job. He lived here his whole life. Y'know that room where we got the mattress? That was where he stayed."

We go upstairs, and I help Bailey put sheets on the bed. When my stomach growls, she hands me what's left of her bag of M&Ms. I'm desperate enough to eat them. At least they've got caffeine.

"Now what?" I say.

"I need to get you some food and stuff. Maybe while I'm gone, you can go online and see if you can learn anything about the disappearances."

The idea gives me a glimmer of hope, so after she spruces up her hair and makeup, tells me the code for the alarm system, and takes off, I fish my backpack out from behind the mattress. When I reach inside for my laptop, my fingers brush against the MedEval. A weird little pulse shoots through me. That part of my life is over now. I'll never get into med school—never become a doctor—because everyone thinks I'm a violent drug addict. Does Dr. Alvarez believe that, too? Shame wells up at the thought. How could everything go so wrong so fast?

I pull out my laptop. The Net service gods smile on me, maybe because I'm not zipping along on the light rail, but panic surges the second my browser pops open. Can the kidnappers trace me through a computer the way they can through a phone? I scrabble through memories of crime shows and movies. I'm pretty sure it's as hard to pinpoint someone on the Net as it is to get a good fingerprint from a crime scene. But to be safe, I don't check my email or go to any sites that'll log me in.

A search brings up a page full of hits. I spend the next few hours exploring them while my stomach gripes about having nothing but M&Ms in it. Every time my thoughts wander off in a pessimistic direction, I rein them in. Breaking down and blubbering like I did last night isn't going to get me anywhere.

My research tanks what little hope I had. I don't learn anything useful. It's all rumors and speculation from secondhand sources—people who say a best friend's boyfriend or a family in their neighborhood disappeared. There's nothing from anyone who was actually abducted.

Why's there no trace of these people? Shouldn't employers and schools be reporting them missing? Who's taking them, and how are they covering their tracks? It doesn't make sense.

The authorities say there's no evidence of foul play—that everyone who's been reported missing moved voluntarily. People who believe in the disappearances argue nobody would leave Cascadia of their own free will. They think poor people are being deported to make room for rich Americans, who are buying their way in.

When I finish my research, I'm tempted to check the news websites to find out what they're saying about me, but I don't have the guts. I'm not sure I could handle seeing people from OHSU spreading lies about me. I fall back on the mattress, my belly gurgling, and wonder what the hell I'm going to do next. How are we supposed to find my family if there's no clue where to start?

I hear something outside the door, and panic explodes through my body. *Crap! Maybe they can track someone through a computer!* I jump up and run to hide in the bathroom, my heart trying to beat its way out of my chest.

The door creaks open. "Piper? Where are you?"

I slink into the main room, my face hot with embarrassment. *Of course it's Bailey. Get a grip, Piper.*

She drops a huge duffel bag on the bed and shucks off her

over-stuffed backpack. "Sorry I was gone so long. I had to go to the house and then hit a couple of stores. And I figured you'd want this." She unzips the backpack, letting the delicious odor of greasy fast food waft out. McDonald's. Judging from the smell, she even sprang for real meat, not the veggie dreck I'm used to.

"I don't suppose you've got a cup of coffee in there?"

"Nope. Sorry."

"That's okay," I say, and take the bag. "This is great." Not bothering to sit down, I tear into the Big Mac and fries as she unpacks everything else. Food, toilet paper, a pillow and blanket, soap, a toothbrush, shampoo, even a few changes of clothing that look like something my little brother would wear.

"Stylish," I say around a mouthful of hamburger.

"Well, if you need to go out for anything, you can't be running around in your regular clothes—especially not those scrubs. You're gonna need a disguise. Which is why I got you this." She pulls a long blond wig out of the duffel bag.

I snicker. Does she really think people will buy that? It might cover my short black hair, but with my dark eyebrows, it'll look about as natural as fried chicken in one of Portland's ubiquitous vegan restaurants.

I swallow my last mouthful of fries and lick salt off my fingers. "So, am I still making headline news?"

"*Oh yeah.* You're supposedly armed and dangerous. A couple of guys have my house staked out, too. I had to sneak in and pretend I'd been there all night. When I left, they ambushed me and tried to follow my car, but I dodged 'em in traffic. I parked at Lloyd Center, turned off my phone, and then took the bus to get this stuff."

"Sheesh, Bailey," I say, shaking my head as I drop into a chair. "How'd you think of all that? It's like you've been leading this secret double life or something."

She shrugs. "I always kind of wanted to have an adventure,

you know? I've been waiting for something exciting to happen since third grade. I thought maybe the secession movement would be my chance, but no, I have to go on leading a boring, pampered-rich-girl life."

My skin flares cold and my stomach tenses around the food I just stuffed in it. For a second, I can't say a word. Then my true thoughts spill out. "So this is all just fun and games to you?"

"Piper, no—" She breaks off, her eyes widening into a boy-did-I-just-screw-up look.

"You realize this is my life we're talking about, right? Not just some chance for you to play hero?"

Bailey sinks onto the bed, her expression sagging right along with her body. "Oh man, I'm sorry. I didn't think about it that way."

Part of me wants to punch her, and the rest is just grateful she's smart enough to have everything figured out. The two feelings wrestle with each other until the second one squashes the first. Bailey might be a little crazy, but she loves me.

"It's okay," I say, forcing some flippancy into my tone. "At least your grandiose delusions came in handy."

She manages a smile, but her eyes are glistening. "I really didn't mean to blow off your problems, Piper. I know this has gotta be hell."

I get up and go over to put my arms around her. "Yeah, but you're going to help me fix it, right?"

"That's right," Bailey says, hugging me back fiercely. "Who-ever took your family better watch their asses, because I plan on kicking them clear to New Seattle."

CHAPTER 5

Piper

Since Bailey's parents are out of town, she commits to spending another night at the White Eagle. But first she abandons me to play soccer.

"I'm sorry," she says, giving me a hug. "But I can't let my team down."

She comes back late that afternoon bearing fast food, coffee, spray paint, and her old tablet, loaded with books.

After dark, we black out all the glass in the doors and windows, which makes me feel more secure. It's not until morning, when Bailey swings the side door open and sunlight peeks inside, that I realize we've turned the already-gloomy tavern into a tomb. It's the first nice weather we've had in days, and I ache to go out and soak up the sun like a lizard, but I can't force myself within ten feet of the doorway. Bailey tries to convince me I'll be perfectly safe in the outdoor seating area—the bushes and vines are so overgrown it would be impossible for anyone to see me—but I can't risk it. I was too scared to even sneak up the back staircase last night to take a shower.

"You're being paranoid," Bailey says.

I know. But I can't help it. It feels like bad guys are hiding everywhere, waiting to snatch me. Even the trucks rumbling by on Russell make me jump.

At noon, Bailey takes off again. She's got another soccer game, plus she needs to finish cleaning up the mess from the party before her parents get home. I'm on my own all day. That's when I find the nerve to look myself up on the Net, using Bailey's tablet, just in case I'm wrong about them not being able to track me on my laptop. I hate that I've waited this long, that I didn't have the guts to face up to things yesterday. But since Friday night, I've been trapped in a soul-sucking fog that's barely left me enough energy to eat and breathe.

The news is as bad as I expected. They interviewed kids in the JSA program, and none of them have anything nice to say.

"Piper was always a little strange," comments one guy I barely recognize. "She never talked much."

"It doesn't surprise me she'd pull a gun on someone," says another girl. "She was kinda creepy, y'know?"

A doctor I've never met claims I held him up and threatened his life, demanding oxycodone. I keep reading, my whole body tense, dreading what Dr. Alvarez might've said, but there's no word from her.

The story goes on to report that my phone was found on the SuperMAX south of Eugene, and that I'm armed and dangerous, just like Bailey said. If anyone sees me, they're supposed to contact authorities immediately. Right. Because if they try to apprehend me themselves, I might blab the truth about the kidnappings.

The only thing I learn on the other news sites is that my family supposedly moved to southern California on short notice when my mom got a job offer, and I stayed behind to finish my junior year. Pretty much what the police said about everyone else who's been reported missing.

It's only ten-thirty when I finish reading. I've still got the whole day to kill. And the one after that. And the one after that. A thick, dark gloom settles over me. Am I going to be stuck in this hellhole forever? Bailey said she just needs time to figure things out, and so far she's been right about pretty much everything. But what if she can't come up with a plan? What if this is all I can expect from the rest of my life?

Longing wells up inside me. A deep need to plunge into the refuge I always seek when things get bad. My future in medicine might be over, but right now, the only thing that'll make me feel better is to lose myself in that world.

I can't risk logging into the Amazon cloud to read my medical books, so I settle for surfing the Net, steering clear of OHSU's student training database. Even if the code Dr. Alvarez gave me still works, using it might be the tip-off that'll get me busted. There are a lot of other good websites, though. I spend hours watching surgery videos on YouTube and trying not to think of my family. But the memories sneak in.

I picture Grandpa, who alternately drives me nuts with his conspiracy theories and cracks me up with his raunchy humor. I think of Nick, who's always living adventures in his head when he's not acting as Grandpa's legs so he won't have to give up on pruning shrubs and planting pansies. I remember Mom, who spends her days teaching kindergarten then wears herself out waitressing at night so we won't lose our house. She insisted on me signing up for a summer shift in the JSA program, even though I could've spent the twenty hours a week flipping burgers to bring in extra cash.

I have to find my family. Failing isn't an option. The idea of never seeing them again snatches the breath right out of my chest.

It's almost eight o'clock when Bailey comes back, bringing a coffee maker, a bag of groceries, and a mocha shake from the new gourmet ice cream shop on Mississippi. She sets everything on the table of the booth I've staked out in the corner opposite the stage. The scent of fresh spring air clings to her. It seems like a year since I've been outside.

"You doing okay?" she asks, flopping on my bed and narrowly missing a bag of potato chips.

I suck on my milkshake, welcoming the merciful rush of sugar and caffeine. "I guess. How was your game?" I'm desperate to talk about something—anything—other than the mess I'm in.

"Good. We smoked 'em, 4-0." Bailey fishes a chip from the bag and pops it into her mouth. Kicking off her shoes, she stretches out on my bed and rests her feet on the brick wall above my pillow.

As she makes her way through my chips, we talk about her soccer club, and that leads to a discussion of how the Timbers, Portland's major league team, are kicking butt this year. I don't give a rat's right foot about this stuff, but it's a distraction.

"They're playing New Seattle next Friday," Bailey says.

Even *I* know this is a major event, since the Sounders—or "Flounders," as Bailey refers to them—are Portland's biggest rival. "You going?"

"Hell no. I heard Jefferson's supposed to be there." Bailey never calls him Cooper, or even the president. With her, he's always just Jefferson, like they're buddies or something. "Not that I wouldn't mind sharing a private suite with him, but it's always a pain in the ass when the Secret Service shows up."

"Just imagine if Sarto went too." Before he was vice president, Sarto used to be the mayor of New Seattle, and he's still a huge Sounders fan. The rivalry between the two cities and their soccer teams keeps him and President Cooper constantly ribbing each other.

"They won't let that happen," Bailey says. "Those two never go to games together. All it would take is one well-placed bomb, and boom, there goes the Cascadian government. . . . Plus we'd lose the Timbers."

"Yeah," I say with a straight face. "That would be just as tragic."

She picks up my pillow and flings it at my head. "It would be!"

I toss it back, and for a few seconds we're engaged in battle, like two normal teenagers on any ordinary day. It feels good to laugh, but Bailey gives up way too soon, letting the pillow lie where it falls.

"I need to get going. My parents just got home, and they're being all clingy." She bites her lip, giving me a look like she's dipping her toe in a lake, debating about whether or not to plunge in. "You gonna be okay?"

Even though there's no difference between night and day with the windows blacked out, the idea of being here by myself after dark feels lonely. "Sure," I say with a shrug. "I better get used to it, right?"

Bailey gives up the lip chewing and moves on to twisting her long, dark hair around a finger. "Why don't you let me talk to my dad about this? Maybe he—"

"No!" As bad as today was, I'm not ready to trust anyone other than her. Just the idea of it sends fear slicing through me.

"Piper..."

"I can't risk it. Anyway, aren't those guys still watching your house?"

"Well...yeah," she admits.

"They've probably got your phone tapped, too. Maybe they've even got the place bugged."

Bailey studies me, her eyes a little sad, and finally nods. "Okay. I'll keep it to myself."

CHAPTER 6

Logan

Chicago, Illinois, Monday, May 21, 2063

The morning we leave, it's seventy-five degrees by eight o'clock. For the past ten days, temperatures have reached the upper nineties, only dipping into the seventies at night.

Zoey's buckled into our SUV with her laptop, and I'm loading up our bags when Dad comes out to tell me to take Mom's duffle back inside.

"What?" I turn to see an uncharacteristically rigid expression on his face. "Why?"

"Don't argue with me, Logan!"

The outburst makes me jump. *Wow.* What's got him so upset? Without a word, I pull Mom's bag out of the Toyota and carry it into the house. Dad stays behind to talk to Zoey.

"Mom?" I call as I close the door behind me. She's standing at the front window, staring out in an absent sort of way, hand at her throat.

"Mom," I repeat, touching her arm. "What's going on?"

She startles and swings around to give me a tight smile. "Just a temporary change of plans. I have to wrap up some loose ends, but I'll join you in a few weeks."

Loose ends? At this point? But as I'm pondering this, my brain strategizes a way to use it to my advantage. "Let me stay, too. I can finish my classes and keep you company." I've made my peace with the move, but I'm not looking forward to plunging into a new school three weeks before the year ends.

Mom's fingers go to my cheek. "Honey—"

"You'll do no such thing." The door slams behind Dad,

punctuating his statement. "Get in the car. We're leaving in two minutes."

My fists clench at my sides, but I've rarely seen him this angry, and I don't want to start a war. With my mouth shut, I follow the order.

Mom trails me outside. Eyes teary, she pulls me into a quick, forceful hug before leaning into the back of the SUV to wrap her arms around my sister.

"What's wrong?" Zoey demands. "Why aren't you coming with us?"

"I will, sweetheart. Just not right now. Don't say anything more to your father about this, okay?"

"But—"

"Please." Mom brushes Zoey's blond hair back from her forehead, giving her a do-it-for-me look.

With an eye roll and an exaggerated sigh, Zoey relents. "*Fine.*"

"I love you." Mom backs out of the car, turning to face me. Her hand finds mine and squeezes. "Take care of her, Logan."

Something as unsettling as it is unreadable hovers in her eyes, but there's no time to decipher it. "Of course."

A door slams behind me and Dad barks, "Let's get moving."

I slide into the front passenger seat while he steps up to Mom, draws her close, and buries his face in her hair.

"I'm sorry, honey."

"We'll work it out," Mom says. They stand like that for several moments before she pulls away.

Neither Zoey nor I say a word as Dad gets into the car and types something into the navigation console, his fingers stabbing the keys.

I sit motionless, trying to process what just happened and afraid the slightest wrong move or word will lead to another explosion. If this is just about tying up a few loose ends, why's Dad so tense?

When I fail to come up with a logical explanation, my mind wanders back to his reasons for making this move. Zoey's a big one, for sure, as is the opportunity at Intel, but I wonder if he might have another motive—if he's hoping it might dissuade me from joining the military.

"The Army's for kids who don't have the smarts for college or can't afford it," he's told me more than once. "You have other options." He's never been able to see how insulting that attitude is, not just to me, but to all the people who put their lives on the line defending his freedom. One thing's for certain—I'm not going to ask him about it now.

Despite Mom's absence, Zoey is soon reclaimed by the raw excitement that's possessed her since she learned we were moving. Cascadia is her idea of the Holy Land. She's probably Jefferson Cooper's biggest groupie, and she has every one of Frequent Deadly Lightning's albums, even though they came out before she was in kindergarten. But her fanaticism is more than just a tween crush. Zoey's way into all things green, and Cooper's energy policies have elevated him to god-like status in her eyes.

"Maybe we'll actually get to meet him, Logan. Wouldn't that be totally prime?"

It's nice to see her so full of zip, but still, I laugh. "I think he'll be a little too busy running Cascadia to hang out with a couple of kids from Chicago."

The stink of dying fish seeps into the car as we head north along Lake Michigan.

"Ugh," Zoey groans. "Look how low it is already. I don't think it was this bad last spring."

The ugly, green water, thick with algae bloom, oozes decay. Despite our blizzards and torrential winter rains, the lake never fully recovers from the summer heat. These days, it seems the dredges outnumber the ships, fighting an endless battle to keep the channels deep enough.

"Fortunately, that's not our worry anymore," Dad says. "Where we're going, the government takes a proactive approach to the climate crisis."

He's plotted a northern route, which he hopes might be a little cooler: I-94 through Wisconsin, Monsantesota (as it's been known since the corporate takeover of the bankrupt government six years ago), and North Dakota. According to the navigation console, the drive to the Cascadian border outside Butte, West Montana, should take less than a day. It's crazy to think that in the 1800s, wagon trains spent months crossing the country. Or that even as little as thirty years ago, before self-driving cars became common, the trip could take days if you stopped to eat, sleep, and fuel up. But that's not an issue for us. Our hybrid SUV will go seven hundred miles on a tank of gas, and Dad brought along plenty of food. He's afraid Zoey will have a medical emergency out in the middle of nowhere, which is a frightening idea, considering her homecare nurse wasn't allowed to come with us.

The road's surface, which hasn't been good since Madison, deteriorates as we head into Monsantesota. The Toyota alternately jolts from hitting potholes and darts to avoid them. We don't see a single living tree the whole way across the plains states. Even grass doesn't grow here anymore. A dust storm scoops up the unanchored soil and scours our SUV with it. Of the few times we stop, twice it's because the grit is so thick it overwhelms the navigation system.

Somehow, the powder works its way inside. A dry, metallic scent fills my nose. I can taste the dust in the air, and it makes Zoey cough. Dad keeps glancing over the seat at her. Each time he asks, "You okay, honey?" she gets a little bit crankier.

But Dad's incessant worrying isn't the only thing bugging her. Even though our Toyota has the Net package, it's not working properly in this godforsaken wilderness.

"Ahhhh!" she yells, pounding a skinny fist against the door

panel. "That's, like, the twenty-millionth time it's dropped."

Something I'm well aware of, since she hollers every time it happens. She's probably on Connect Me, engaging in social network repartee as one of her many personas. She has at least three in addition to her real self, and probably more. A staunchly conservative widowed schoolteacher in South Florida. An elderly Canadian environmental activist. A high school sophomore in a small town outside New Seattle, who's a huge fan of Japanese anime. Sometimes she gets into arguments with herself, which is a real crackup. Even though fictional personas are against the site's rules, she's found a way around the barricades that keep most people from doing it.

"Which one of you got dropped this time, Sparky?" I crane my neck to look at her between the seats. Zoey glowers, jerking her chin toward Dad. He doesn't know about her Connect Me mafia. I grin and shake my head. Whenever I'm on the site, I worry I might be talking to one of my sister's yet-to-be-discovered secret identities.

As we make our way across the country, Dad's mood improves, and he begins commenting on the view outside the grit-caked windows. Probably the most unsettling things we see are the ghost towns. Big cities like Minneapolis and Fargo have become nothing but block upon block of abandoned buildings. Garbage, shattered glass, and derelict cars litter the streets, and the drifts formed by the incessant dust are so big our SUV has to swerve to avoid them.

There's one sign of hope as we drive through Bismarck at sunset. A new factory, built by FreedomCorp. It's huge and looks like a fortress, with high brick walls topped by razor wire. Dad says they manufacture telecommunications equipment and need the walls to keep out looters. Zoey looks them up online during one of her computer's rare moments of Net lucidity.

"'FreedomCorp believes in the future of America,'" she

reads. "'While other companies are closing their doors and leaving communities high and dry, we're making a concerted effort to breathe new life into these troubled towns. We offer not only steady employment at a great wage, but also family lodging in our clean, friendly, state-of-the-art facilities. Anyone seeking employment in the cities of Bismarck, Cleveland, Houston, or Tulsa should be sure to apply. We have many exciting positions available.'"

"Lodging?" I say.

"It's not a new concept," Dad replies. "A lot of companies have done it. Vanport, for example, just outside Portland. The entire town was built to house the families of shipbuilders during World War II. It makes sense to resurrect the idea. Some of these cities have horrible problems with crime, black-outs, and food shortages. If they're going to survive, someone has to step up to solve those problems."

As a fan of political and military history, I'm familiar with Vanport, but I let Dad believe he's educating me. It's rare that we can find a topic we're both interested in, and I don't want to ruin the moment.

"What amazes me is that something like Cascadia could happen," Dad says, shaking his head. "Who'd have thought a secession was possible, let alone a peaceful one?"

I've speculated about this quite a bit. "The only reason it worked is because Cooper was willing to trade water and electricity for the equipment on those military bases. If he hadn't done that, we'd have wound up in a civil war that would've wiped us all out."

Dad glances at me, a rare light of respect in his eyes. "I think you're right."

In my opinion, the compromise was a brilliant tactical maneuver. Cooper realized the United States wouldn't be able to cope with a sudden loss of resources from the Northwest, so he proposed a grace period of five years in which they'd continue to receive water and electricity at no cost. When that didn't fly with his co-conspirators, he amended the idea. Cascadia needed a military, and simply taking over the bases in their territory would have been a slap in President Goldstein's face. But a trade gave him an out.

"What *I* find fascinating is Cascadian politics," I say, since further talk of the military could easily lead to an argument. "The Northwest is known for being liberal, yet Cooper's taking a middle-of-the-road approach. I mean, sure, he's into green energy and regulating emissions, but he also pushed for a closed border. Plus he rolled back Goldstein's latest gun-control law."

"Lots of hunters in the Northwest," Dad says. "It's one thing to give up semi-automatic weapons and another not to be able to buy ammunition for your deer rifle. Cooper's no fool. He's not going to alienate half his constituency. And the Cascadian Party's a good compromise after years of gridlock between the Democrats and Republicans."

I settle back in my seat. This is something I could talk about all night. "True. But there's division even within that party. I mean look at the vice president. He thinks Cooper's energy infrastructure projects are too big a financial risk. And then there's the issue of water rights. If Sarto had his way, there wouldn't be equal distribution between cities and farmland."

"I think that's the point," Dad says. "I guarantee you, the Cooper/Sarto ticket pulled more votes because of that diversity."

He's got me there. It's a political strategy that's been used forever.

Once dusk has given way to night—after nine, because it's almost summer and we're so far north—I climb in back and fold down the seats so Zoey and I can get some sleep. It's eerie to hear the dust scratching against our SUV in the darkness. I wake at sunrise and crawl up front to sit with Dad.

"Did you get much sleep?" I ask. Even though he doesn't need to pilot the car, the driver's seat couldn't have been comfortable. But it would've been even more cramped in the back with us.

He sighs and rubs a hand across his stubbly face. "Enough."

I scrounge in the bag at my feet for some energy bars and hand him a couple. Silence hovers between us as we eat. Despite last night's discussion, the two of us aren't very good at communicating. Zoey is the one he understands. She's as smart with computers as he is, and none of my efforts to please him can compare to her just being herself.

I pull out my iPad and bring up my favorite book, *The Art of War*. It's an ancient Chinese work that's been used as a military training guide for centuries, but Sun Tzu's wisdom can be applied to anything strategic—law, business, sports. I use it regularly on the football field.

Zoey wakes up an hour after I do. Like a magician performing some slight-of-hand, she works a pain pill out of the bottle in her backpack and slips it under her tongue. She wouldn't be taking one if she wasn't feeling awful, but she doesn't look any paler or shakier than normal. I don't want a repeat of yesterday's grumpiness, so I pretend I didn't see.

"How ya doing, honey?" Dad asks, turning to flash a grin at her. He must not have noticed her covert maneuver, or he'd be fussing.

"Great." She gives him a thumbs up. Her own smile looks only slightly forced. She's spent years perfecting that please-don't-notice-me-I'm-fine expression.

I dig into the food bag for some of my homemade trail mix and hand it to Zoey. Even though we can afford the meat many people do without, she refuses to eat anything with a face. Since this is one area where Dad won't humor her, I've learned to run interference, taking over the cooking that he and Mom are too busy for anyway.

Dad's sketchy mood has returned by the time we stop in Bozeman to find a bathroom. I hurry back to the car, not wanting to set him off. I have no idea what's bothering him now. We're only eighty miles from Cascadia. He ought to be happy.

The last stretch passes quickly, and as we approach the border, we begin to see trees. Real trees. I've spotted a few patches of forest high up in the mountains since I woke this morning, but they were graveyards. Dark, brittle skeletons ravaged by fire, and sickly stragglers fighting for any drop of moisture that might make it over the Rockies.

Zoey presses her forehead against the window. "Logan, look at the trees."

"That's nothing," Dad tells her. "Just wait until we get to Idaho and Oregon."

"I *know*, Dad." Zoey's passion for research is exceeded only by her love for all things electronic, and she's no doubt thoroughly studied the subject. Besides, she'd be the ultimate tree hugger if there were any trees left back home to hug. Most of them died after the anti-watering laws went into effect.

We top a crest and the border crossing at the Continental Divide comes into view. A couple of trucks are lined up at the gate, but judging from how deserted the interstate has been, I suspect most freight is shipped in and out through North California and the southern part of Idaho. I've hardly seen any other cars since I woke up. Only limited travel visas are issued for Cascadia. The official word is that regulations will relax in the future, but for now, they want to keep everyone out.

The checkpoint, which looks like something you'd see in photos of concentration camps, makes that clear. An imposing steel and concrete structure, complete with roll-down gates, blocks all four lanes of traffic. A fifteen-foot chain-link fence extends from it, the top angling back over the U.S. side with looping strands of concertina wire. Underneath, signs read,

"Danger. High Voltage." The fence runs as far as I can see in either direction, disappearing among the trees. Guards armed with assault rifles stand at each of the gateways.

"Damn, look at all those guns," Zoey says.

Dad pulls up behind one of the trucks. "Language, Zoey."

"Remind me again of why Mom couldn't come with us?" It's her way of sticking it to Dad for reprimanding her.

"Like I told you, she had some important matters she had to finish up at work."

"So when will she be done with all that?"

"I don't know!" Dad snaps.

Zoey flinches, staring at the back of his head with wide eyes. I don't think he's yelled at her more than a dozen times in her entire life.

"Probably in a few weeks," Dad continues, his tone more reasonable. He runs a hand through his hair and looks at her through the rear-view mirror. "You have to remember, her career is just as important to her as mine is to me."

I glance at him. Since when? Mom's a journalist, and even though she enjoys her investigative environmental reporting, she's been threatening to quit for years because she's sick of the stress and deadlines. Besides, I can't see her allowing work to come between her and Zoey. This is the woman who, every time Zoey's been in the hospital, has spent the nights camped out in a chair beside her bed.

The trucks are ushered through, and then it's our turn. The guard steps close, rifle at the ready, to look through the driver's window of our SUV. "Passports and visas?" he barks.

If we'd had any doubts, he makes it clear this is no friendly weekend trip to Toronto.

Dad hands over the official papers from the Cascadian government then holds out his wrist phone. The guard bumps it with his tablet to transfer the digital version. He glances at the readout. "Carl Voigt?"

"Yes, sir."

"And you have two children? Logan, age sixteen, and Zoey, eleven?"

"Yes, sir." Dad's tone brings to mind the way a soldier would speak to a superior officer, another thing that's totally unlike him. In his world, he's used to being pack leader.

The guard peers around Dad, dispassionately appraising my sister and me. "Wait here while I check this out."

He walks over to consult with someone in the booth, keeping an eye on us the entire time.

After five minutes, Zoey starts fidgeting. "What's taking so long?" She leans between the front seats to look around Dad's shoulder. "He should be able to check everything on his tablet. It's like he's—"

"Hush, Zoey." Dad's fingertips drum out a beat on the side of the navigation computer. He darts a glance toward the booth, releasing a long breath through tight lips.

After ten minutes, the guard comes back. He hands the papers to Dad. "You can go."

The roll-down gate creaks skyward with a rattle. The Toyota's hybrid engine engages. We drive through the checkpoint, out of the United States and into our new life.

CHAPTER 7

Logan

We spend the night in Cascade Locks because Zoey is enamored by the sheer majesty of the Columbia River Gorge. I am too. Raw basalt cliffs, cloaked in stunning evergreens, tower high above the river. Wispy, low-hanging clouds shroud the cliff-tops, giving the place an other-worldly aura. The air, cool and moist, soothes my lungs after the hot, dry dust we encountered on the Great Plains. I feel like I've been transported to some surreal alternate universe, more amazing than any I've encountered in my virtual reality games.

Wednesday morning, we drive along the Columbia. The fresh, clear water is such a contrast to the murk of Lake Michigan. Zoey's torn between staring out the window and using the Net to look up everything she sees. She finds a video of one of Jefferson Cooper's speeches from his first campaign, four years ago, and plays it.

Standing in front of the green, white, and blue Cascadian flag with its Douglas fir tree silhouetted in the foreground, Cooper looks more like a rock star than a president. "Whether climate change is man-made or naturally occurring is of no consequence," he says. "What matters now is how we respond to it. If we're to leave anything to our children, we need to make changes. We need to harness the power of the wind and sun—to build dams to collect the rain, since we can no longer rely on snow pack. Urban and rural citizens must put aside their differences and work together to ensure there's enough water for everyone. It's only if we come together as a community that we can build a nation that will not only survive, but also thrive in the decades to come."

Even though I've been in Cascadia for barely a day, Cooper's passion wakes a sense of patriotism in me. My own leadership abilities are limited to a quiet, behind-the-scenes approach, and I'd never be comfortable speaking to the masses, so I can't help but admire his charisma.

"Too bad someone didn't have that much sense fifty years ago," Zoey says. "Then we wouldn't be in this mess."

We arrive in Portland by mid-morning, but our house isn't ready, so we stay in a downtown hotel. I'm astonished by how friendly the people here are. When you pass them on the street, they meet your eye and smile, rather than looking away as they would back home.

Dad, who won't start work until next Tuesday, takes us on multiple tours of the city and surrounding valleys. Portland is a smorgasbord of colorful sights. Food carts offering vegan, organic, and GMO-free options. Street musicians in dreadlocks and tie-dyed hemp clothing. Bubbling drinking fountains, right out on the sidewalk, that never stop running.

I'm struck by the irony of this last wonder, since signs everywhere pay testament to Cascadia's progressive stance on the shortages caused by the climate crisis. "Supplement with solar." "Power down for a strong future." "There's enough for everyone if we water on assigned days." My cynicism spurs Zoey to research the issue, and she learns the water in the fountains is recycled. I should have known better than to get between her and her hero. She's already gone loopy over Jefferson Cooper's re-election billboard and forced us to listen to every Frequent Deadly Lightning song in existence.

It blows my mind to be in the midst of so much lush, fragrant vegetation. Trees, shrubs, grass, and flowers—I see more green in a few days than I have in my entire life. And it drizzles the whole time, something just as astounding. I swear, heaven itself couldn't be as stunning as the state of Oregon.

By Friday morning, the movers have everything unloaded, so we're able to leave the hotel. Our new house is actually an old one, built in 1908. It isn't very big, but compared to our utilitarian place back home, it has character. And the small yard is a mass of raised beds, filled with blooming plants, something Mom will appreciate. It seems so strange to be here without her, and I can tell from Zoey's waning bubbliness that she's feeling the loss: For her sake, I hope Mom ties up the lose ends that kept her in Chicago soon.

We spend the weekend getting our furniture situated and belongings unpacked. This is followed by Memorial Day—which they continue to celebrate in Cascadia—so I get one last reprieve from school. I try to talk Dad into letting us study online for the rest of the year, since we only have a few weeks left, but he tells me it's best to get a head start on making new friends.

When I arrive at Cleveland High Tuesday morning, I'm given the option of going straight to class or watching a series of videos on Cascadian history. Even though I've studied the subject in depth, I opt for the videos. Better than having to face a crowd of strangers first thing in the morning.

I'm led into a small room at the back of the office. The half-dozen desks have tablet-style computers imbedded in the tops, just like back home. I suspect the entire system is the same, with teachers only through sixth grade, at which point the desk-vids, with their access to the cloud-based curriculum, take over.

The reasoning is that only little kids need nurturing, and discipline can be maintained without teachers in the upper grades. Sensors in the desk-vids detect if a student's gaze strays for more than fifteen seconds and give a warning beep. That's usually enough to keep me focused, but some kids aren't as able to stay on task, so cameras are used to monitor what's going on in the classrooms. If anybody causes trouble or refuses to do the work, someone's sent in to handle the situation. Dad thinks the whole system has an Orwellian reek—and I've heard President Cooper agrees—but I'm used to it. It's not like we don't still have advisors and a tutoring center.

I power up the desk-vid and log onto the cloud.

"In October 2057, Jefferson Cooper, singer/songwriter and leader of the indie rock band, Frequent Deadly Lightning, composed *The Tom McCall Song*. The lyrics outlined his disdain for the U.S. policy of diverting power and water from the Pacific Northwest to the rest of the country. It was a sentiment shared by many in the region, and the song went viral, resulting in Cooper being inundated with requests to speak out about the climate crisis."

It's nothing I don't know. In fact, the video leaves out a lot of details, like the fun the media had when Cooper appealed for someone to take charge and become a champion for the Northwest, and his bass player pointed out he was already filling that role. But it's a quality production that provides a good glimpse of Cascadian pride, and it's better than sitting in physics class.

"Cooper's grassroots efforts to form Cascadia, a country named in honor of a populist movement dating back to the 1970s, met with wide approval. The area would include the bioregion of the Columbia River Basin—Oregon, Washington, Idaho, western Montana, and southern British Columbia—along with northern California.

"Though the campaign was popular, it didn't gain steam until retired U.S. Senator David Daskalov, impressed by Cooper's passion and charisma, took the budding young leader under his wing. With Daskalov providing legal advice, Cooper drew up the McCall Initiative, a petition for secession named for 20th century Oregon governor Tom McCall. Cooper went on to approach the leadership in the various state and provincial governments, persuading them to hold special elections to vote on the issue."

The next part candy-coats things, making the call to secede seem simple. But my reading has told me it wasn't that easy.

Even though the measures passed with overwhelming majorities, the state governments were so busy bickering over their liberal vs. conservative agendas that the movement stalled. Cooper had to go over their heads, recruiting the U.S. senators and congressmen from the area to form a committee.

"The first meeting of the Cascadian Congress took place in Portland, Oregon's, Benson Hotel in January of 2059. A constitution was drawn up, and a declaration of secession filed with the government."

The video goes on to explain Cooper's bargain with the U.S. and how he got nominated for the presidency, another thing Daskalov had a hand in.

"In a grand address, Daskalov outlined the qualities and values needed in the first leader of this new nation, concluding that Cooper, who had done much of the hard work already, was the ideal man for the job.

"By this time, Cooper was ready to step down and go back to his music. But public outcry became so strong that he agreed to run for office, forming the Cascadian Party."

The video glosses over the protests of people who doubted a 28-year-old rock star with no previous political experience had what it took to be president. It mentions Daskalov's death from a heart attack, but not the speculation that the loss would make Cooper crumble. However, it does cover one of the biggest surprises of the campaign.

"Rick Sarto, mayor of New Seattle, who had initially opposed locating the Cascadian capitol in Portland, abandoned his own bid for the presidency to align himself with Cooper. Though they differed on several positions, Cooper was impressed enough with Sarto to select him as his running mate."

The presentation ends with a summary of the landslide victory, and just like in 2059, I'm gratified by Cooper's ability to rally and prove his opponents wrong. It's nice to know that, in Cascadia at least, the majority of citizens realize youth doesn't necessarily equal incompetence.

The desk-vid shows me several more videos, one of which details how, after the military bases in the region were secured, troops were given the option of returning to the U.S. or re-pledging their allegiance to Cascadia. This is of particular interest to me, considering my career goals, but I'm not sure I'm ready to dedicate my future to this brand new nation.

After I finish watching, I have to face the inevitable—finding my way around in an unfamiliar school. As a football team captain and leader in JROTC, you wouldn't think this would intimidate me, but the truth is, I'm not good with crowds. The desk-vid won't allow me to stall, so I proceed to my regularly scheduled class, English.

Academically, changing schools is not an issue. All the ones in America use the same government-mandated curriculum. Apparently those in Cascadia do, too. Cleveland High appears to be on a lesson plan identical to that of my old school, down to the day. Which means I have a week's worth of work to catch up on. I should have anticipated this and studied on my own, but the landscape unfolding around me has been a lot more interesting than homework.

After English, I go to lunch, which is equal parts loud and lonely. At home, I was always surrounded by friends. Here, I'm invisible. I thought I'd prefer that to having to deal with a mob of strangers, but I was wrong.

When lunch is over, I consult my schedule and head for trigonometry. The desk-vids make it so there's no need to move from room to room, but years ago, a panel of experts argued that if kids don't get exercise and social time, they're more likely to become disciplinary problems. As an athlete, I laugh at the idea that walking from one class to another constitutes real exercise, but I'm glad they're not allowed to park us in one place for seven straight hours.

The rest of the students in trig are taking a quiz I haven't studied for, so I spend the period catching up on some of the lessons I missed. I'm in the middle of a problem when the intercom blares. "Logan Voigt, please report to the main office."

My stomach instantly goes into lockdown. *Zoey.* I switch off the desk-vid and head for the door.

In the office, I receive the news I'm expecting: I need to go pick up my sister because she's sick.

"We couldn't get a hold of your father," says the secretary, who has purple hair and two piercings in her left eyebrow.

I'm not surprised by the news. No doubt, he's busy going through company orientation. What annoys me is that they'd try to call him when I'm clearly listed as the emergency contact in Zoey's paperwork. My school is only a few blocks from hers, so they've got no business disturbing my father on his first day at a new job.

"Do you have a vehicle?" the secretary asks.

"Yes, ma'am."

Dad prefers public transportation, and Portland's light rail goes straight out to the Intel campus, so he let me use the Toyota this morning. The secretary signs me out, and I jog to the parking lot. I know the situation can't be desperate, or the nurse at Zoey's school would've sent her straight to the hospital, but my heart still pounds as if I've narrowly avoided fumbling a perfect pass.

At Winterhaven School, the secretary directs me to the nurse's office, where I find Zoey lying on a cot. She's about two shades paler than her normal ghostly hue, and I know what this means. Why can't the poor kid catch a break?

"Hey, Sparky," I say, sitting down beside her and squeezing her shoulder. "You okay?"

"Yeah." She sounds as pale as she looks. "I just wanna go home."

"She lost consciousness in her classroom," the nurse says. "But she was at her desk, so fortunately she wasn't hurt."

"No, I just made an idiot of myself in front of thirty kids."

"You can always blame it on the school food," I suggest.

Zoey doesn't even attempt a smile. I feel for her. I'd be disgusted with myself, too, if I'd made that sort of entrance at Cleveland.

"I wish Mom was here," she says.

"So do I." She'd be able to get a smile out of Zoey, or at the very least, coax her into accepting the hug she so obviously needs. Mom calls every day, but it's just not the same as being with us.

"Let's go." Zoey pushes herself up off the cot, and I help her to her feet.

"Do you think you can make it to the car on your own, or should I carry you?"

She gives me the evil eye. "If you try, I'll bite you."

Hearing that much fight in a voice that's so weak twists at my heart.

I make things easier on both of us by starting Dad's SUV with my phone and directing it to meet us at the front entrance. Zoey insists on taking every step herself, but she leans on me heavily. When we get to the car, she collapses into the front seat.

"I'm *never* coming back to this school."

"Can't blame you there," I say. And Dad won't make her. She's missed more classes than she's attended, but it hardly matters when she's smart enough to teach herself.

At the house, I carry Zoey inside because she's short of breath now. There's only so much damage I'll allow her to do in the name of preserving her dignity. Denise, the new homecare nurse, shadows us down the hallway. She's older than the one we had back in Chicago, about our grandma's age, and her eyes are kind.

After a quick evaluation, she gives Zoey the news we're both expecting. "We're going to need to put you back on your PVAD, honey."

Zoey groans and scowls at her. She made it clear on Sunday she has no use for Denise. But then, she's never liked any of her nurses. It has nothing to do with how competent they are, or even if they're friendly. They're just one more reminder of how she's not like other kids.

I leave the room while Denise attaches Zoey's ventricular assist device to the port implanted below her collar bone. She's not a baby anymore, and she won't put up with her older brother seeing her bare chest.

When Denise is finished, she lets me back in. Zoey's sitting up in bed wearing her pajamas, a scowl, and the PVAD vest she hates. It has a hidden pocket to hold the pump that helps her failing heart do its job. The device isn't very big, but when you're in the fifth grade, anything that makes you stand out is social suicide.

Denise scrolls through Zoey's records on her MedEval then turns to me with a puzzled look. "According to this, it's been less than a month since your sister last used her PVAD. Could this date have been entered wrong?"

I think back. "No. I remember she was upset because she had to wear the vest to Mom's birthday dinner. That was May second."

Denise consults the MedEval again. "Zoey, how long has it been since your doctors mentioned an implanted device to you? Most MB kids your age have one."

"No!" Zoey's eyes go wide. I wouldn't have thought she could get any paler, but she does.

Denise turns to her, full of grandmotherly charm. "Honey, it would make your life so much easier. You wouldn't have to worry about episodes like the one at school today. You understand it would be completely hidden, right?"

"I'm not your honey," Zoey says, her voice as jagged as shrapnel. "And I don't need a . . ." she stops to catch her breath, ". . . damn implanted device."

"Can we talk a second?" I motion Denise toward the door with a jerk of my head.

She follows me into the hallway.

"Look," I say. "We all know Zoey's going to need that surgery eventually, but you're not going to earn any points by arguing with her. She's scared to death of the idea." I explain how the last time, when she got her port, she had a near-fatal reaction to the anesthetic, and what should have been outpatient surgery turned into a month-long hospital stay.

"I know, Logan. I've read her medical records. And she isn't the only MB patient who's had such a strong reaction. But that was almost four years ago, and we've learned enough about the disease since then to prevent that sort of thing in eighty percent of cases. It's in her best interest to have the procedure."

"It's in her best interest not to be terrified."

"Of course." Denise nods and softly touches my arm. "But it's my job to work with your sister's medical team to educate her and your family about her options. We have a duty to keep you updated about the latest medical advances. And we'll do that, but you need to do your part. Zoey's just a little girl. Your family can't keep allowing her to dictate her own medical care. You have to stand up to her and do what will keep her as healthy as possible."

I know she's right, but I also know how hard it is to see my tough, sassy little sister scared half out of her mind. And that kind of stress can't be good for her.

"Please," I say, "don't mention it again until you've talked to my dad."

Denise agrees, and I go back into Zoey's room to cheer her up. But by now she's got her laptop out and is lost in another world.

I take pity and don't try to bring her back to ours.

CHAPTER 8

Piper

Despite Bailey's determination to help, her efforts to find my family go nowhere. I spend the next ten days hiding out in the White Eagle, lost in a daze while she tries to come up with a plan. Even though I can't blame her for running smack into the same brick walls I did, I feel cheated. She seemed so sure of herself in the beginning—so confident she could fix things.

The first few days, I'm anxious about missing school, hoping there might still be some way out of this mess and not wanting to get behind. But eventually I stop caring. I fritter away my time reading Bailey's books, watching surgery videos, and trying to shut out the construction noise from the condo going up across the street. I'm not any more successful at that than I am at shutting out the memories of my family. Crazy little snippets hit with no warning: Nick leaving buckets on the lawn in summer because Grandpa's got him convinced the Groundwater Fairy will fill them up. Dad telling gruesome stories at the dinner table about his last shift while Mom shushes him, worried it'll scare Nick and me. As if I'd be anything but fascinated by something like that.

The memories are as much a curse as a blessing. I'm desperate for every detail I can dredge out of the swirling chaos of my brain, but each one makes me feel worse. Deep down, I know I'm never going to see my family again.

Being socked away in this crypt doesn't help. Bailey nags me to go out for some fresh air, but whenever I get close to either of the doors, my heart starts to race. The constant darkness has screwed up the calendar in my head, and I have to use the one on her tablet to keep track of how long I've been here. Not that it makes any difference. By Memorial Day, I'm spending most of my time lying in bed, staring at the ceiling.

Bailey sneaks in that evening, the way she has every night, bringing me food and coffee. This time, she also brings news.

"I went by your house," she says. "Somebody's moved in. There's an SUV in the driveway and a bunch of broken-down boxes on the porch."

Anger and loss ricochet through me, doing major damage to everything they hit. But it's not like her news is any surprise. If people are buying their way into Cascadia, it only makes sense someone would take over our house. I want to ask for details, but I can't. It's easier to lie back and listen as Bailey recounts the two soccer games she played today, wrapping up a successful tournament weekend. My life has been reduced to living vicariously through a jock, and I don't even like sports.

Tuesday morning marks the beginning of my eleventh day in captivity. I spend it picking through the teen romances on Bailey's tablet, trying to find something I haven't already read. I'm getting sick of books where the love interest's only redeeming quality is being scorching, but it's not like I've got room to be picky.

It's noon before I realize I haven't eaten anything. I drag myself into the kitchen to make lunch. A simple box of macaroni and cheese—Grandpa's favorite—makes my eyes load up with tears. I blink them back, too exhausted to flog myself for being such a wuss. Why does every stupid little thing have to rip me into a million pieces? As I put water on to boil, I think of how he liked to mix peas and faux-tuna in with the noodles. And then I remember—*his notebooks!*

Out of nowhere, Grandpa's voice fills my head. "When I kick off, I want you to have my journals. There's a loose board in the hardwood floor under my bedroom window. Pry it up, and you'll find a cubbyhole. That's where I stash them."

Hope flares hot across my skin for the first time in over a week. Maybe they're still in the house. All the rest of our belongings have no doubt been hauled away, but how would the kidnappers find something like that?

An all-consuming need swells in me. I've *got* to have those journals. They're the only thing left of my family. A pulse of fear threatens to snuff out my excitement, but I squash it flat. Nothing is going to stop me from finding this one last link.

I think up a plan as I eat my lunch. It's a weekday, so the new people are probably at work or school. The windows in that house were replaced decades ago with the cheap vinyl kind, the ones with the little flip latches nobody in our family ever bothered to secure. It's easy to pry them up from outside. I should know, since Bailey snuck in that way often enough. That'll give me a direct route to Grandpa's room, and if I come and go through the backyard, anyone who might be watching the place won't see me.

It's a wonder I haven't thought of the journals sooner since I still have the notebook I bought Grandpa the night of the kidnapping. But it's been stashed in my backpack, along with my laptop, MedEval, and scrub shirt, and I haven't been able to bring myself to touch any of that stuff since the first morning I was here.

I unload the pack now and cram everything into the space between the bed and the wall. Sucking up my courage, I tuck my hair under the blond wig and sling my empty backpack over my shoulder. As I reach for the door, my fingers freeze on the handle. A flutter of palpitations takes over my heart. What if I get on the MAX and someone recognizes me? What if the kidnappers are waiting outside? What if someone thought to flip that stupid little latch on Grandpa's window?

For almost an hour I waver, changing my mind, sitting down to mess with Bailey's tablet, and then getting up and wandering back to the door. The indecisiveness makes my brain ache. I want those journals so bad I can practically feel them in my hands. But what if I get caught?

Damn it, Piper, stop being so paranoid! It's Bailey's voice I hear as much as my own. And it's right. I can't hole up in here forever. At some point, I'll have to do something. It might as well be now.

Before I can stop myself again, I take a deep breath and dart through the door into the cool, damp afternoon. The construction noise amps up my heart rate. I peer through the break in the shrubbery, step out into the parking lot, and slink along the overgrown vegetation until I'm near the sidewalk. A peek across the street tells me none of the workers are out in the open.

Act like you belong here, I tell myself. And then I do it. Ignoring my fear, and the wig's incessant itching, I walk to the MAX station. When the train comes, I use some cash Bailey gave me, rather than my transit card, to pay the fare. It feels like I'm wearing a giant neon "WANTED" sign, but no one looks twice at me the whole ride.

To get to the house, I cut down Woodward and sneak in the same way I got out the other night—through the yard that backs up to ours. Panic needles me the entire time, but I keep telling myself not to psych. I slink along the bushes that edge the yard and duck low to dash across the wet grass. Finally, I'm under Grandpa's window. A glance tells me no one's inside.

Without giving myself time to think, I pry off the screen, place my hands against the pane, and lift. My sweaty palms squeak uselessly against the glass. Crap. It must be locked. Now what? I give another desperate shove, and this time the window slides upward. *Yes!*

I boost myself onto the sill and drop down to a bed that's been pushed to within a foot of the wall. Glancing around, I step to the floor. The room is done up in purple, the walls plastered with posters of Jefferson Cooper's band and that anime character, Jyunsui, who's so popular with tween girls. A guitar rests on a stand in one corner. Stuffed animals—mostly frogs—line the shelves and desk, with one even snuggled up against an oxygen tank that sits on the side table.

That snags my curiosity, but there's no time to speculate. I move the end of the bed away from the wall, lifting so the feet won't screech against the hardwood. My pulse pounds as I crouch in the narrow space, feeling along the floorboards for a crack. With shaking hands, I pull out the pocket knife Bailey left me and use the screwdriver blade to pry up the board. Hair from the wig falls in my eyes. When I shove it back, I still can't see into the dim cubbyhole. *Damn.* I reach inside, scooping out everything my hand falls on. Eight notebooks, each about seven by nine inches, and a wad of cash wrapped in a fat rubber band. I stuff everything into my backpack and run my hand through the space one more time. Nothing left but the dusty wooden sides and bottom of the compartment.

I can't believe how easy this has been. Maybe Bailey's right, and I'm being paranoid. I fold up the knife and slip it into my pocket. As I'm replacing the board, the floor creaks outside the door. *Crap!* My heart slams into freak-out mode.

There's no time to scramble through the open window. All I can do is drop to the floor behind the bed and hope whoever's out there will go away.

No such luck. The door swings open. Someone steps into the room.

"What the hell?"

I lie on my stomach, holding my breath, willing myself to be invisible. *Go away, go away, go away.*

The silent prayer doesn't work. Footsteps cross the floor and stop at the end of the bed.

"What are you doing in here?"

The wig twists off my head as I roll over and glance up. A pale, skinny blond girl, who looks maybe eight or nine, stands at my feet.

"Please don't scream," I say, my voice low.

The girl rolls her eyes. "Do I *look* like a screamer?" She pauses to take a breath, and I realize she's wearing a PVAD vest. Well, that explains the oxygen.

"You're that girl from the news ... aren't you?" she asks. "Piper Hall?"

She knows that and she's not scared? "Yeah," I say. "But I'm not armed and dangerous, and I didn't steal those drugs." I lift my hands so she can see them, using my elbow to leverage myself against the bed as I get to my feet.

She stares at me—a challenging look without an ounce of fear in it. "Well, I guess that means I can't ... count on you to put me out of my misery."

"Magnusson-Bell?" I ask, nodding at her vest. The syndrome has a cyclical nature, so a portable ventricular assist device was designed specifically for kids who have it. Their hearts go through periods of recovery where they don't need the boost of a regular VAD.

"Yeah." The girl scowls, flipping long hair out of her face.

"That's rough."

"It's none of your ... business." Willpower alone seems to be keeping her upright. She's trembling—her body rigid with the effort to hide it—her breath quick and shallow and her lips slightly blue.

"Shouldn't you be using that oxygen?"

The girl glowers at me. "I've been a medically fragile child ... most of my life. I think I ... know what I can ... get away with. And if you're going to nag me ... I *will* scream." She has to stop to catch her breath. "What are you doing in my house?"

I'd like to sweep this kid into bed before she collapses, but she'd definitely make me regret it. "It used to be my house. I'm on my way out. I just needed to get something my grandpa left here."

"Why didn't he ... take it with him?"

"He didn't have time. Someone—" my voice catches a little, but I go on, "kidnapped him, along with the rest of my family."

"Really?" It's the only word the girl gets out before a fit of coughing chokes her. She grabs at the wall for support, her already-pale face blanching.

I step forward, hooking my arm around her shoulders to steer her into bed.

"Zoey, are you okay?" a guy's voice calls.

"You've gotta . . . get out of here!" the girl gasps. She tries to wiggle free to push the bed into place, but I don't let her. Shoving it back with one arm, I scoop her down on top of it with the other. I snatch up my wig and backpack, but before I can get to the window, the door squeaks open.

"What's going on in here?"

The only cover available is a chair in the corner. I make a dive but only wedge half my body behind it before a guy my age comes into the room. From his tousled blond hair and blue eyes, I can tell he's the girl's brother, even though he's got the firmly muscled body of an athlete, while she's a skinny twig.

Fortunately, it's her he focuses on. "Zoey—oxygen," he orders, shooting her a stern look that barely covers up the worry in his eyes. She scowls and reaches for the tubing on the table beside her bed.

I hold my breath, fists clenched, hoping he'll slip right back out that door. Instead, his gaze flicks toward the open window. When it comes to rest on me, he jumps but quickly gets a grip, hiding his surprise behind a perfect poker face.

"Who are you?" he demands, edging toward his sister.

Now that he's looking my way, it's obvious he's scorching. That messy blond hair, the smoldering, protective look on his face. Hell, I'm as bad as Bailey. My life is at stake, and my hormones decide to kick in?

"Nobody," I say. "I was just leaving." I slink out from behind the chair.

"Wait! You're that girl from the emergency alert." He sweeps across the room in one swift, fluid motion, grabbing my wrist. "What are you doing here? I'm calling the cops."

"Logan, no!" Zoey sits up, eyes big. "We have to help.... Someone took her family."

He turns toward his sister, his fingers solid as a handcuff around my wrist. "Are you crazy? She's a fugitive. They say she's armed and dangerous."

If I hear that line one more time, I swear I'm going to punch someone. "I just came for my grandpa's journals," I say, holding up my backpack. "They're all I have left of my family."

Logan swings to face me, his grip relaxing. "Okay, fine. Climb out that window right now, and I won't say anything. But I don't want to see you around here again."

"You've got it." I back away.

"Wait!" Zoey scrambles up to dig through the drawer in her bedside table.

"Damn it, Zoey," Logan says, going after her.

"She needs our help." The girl pulls something out of the drawer, pushes past her brother, and presses it into my hand. "Plug that into your computer and fire up ... Carrier Pigeon. It'll ask for a ... transport passphrase. Type in 'Frequent Deadly Lightning rocks.' I'll be in touch."

Logan scoops her off her feet. "No, you won't," he says as he puts her back in bed. He turns to me. "Get out of here."

"No," Zoey says. "I want to know ... what happened to her family."

I hesitate only a second before telling them what I came home to eleven days ago—the empty house, the guy chasing me. "We didn't do anything wrong, I swear. Not any of us."

For the first time, Logan's expression melts into something kind. "I'm sorry. But you need to go. Coming here was crazy. It's the first place they'll look."

He's right. I hitch my backpack over my shoulder and crawl out the window. I got what I came for, and that's all I care about.

CHAPTER 9

Logan

The moment the girl slips out of the room, Zoey starts in on me. "You shouldn't have ... made her go, Logan. I can help. ... If there's any trace of her family online ... I can find it."

I slide the window shut, cutting off the flow of moist, cool air, and turn to face her. "She wasn't safe here."

"She's not safe out there!" Zoey bolts upright in bed, her expression fierce. "We could've ... hidden her in the attic or something. She's probably ... living on the streets."

Typical Zoey—always eager to save every homeless soul, mistreated individual, and orphaned chipmunk.

"I'm sure she's got a place to stay."

"Yeah, right." Zoey rolls her eyes. "Like the Cascadian federal prison."

"You need to calm down. It's not good for you to get this excited."

Her gaze narrows and her lips scrunch into a pucker. "Maybe you should've thought about that ... before you kicked Piper out."

I fold my arms across my chest. "Do you want me to tell Dad about her?" I ask, giving her my best big brother glare.

If Zoey could breathe fire, I'd be a pile of ash. But she doesn't seem to realize I'm bluffing, and she settles against the pillows. "This isn't over, Logan."

I'm sure it's not. If I know my little sister, the second I leave, she'll be on her computer, sending a message to Piper Hall.

I go to my room to start my homework, but I can't get the girl out of my head. Her sad and desperate eyes, so dark brown they look black, still cut into me. Common sense dictates I should believe the emergency alert, but instinct tells me she wasn't lying, that she really did live in this house up until a little while ago. And that's what's so disturbing. If someone's snatching people out of their homes, the rumors I've heard are true. And maybe not just the ones about poor people being displaced.

I try to concentrate on trigonometry, but the numbers merge into an indecipherable jumble of sines and cosines. Did Dad lie to me? Is it possible he bought our way into Cascadia? I can't imagine that. He's so honest that when he works on his friends' computers, he claims the income on his taxes.

There must be some other explanation for what happened to Piper. Maybe it's a coincidence. After all, they wouldn't have orientation videos for new citizens if there wasn't a legitimate immigration policy, would they?

I've almost got myself convinced of this when I realize Piper's story solves a mystery that's nagged at me since we left home. If her family was deported, and she escaped, one less person left Cascadia than should have. Is that why Mom had to stay behind?

I click the Net icon on my laptop, bring up Google, and type in "Piper Hall." Each of the dozen hits repeats the story I already know, adding only that Piper's mother, brother, and grandfather recently moved to California and weren't available to comment. This last part immediately raises my suspicion. What parent wouldn't have something to say about an accusation like the one leveled against Piper? I enter her mother's name into the search box. Plenty of links come up, but nothing connected with California. Further research fails to reveal records of address, utility usage, or place of employment for Piper's mom or grandfather. Neither are registered to vote, and the younger brother, Nick, isn't enrolled in school. I know it's only been eleven days since they allegedly moved, but there should be something. What does this mean?

There's only one person who might have an answer, and he's

not home. But maybe there's another way to learn something.

I tell Denise, who's in her basement room absorbed in an online soap, that I'm going for a jog. After changing into sweats and running shoes, I head out into the mist.

At the end of the driveway, I stop to tighten a shoelace, discreetly glancing up and down the block. Whoever took Piper's family must still be watching the house, hoping she'll come back. That's what I'd be doing.

It's not as simple as spotting a sinister black surveillance van with tinted windows. I'm just hoping to see something that looks out of place. The street is lined with parked cars and trucks, all innocuous-seeming. I haven't been paying much attention, so I'm not sure which ones belong in the neighborhood.

Chances are, whoever's watching will be across the street where they'll have a better view, so I jog to that side and start down the sidewalk. All the vehicles I run past are empty, and none look unusual. Could they be monitoring the place remotely? I suppose it's a possibility, but it wouldn't be practical. If Piper showed up, they'd want someone on site to apprehend her. She must be smart to have snuck in and out of the house without being noticed.

With the fresh, sweet scent of blooming things drifting from people's yards, I jog down the block, enjoying my workout. This is the first real exercise I've had since we left Chicago. I've missed the fluid feeling of my muscles warming up and working together. As I round the corner, I pour on the speed, letting my worries fuel me.

The block we live on is as long as four regular ones, but for whatever reason, the numbered avenues don't bisect it. It takes me a few minutes to circle back around to our street. And then, as I'm closing in on the house, I see it. A non-descript silver Ford sedan. The lightly tinted windows barely allow me to discern a figure in the front seat. I note the model and plate number. This could just be some random person, sitting in his car for a moment after returning from an errand, but at least now I know what to watch for.

The run feels good, and Dad won't be home for a while, so I take a few more laps. The light rain soothes the heat from my face and arms. Back in Illinois, jogging anytime after the end of March was not for the faint of heart. I think I'm going to like this country—if I can just figure out what to do about my future.

Each time I pass the silver Ford, the man is still behind the wheel. It looks like my suspicions might play out. I'll have Zoey run a check on the plate number to see if she can learn anything.

As I go inside and resume my homework, I leave my bedroom door open so I'll know when Dad comes in. My head is clearer now. I make it through trig and English with no trouble. And then the front door creaks open.

A sick feeling wells up in me. I'm going to have to confront him. I thought I was ready, but I'm not. Despite the difficulty I've had winning my father's approval, I'd much rather go on being a disappointment than learn he's not who I've always thought he was. But I can't hide from the truth.

The short trip down the hallway feels longer than all the blocks I just jogged. I want to believe Dad will have a logical explanation, but deep down, I know he won't.

He pulls off his rain-slicked windbreaker and hangs it on a peg by the door. "Hey, Logan," he says, tossing me a perfunctory look that makes it clear he isn't really seeing me. "How's your sister? I got a message from the school and another from Denise. She said everything's okay, but she doesn't know Zoey the way we do."

"Zoey's fine."

Dad has those creases in his forehead that tell me he's worried. Usually, I'd go out of my way to reassure him, but this time, I don't care.

"Are you sure?" he asks. "She's not scheduled for her first

appointment at Doernbecher until next week, but if there's a problem, maybe they can get her in sooner."

"It's not an emergency. She just had to go on her PVAD, same as the last half dozen times. She'll feel better tomorrow." I can't keep the annoyance out of my voice.

"Then what's wrong? Why are you looking at me like that?"

For once, I have his full attention, but it only makes my resolve falter and my tongue freeze. I swallow, calling up the focus I learned on the football field. It doesn't matter how badly a botched play rattles you, you can't let yourself get flustered.

I clear my throat and stand up straighter. "Today I found out Piper Hall, the girl who's been in the news, used to live in this house." It takes all my willpower to keep my eyes locked on his.

"Is that so?" Dad glances beyond me toward the hallway.

"Yes. Up until a couple of weeks ago, in fact." Though the statement isn't quite an accusation, my pulse thuds in my ears.

"Interesting." He fidgets with his phone, twisting it on his wrist.

"Do you know anything about that?"

Dad tenses almost imperceptibly, his fingers going still. "Of course not."

I hate what I'm about to do, but there's no getting around it. Drawing a deep breath, I steel myself against the knowledge that my next question will change everything.

"Are you telling me the truth?"

"*What?*" His eyes snap up to bore into mine. "Just who do you think you're talking to?"

The evasion tells me what I need to know. "I *thought* I was talking to my father, the man who raised me to be honest and ethical. Maybe I'm wrong."

Dad's face flushes. "I'm not sure what you're getting at," he hedges, crossing his arms over his chest. "But I can say one thing. I'm not going to put up with this attitude."

I should be angry that even though he's the one at fault, he's trying to shift the blame to me. Yet the only thing I feel is disappointment. A deep, overwhelming sense of loss. All my life, I've looked up to my father. I'm not ready for that to change.

Calling up every bit of my courage, I venture the incriminating words. "I don't believe what you said about that headhunter recruiting you. Or why Mom had to stay behind." My nerve falters, but I force myself to press on. "I think you bought our way into Cascadia."

"That's ridiculous."

"Is it?" My voice sticks in my throat, a jagged lump that feels like it might tear a hole through me. I'm not sure what upsets me more, that he did something so dishonorable, or that he lied about it. "Just tell me the truth."

He shifts his weight, eyes focusing somewhere around my knees. "I don't owe you an explanation, Logan. I did what I had to for your sister."

"What the hell, Dad?" Despite my suspicions, the confession hits with the force of a grenade.

"You'd have done the same damn thing, so lay off," he barks, shouldering past me toward the kitchen.

And now I have my answer.

The question is, what am I going to do about it? Even if I had the courage to turn my father in, how could I? He's right. Zoey's better off in Cascadia, and I can't throw away the one chance she has.

But there *is* something I can do to counterbalance this injustice.

I have to help Piper Hall find her family.

THE McCALL INITIATIVE

EPISODE 1.2: REVELATION

LISA NOWAK

CHAPTER 1

Piper

As I jog down Woodward, my backpack, filled with Grandpa's journals, bounces against one shoulder. My breath rasps in my throat and uneasiness pinches my gut. Zoey's obviously no threat, but I'm not so sure about Logan. He could be on the phone right now, supplying the cops with a detailed description. Since there are only so many bus lines that cross through the Hosford-Abernethy neighborhood, the thought's almost enough to spook me out of taking public transit.

My brain gnaws on the problem as I zigzag back to 12th Avenue, where I decide to take my chances. It's a long walk from my former home to the White Eagle—over three miles—and as jumpy as I felt earlier riding the bus and the MAX, it would be a thousand times worse hoofing it out in the open.

I catch the 70 and find a seat, sweat trickling from under my wig and making my neck itch. I'm desperate to scratch, but force myself to sit still, one hand clamped around the other in my lap. Even though it's cool and damp outside, the bus feels stifling. I flinch with every pothole we hit. The only thing keeping my nerves from nuking out is the firm grip my teeth have on my lower lip.

Apparently, Logan's a true Boy Scout because I don't hear the *beep-beep-beep-squeal* of an emergency alert being posted to the cell phones of the numerous people around me. I don't see a flash of red and blue light signaling the bus to pull over. At Lloyd Center, I transfer to the MAX, like any normal person on any normal day, and in a few minutes, I'm at the Albina stop.

On Russell, the condo construction guys are milling around near the sidewalk. It's not even four. It'll be at least an hour until they go home. Heart thudding, I walk by, pretending I'm just passing through as I size up the situation. I swear, once I get inside that building, I'm not coming out until my name is cleared.

Except for the entrance to the parking area, the White Eagle's lot is fully fenced. No other way in unless I climb. Bailey's come and gone plenty of times, but mostly on weekends or in the evening when there's no construction. Still, I know she's been here during business hours, checking on the property for her dad. I'll probably be less of a sore thumb if I walk in like I belong, instead of scaling the fence in a ridiculous wig that might take a hike at any second.

I circle the block—like *that's* unobtrusive—and notice the condo guys aren't even looking at me. No one hollers when I cut into the lot. So far so good. I punch the code into the keypad with a spastic finger and duck inside. When the door shuts behind me, it muffles the construction noise, letting the jackhammer in my chest drown out the one across the street.

After wiggling out of my backpack, I collapse on the bed, totally whupped. Never again. This bar might be a dark, musty hole, but at least it's safe.

When I can breathe normally, I sit up and unzip my backpack. Along with Grandpa's eight journals, I pull out a wad of cash—fives, tens, and an occasional twenty. All told, it's just over $300. Even though it would barely be enough to pay a month's water bill, it must've taken Grandpa forever to sock it away. Maybe I should use it to help offset the cost of the food Bailey's been bringing me, but it's not really mine. Spending it would be as much as admitting Grandpa's gone for good. I stick it under the mattress before sorting through the journals.

Each of the seven-by-nine spiral notebooks has a date printed neatly on the cover, starting with 2057. I'm surprised they're so recent. I figured Grandpa had been keeping them all his life. After putting them in order, I open the earliest one: January 2057 – September 2057.

The very first words are pure Grandpa:

January 8, 2057 – What's the matter with this world? You'd think a man could find a spiral notebook. But no, I've gotta traipse all over the damn city, go to a dozen different stores. And when I finally find what I'm looking for, there's a paper surcharge. What the hell? This notebook's not even made from wood products. It's hemp. And where does that bozo in the White House get off thinking he's got a right to tax wood, anyway? Son of a bitch probably wouldn't know a tree if one fell on his head.

I grin, my eyes tearing as he goes on to complain about how the country's in a buttload of trouble: nobody's doing anything about the climate crisis, and all the politicians are idiots. Yup, that's Grandpa. He might have a screw loose when it comes to conspiracy theories, but at least he makes people laugh.

Mostly, the stuff he's written isn't personal. Just like his conversations, Grandpa's journals are crammed full of his opinions. He might go weeks without making an entry, and then he'll let loose with a five or ten-page rant. It's always something in the news that sets him off. The new pipeline authorized to carry water from the Columbia into Southern California. Overseas troops getting called home to help the National Guard deal with the superstorm-ravaged Gulf Coast. The government rushing approval of crops and cattle engineered to resist drought, in spite of the Magnusson-Bell disaster. One of his biggest beefs is companies taking over state governments that have gone bankrupt.

Haven't the corporations done enough damage in this country? I guess they couldn't be satisfied with pulling government strings behind the scenes. Now they've gotta outright run things. What's a name like Monsantesota supposed to mean, anyway? Land of 10,000 Chemicals?

I'm several entries into the journal before I come across something personal. My breath catches in my throat as I read a memory about my dad.

March 5, 2057 – Had dinner with Adam tonight. It's always a treat to spend time with him and his family. He's as worried about the mess we're in as I am. Says every time the East Coast hijacks our power, he sees more accidents. I guess those almighty self-driving cars don't like it so much when the traffic guidance beacons go down.

I remember Dad talking about that. He had nearly as many gripes about the government as Grandpa did, but at least he didn't think top-level scientists were plotting ways to divert rain clouds from the Pacific Northwest to the Great Plains.

Now, that Piper, she sure is a smart one. Ambitious too. Got all her daddy's brains and twice his drive. Barely eleven years old, and already has her heart set on being a doctor. When we got there this afternoon, she was sitting at the kitchen table, practicing stitches on a pig's foot. Even gave me a lesson on how it should be done. If there's any hope for our future, it's gotta be kids like her.

Tears fill my eyes, spilling out to drip on the page. My vision blurs, and I drop my head to my arms as shame rushes in and makes me bawl harder. I don't deserve his respect. I'm not the tough, spunky girl he thinks I am. I'm a pathetic mess. All I've done these past eleven days is feel sorry for myself. I'm not one step closer to figuring out what happened to him, Nick, and Mom, let alone saving them.

But as disgusted as I am with myself, I'm not ready to face the problems I have no idea how to fix. I sniffle, wipe my eyes, and go back to reading.

Not that there's a lot of hope. Take that jackass Goldstein. How he got re-elected, I'll never know. Son of a bitch treats the Northwest like a giant battery put here for his convenience. He never gives back a thing. Couldn't be bothered to help Seattle after the Great Quake. I know the country's in deep shit, but you don't just leave folks to drown in rubble and seawater after an 8.7 quake.

Much as it kills me to say it, if it weren't for Sarto, there probably wouldn't be a New Seattle. He might be an asshole, but as police chief, he took care of business after the quake. Not that I'm saying I agree with the fools up there, tossing out their mayor and giving him the job. Once a snake, always a snake, no matter how good you are at putting a nice shine on things for the public.

Huh. This makes it sound like Grandpa somehow heard about Sarto even before the guy was mayor. But that doesn't make sense. Grandpa was a grunt in the Army for twenty-five years, and when he got out, he worked in a hardware store. He never lived anywhere close to New Seattle.

The keypad outside the door beeps, and I jump. Bailey steps inside, wearing her blue and gold soccer uniform. With my phone gone and the windows blacked out, it's hard to guess what time it is, but my stomach tells me the thermo bag she's carrying probably holds our dinner. Bailey reaches into it, pulls out a huge burrito wrapped in plain white paper, and hands it to me.

"Chicken," she says. "I hope that's okay."

Sure. It just costs twice as much. I peel back the wrapper, letting out a delicious aroma. "Bailey, you've got to stop spending all this money on me. I'm fine with veggie beef or a chili relleno or something."

"Chicken's good for you," she says, taking a seat at our table along the back wall opposite the bed. "Plenty of protein. You'll probably get anemic hiding out here in the dark."

"You don't get anemic from a lack of sunlight. Vitamin D deficient maybe, but not anemic. Anyway, there's just as much protein in the fake stuff."

"Whatever." Bailey digs her own burrito out of the bag and unwraps it. "What's all that?" she asks, waving at the bed.

"My grandpa's journals." I take a bite. *Mmmm.* Pure burrito bliss. Food hasn't tasted good in a week, so I guess my terrifying ordeal must've done something for my appetite.

"Haven't seen those before. Where'd you get 'em?"

"I went back to the house. He had them stashed under the floorboards."

"What?" Bailey sits forward, nearly choking on a mouthful of burrito. "Are you completely whacked?"

A weird mix of shame and annoyance floods through me. "You're the one who was telling me I should go outside."

"Yeah, like out there," she jerks a thumb over her shoulder toward the jungle on the other side of the door. "I didn't say you should return to the scene of the crime. That's twenty kinds of stupid. You know that, don't you?"

Maybe. But I don't care. "I've been here eleven days, Bailey. We haven't made any progress. I'm sick of this place—sick of being such a damn coward. I can't sit here forever."

It's not exactly a fair thing to say. She's got to feel craptastic about telling me she was going to fix everything then smacking head on into a brick wall when it came to making it happen. But she doesn't tear me one for pointing it out. She just shakes her head.

"At least you didn't get busted."

Right. "Actually ..." I take a bite to give myself an excuse not to finish the thought.

Bailey's hand halts halfway to her mouth, tomato chunks spilling from her burrito. "Huh? Piper, what are you talking about?"

"I didn't exactly get away free and clear."

She stares, her mouth working silently, like she can't quite figure out which question to ask. "But ... you're here."

"Yeah. Because it wasn't the cops who caught me. It was a couple of kids—a little girl and her older brother."

"Are you kidding?"

I don't answer.

"So what did they do?" Bailey seems to realize her burrito is puking all over the scuffed-up floorboards and she takes another bite.

"Nothing. The brother threatened to call the cops, but the girl just wanted to help. She talked him out of turning me in." I remember the little device she shoved in my hand and dig it out of my pocket. It looks kind of like a flash drive. "She gave me this."

Bailey squints across the dimly lit room. "What's it for?"

"I'm not sure." I get up and join her at the table, where I left her tablet. Remembering Zoey's orders, I stick the device in one of the ports and fire up Carrier Pigeon, the chatware that comes factory-loaded onto most computers.

When I'm asked for a passcode, I type in, "Frequent Deadly Lightning rocks." Fortunately, the characters are hidden. If Bailey saw them, she'd never let me hear the end of it. I'm not exactly Jefferson Cooper's biggest fan. If it wasn't for the secession, Dad's hospital bills would've been paid by the National Health Service. And while Cooper probably didn't see that coming, he also didn't step up to help anyone in my family's position.

When I tap "enter," a chat box pops up. There's already a message, but the sender is no longer online.

Greengirl007: *I can help if you'll let me. You probably think I'm just a little kid, but I know a lot more than most people give me credit for.*

In case you're wondering, it's perfectly safe to communicate with me. The NetMax dongle encrypts everything. Just keep your computer on and logged into Carrier Pigeon, so you'll hear when I send you messages. Think it over and let me know what you want to do.

"How little is she?" asks Bailey, who's been reading the note upside down from across the table.

I shrug. "She looks eight or nine, but she's got Magnusson-Bell, and that stunts growth, so I'm guessing she's probably eleven or twelve."

Bailey eyeballs me like I suggested Zoey's going to sweep me off to safety on a magic carpet. "So some sick little kid is supposed to rescue you?"

"I never said that."

"What about her brother?"

"He's our age. And he's scorching. He'd probably willingly line up to be another of your conquests." I've never had a boyfriend, but Bailey collects them the way some people collect gasoline credits. Even though she's never serious about any of them, when they part ways, it's usually friendly.

"I'm perfectly happy with Simon."

I smirk. "At least until next week."

Bailey threatens to lob the remains of her burrito at me, but I know she'd never do it. All that soccer playing gives her the appetite of three teenage boys.

As if to prove my point, Bailey takes another bite. "So what are you gonna do?" she asks around a mouthful of chicken and refried beans.

I shrug. "Who knows? Guess I'll have to think about it." I'm not any more convinced than she is that a sick little kid can save me, but something has me feeling less defeated. I set up Carrier Pigeon to beep when I get a message and lay the tablet aside.

Bailey and I chat until she says she has to leave to do her homework. The mention of school sends a twinge through me. Now that I've got a hint of a chance—even if it's in the form of an 11-year-old girl with Magnusson-Bell—the idea of bailing on my junior year makes me want to bite my nails clear back to my wrists.

Once Bailey's gone, the quiet looms in to smother me. I satisfy myself with listening to the TuneZone station she's got set up on her tablet—all the latest hits—because I don't want to put up with the grief she'll give me if I start my own. "Why do you listen to that old man music?" she always teases. "It's depressing." She's only kidding, but it makes me feel like a freak. So what if I like blues? After Dad died and Grandpa moved in with us, that's what I heard coming out of his room. Somehow, it just felt right. I've got a ton of Buddy Ray Tompkins and Mama Dupree on my laptop, but I'm still worried pressing the power button might bring a SWAT team swarming down on me, so I can't get to it.

Since I've finished all the decent books on Bailey's tablet, I go online using her Amazon account and download a few more. Even though she's given me permission to buy whatever I want, I limit myself. I already owe her a ton, and that's just counting the physical things she's given me, like food and clothing. But there are only so many teen romances I can stomach.

I'm just getting into the latest Stellinger medical thriller when the tablet beeps and the Carrier Pigeon box pops up, displaying a new message from Zoey.

GreenGirl007: *My brother finally came around. He's got a good plan. Can you meet us tomorrow after school? You name the place.*

A whisper of hope sweeps through me, crashing right into a rush of foreboding. Maybe Zoey and Logan can help, but why would they? If we find my family, won't it mean they'll get deported? Maybe they're setting me up so they can turn me over to the cops.

Since I'm not sure how to answer, I ignore the message. What can these two do anyway? They're just kids. Kids I have every right to resent, considering my family would still be around if it wasn't for them. Besides, the thought of leaving the White Eagle again sends a 6.0 aftershock through my gut. Look what happened this time.

But the idea won't leave me alone. After I go to bed, I lie awake thinking about it. And about them. Zoey's brash and snarky, nothing like my little brother, who's a cut-up with a wild imagination. But somehow, she reminds me of him. A memory from a few years ago sneaks past my defenses.

It's summertime, and Bailey and I are camping out in the backyard. Nick's there too, jammed between us because he always has to be in the middle of whatever we're doing. As we lie in our sleeping bags, staring up at the tree branches shifting in the wind, Nick says, "What if there is no wind? What if the trees are moving all on their own?"

A chill goes through me. Now the branches are arms, thrashing in a furious tantrum.

"Nick," Bailey says. "You are one spooky little dude."

I shine my flashlight on the big Doug fir in the neighbor's yard. "Hey, tree," I yell. "Can you hear me?"

Bailey slaps my hand. "Quit that, Piper! You're gonna piss it off."

My lips twist into a smile, but that doesn't stop the tears from filling my eyes. Nick was always coming up with crazy stuff like that. Seeing things no one else did, or telling stories that cracked everyone up. The one about Bigfoot skateboarding through Washington Park in swim trunks was so funny it made Grandpa snort beer out his nose.

I take a deep breath and wipe the tears away with the back of my hand. The sad truth is, unless I trust Logan and Zoey, I have no chance of seeing Nick again. Maybe they're trying to trap me, but if there's even a remote possibility they can help, I can't afford to pass it up. No matter how scared I am, I owe it to my family to try.

I get out of bed, wake Bailey's tablet, and type a message to GreenGirl007 – *Meet me at Coffee Madness on Broadway at four o'clock.* After adding a link to the café's website, I hesitate a second before sucking up the nerve to press "post" with a shaking finger.

There. It's done. I might be signing my own death warrant, but at least this way I'll be able to meet my fate without feeling like a wuss.

CHAPTER 2

Logan

It's after eight, and I'm still wrestling with the enormity of Dad displacing a family to make room for us in Cascadia, when he knocks on my door.

"Logan, may I come in?"

I'd like to growl at him to get lost, but arguing will only keep the issue on his radar. Leading him to believe he's won might make him drop his guard. If I want to help Piper, it's important to have him looking the other way.

"Sure," I say, careful to keep my voice neutral.

Dad eases the door open and steps inside. "Someone at work told me about a pub up on Powell. I'm heading over there for an hour or so."

Zoey's sick and he's going out for a drink?

The look he gives me suggests he's read my thoughts. "Your sister's fine. Denise is in the living room, and I'll be less than ten blocks from here."

I nod. This shouldn't surprise me. He skulks away from conflict whenever possible. "Of course. I'll give you a call if anything happens, but I'm sure she'll be fine." It takes all my composure to make the statement sound both civil and believable. I don't want to do anything to discourage him. I need to talk to Zoey, and with Dad out of the house, there's less chance of being overheard.

He meets my gaze then looks away, running a hand through his hair. "I'm sorry, Logan. The move—it wasn't a decision I made lightly. But you know I'd do anything for your sister. For you, too."

These last words stir something inside me, even though I'm not sure I believe them. "I guess you did what you had to."

Dad nods. "I'll see you in a while."

I listen as his footsteps fade down the hall. The front door closes, and I wait for the Toyota's engine to start. When it doesn't, I sneak a look out the window. He's walking. As soon as he rounds the corner of 21st, I go to Zoey's room and knock.

"Enter," she says, as though she's royalty.

I slip inside. Zoey looks like royalty, too, sitting upright in bed, her purple robe draped over her shoulders to hide the hated PVAD vest.

"I've been doing some research," I say, keeping my voice low and pulling the door fully shut behind me. "I think you're right about Piper. We need to help. Can you send her a message?"

"Already done." Zoey drills me with a look that says I'm not entirely forgiven. "I'm just waiting for her to get back to me."

"Good." I take a seat on the edge of her desk. "When she does, see if you can get her to meet us someplace after school tomorrow."

The hostility begins to fade from my sister's expression. She reaches behind herself to adjust the pillows. "Why'd you change your mind?"

"Because of Mom. I never fully bought into her reason for staying in Chicago. Since Piper was obviously supposed to be taken the same night as her family, it made me think there might be some sort of one-on-one trade to get into the country. When she didn't go, Mom had to stay behind."

The last of Zoey's anger evaporates as the implication sinks in. "So she's not coming."

"Probably not." My throat tightens around the words. The more I recall of our mother's behavior, the more certain I am of my theory. Every time she's called or emailed, I've sensed something dark in the background. Something hiding behind her upbeat words. Is that simply because she knows she'll never come to Cascadia, or is she complicit in Dad's plan? I can't stomach the idea. It's unsettling enough to learn that the father I've always respected is capable of deceit.

Though I suspect Zoey understands what she's committing to, I have to be sure. "If we were to turn Piper in, they might let Mom into the country," I say, "but—"

"It wouldn't be right," she interrupts. "Piper belongs here. Her whole family belongs here."

"Exactly. You should know what we're getting into though. If we get caught, we could be deported."

Zoey's chin juts out and her voice goes sharp. "We have to do it, Logan. At least we've got each other. Piper doesn't have anyone."

I've thought about that, too. Even though I only saw her for a few moments, my mind's eye is branded with Piper's expression—so scared, and yet so determined. I feel as compelled as Zoey does to help her. And not just because it's the honorable thing to do.

But there's one detail I haven't mentioned. I run my fingers along the desktop, debating whether or not I should tell Zoey the rest. "Look, Sparky," I finally begin. "There's something else."

"Okaaay . . ." she says, waiting.

I draw a deep breath. Zoey worships our dad. If learning the truth shocked me, what will it do to her? But it's only a matter of time before she adds it up, and I'd rather that happen when I'm around to handle the fallout.

"We didn't come here because Dad got recruited by a head-hunter," I say, pausing as I gather the courage to voice my next words. "He bought our way in."

Zoey gasps, her eyes wide, and I can see the gears turning, the switches flipping one by one until she's put it together. Her face goes red, her fists clenching handfuls of purple comforter. "He did it because of me, didn't he?"

She's about to go nuclear, and I can't blame her. I also can't let it happen. "I know that's got to frost you. But if he finds out you know, he'll be watching even more closely than usual, and that will make it harder for us to help Piper. You've got to keep this to yourself."

At some point, she's going to be devastated. Right now, she's just furious. A battle rages in her eyes, and for a moment, I'm afraid she's going to scramble out of bed to grab her phone and give Dad a piece of her mind. But her true nature wins out, a glimmer of determination sparking behind her barely controlled fury. "So you have an idea? Because I don't. I had zero luck searching the Net, and without any leads, there's nothing I can do."

"Actually," I say, "there's *plenty* you can do." I move over to sit beside her on the bed while I outline my plan.

CHAPTER 3

Piper

Wednesday morning, I read the rest of Grandpa's first journal. When I'm finished, I reach for the second, but my hand stops halfway. These notebooks are the only connection I have to my family. When I come to the final words, that'll be it. I grab Bailey's tablet instead and go online to research Magnusson-Bell.

I already know the basics: the syndrome first showed up about twenty years ago, the result of an experiment gone wrong. Scientists were trying to create a breed of cattle that didn't need as much water, but the virus they were using for the gene-splicing mutated and went airborne.

At first, no one noticed. The symptoms of the disease it caused were a lot like those of the common cold. But a percentage of the population—old people, little kids, and anyone with a compromised immune system—went on to develop slow but progressive heart failure. By the time someone figured out what was going on, hundreds of thousands of people had been infected, with the largest population being babies and toddlers. Most of these kids wound up dying between the ages of ten and fifteen.

They've been working on a cure ever since, but the efforts haven't gotten far. The kids aren't even good candidates for transplants because the virus stays in their system and goes on to attack the new heart. But that's not the worst of it. They also metabolize medications differently, especially anesthetics and anti-rejection drugs, so early attempts at transplants didn't go well.

What I'm interested in now is the latest advances. The study at Doernbecher seems to be getting the best results.

They've developed a drug that extends the periods of remission MB is known for. If Zoey can get in, she might have a chance of at least making it into her twenties, and by then, there might be more options. Of course, if she's still using a PVAD rather than an implant device at her age, she's doing better than most.

I read until three, when it's time to leave for Coffee Madness. It takes me another fifteen minutes to fire up my courage. I can't believe I'm doing this again—leaving my safety zone. What kind of idiot am I? Every ounce of sense and self-preservation tells me to stay right where I am, but I need to know if this plan Logan's supposed to have might work. And I'm sure as hell not telling the two of them to meet me here.

My heart starts hammering before I even step out the door. I force myself to take long, deep breaths and concentrate on the pride Grandpa has in me—pride I've done absolutely nothing in the past twelve days to earn. Somehow, I manage to get outside and make the trip without fainting dead away or going into cardiac arrest.

Since I want a chance to scout out the situation, I show up fifteen minutes early. The rich scent of coffee fills my nose when I walk in, making me feel better and worse at the same time. It's been almost two weeks since I've been in a place like this.

I try not to psych as I order my drink and give my name as Cindy. Nobody seems to notice that my dark eyebrows don't match my blond hair, or that my face belongs on a Cascadia's Most Wanted poster.

Once I have my coffee, I choose a seat facing the door. My fingers rattle against the tabletop in quick succession as I stare at the entrance. After about ten minutes, Logan and Zoey come in. He goes up to the counter to order while his sister walks over to me. Even though it's seventy outside, she's wearing one of those jackets with the animated graphics on it. Jyunsui—the character who was on the posters in her bedroom—now doing some kickass ninja move, over and over.

"Hey," Zoey says, pulling out a chair and sitting down.

I gulp out a "hi." Small talk has never been my forte. Do they plan on discussing everything right here? Nobody minds anyone else's business in a coffee shop, but it's not like we're going to be gossiping about my neighbor's affair with the pizza delivery guy.

Zoey sinks back in her seat, zipping her jacket up further over her PVAD vest. She's still pale, but she's not having trouble breathing today. I don't comment on that. Not after the way she tore me one when we first met.

"You think this rain is ever going to end?" she asks.

Easy topic. Any Portlander could write a thesis on the subject. "Sure, probably in a couple of weeks. Then we'll barely see another drop until the middle of October." I want to ask her where she's from, but I figure that'd be almost as suspicious as talking about my own problems. From what I've heard, only a few people with specialized skills have been allowed to immigrate into the country.

Zoey asks if I know about the anime character, Jyunsui, and when I say I don't, she fills me in. Half-listening, I glance at Logan, who's now waiting for the barista to whip up his drinks. Bailey would consider him a particularly tasty variety of eye candy.

The barista calls out the name "Bobby," and Logan goes up to collect two cups. Interesting. He doesn't want anyone to know who he is either.

He comes over to our table and gives one of the drinks to Zoey. "Let's go."

"So we're not going to talk here?" That's a relief. Sort of.

"Are you kidding?" Zoey reaches inside her jacket to pluck at her PVAD vest. "I hate people seeing me in this thing. Anyway, it'll be more private in the car."

She stands up, and for a few seconds, I stay where I am. Are they messing with me? Trying to get me into their vehicle so they can cart me off to the nearest police station?

"I know it's asking a lot, expecting you to trust us," Logan says. "Nothing I can say is going to change that. But we really do want to help." His blue eyes cut into me, Boy Scout honest. This guy's either one hundred percent trustworthy or the world's best con artist.

He doesn't convince me, but I've come this far, and if I wasn't willing to take a chance, there was no point leaving the White Eagle. I grab my drink and stand up.

Zoey and Logan lead me out through the rain to a metallic gold Toyota Cypress that's sporting a "Cooper '63" bumper sticker. No surprise there. The president is practically the patron saint of Cascadia. The other candidates might as well give it up now and save themselves the headache of another five months of campaigning.

Zoey gets in back, so I reach for the front door handle. I only debate a second before pulling on it. Maybe it's crazy to get inside, but it's even more whacked to stand in the middle of an open parking lot where everyone and their dog can get a good look at me.

I feel a little better after I've closed the door to shut out the world, but I can't make my fingers release their death grip on the armrest. Logan programs something into the navigation console. The SUV pulls onto Broadway. A few blocks down the road, we merge onto I-5 south.

"Where are we going?" It's taking everything I've got to keep my anxiety in check. But if they wanted to bust me, wouldn't we be heading downtown?

"Nowhere in particular," Logan says. "We're just driving."

I manage to let go of the armrest, and that hand immediately joins the other, clutching my coffee cup like it holds the key to my salvation. Maybe it does. I take a slug, letting the caffeine rush in to comfort me.

Logan types one more thing into the console before turning in my direction. His blue eyes are kind and steady. Not the eyes of a guy who tricks people into trusting him. "I have to say, you've really impressed me, Piper. I'm not sure I'd have the courage to get into a vehicle with a couple of strangers if I were in your position."

His approval feels strangely satisfying. "It's not like I have a lot of options."

"Well, I want to put your mind at ease." He clears his throat and looks away, taking a long breath before he goes on. "Our father has as much as admitted he bought our way into Cascadia. Our mother was supposed to come with us, but at the last minute she couldn't. I suspect that's because you escaped when the rest of your family was kidnapped." He hesitates again, staring at the navigation console, his thumb going back and forth over the corner of it. "Zoey and I don't condone what our father did. We want to try to make it right."

Whoa. This is definitely not what I was expecting. "How?" I ask, risking a peek out the rain-spattered window. I feel like I'm in a rolling display case. Like at any second, someone might glance over and recognize me.

"Good question. The way I see it, the problem is that no one believes in the disappearances. We have to convince people they're real. The best way to do that is to go public with a statement straight from the mouth of someone whose family was abducted."

Right. Simple. No problem at all. "And how are we going to do that?"

"We'll make a video. Zoey here," Logan hitches his chin at his sister, "is a computer genius. She's got the equipment and the know-how. For the first broadcast, we'll use the Emergency Alert System. But that will only work once, so we'll have to follow up on Connect Me and YouTube."

Is he serious? "How's that even possible? Hasn't everything

been hacker-proof for, like, thirty years?" Grandpa used to talk about people who'd Houdini their way into government websites or broadcast stuff that made the public believe zombies were taking over the world. But that was a long time ago.

"There are two kinds of hacking," Zoey says. "You're right about the technical stuff. It's nearly impossible. But there's also social engineering."

I turn to look over my shoulder. With my back to the window, I feel a little less exposed, but I'm still itching to escape to the safe darkness of my hideout. "What's social engineering?"

"Tricking people into giving you what you want. You know, like phishing. It'll actually be pretty simple to put this together, but we'll need someplace to do the filming. Not our house—Logan says someone's watching it. Plus, there's my nurse." Zoey stops talking, like she's waiting for a response. I don't have one to give her.

"How about your place?" she asks after a few heartbeats. "Where are you staying?"

A needle of panic jabs me. "You think I'm going to tell you?"

Zoey gives me a why-wouldn't-you look.

"It's not necessary," Logan says, shooting a warning glance over the seat. "We can figure out something else."

She answers with a belligerent glare. "What's the big deal?"

"The 'big deal' is Piper's already taken a huge chance by trusting us. We can't expect her to give up the only security she has." His eyes shift from hers to mine, and the understanding in them totally derails me.

"But we're trying to help," Zoey says. As if that should be enough to make me follow her to the ends of the earth.

"And she doesn't know us. Look, Sparky, I might be privy to the fact that you're the most awesome individual on the planet, but Piper hasn't had the benefit of being around you for the past eleven years. You need to give her a break."

"Fine." Zoey slumps in her seat, arms across her chest, and

scowls out the window.

One corner of Logan's mouth twitches. He shakes his head and turns back to me. "Do you have any idea where we could do the filming?"

"No." Even if I did, there's no way in hell I'm leaving my sanctuary again. The sooner I get back to the White Eagle, the better.

"Okay. Well, let me give it some thought. I'm not that familiar with Portland, but maybe I can come up with a place."

There's something calming about Logan. Like he's aware of everything around him and has complete control of the situation. Dad was that way. When the neighbor kid cut off half his foot with a lawn mower, Dad not only handled the first aid, but also calmed him down and kept his parents from freaking out.

I want to trust Logan. I'm tired and broken and ready to hand this whole damn problem over to someone else. Maybe he's using social engineering to con me into doing what Zoey wants, but I don't think so.

"Do you really believe this broadcast idea will work?" I ask.

He nods. "Yeah."

I let my head fall back against the seat as I look out the windshield at a city full of people who want to lock me up. Only three are on my side, and I'm not really sure I can trust two of them. But I'm sick of being so damned scared and helpless.

"Okay," I say, pausing to pull in a breath that doesn't do a thing to settle my nerves. "I'll show you where I've been hiding."

CHAPTER 4

Logan

Piper says she's staying at the White Eagle Saloon, so I type that into the navigation console. The Toyota takes us to a derelict brick building not far from the waterfront on the east side.

"Don't pull into the parking lot," Piper warns. "Just drive by."

When I do, she glances at a construction site where a new building is going up across the street.

"Good," she says. "Everyone's gone home. Find someplace to park a couple of blocks from here, and we'll walk back."

"Zoey's not good for long distances," I say.

"Speak for yourself!" grunts my sister.

"Oh, right." Piper nods. "Just let us out around the corner then."

I program the Toyota to drop us off half a block away and then find itself a place to park. Piper leads us through the White Eagle's empty lot to an entrance near the back which is concealed by an overgrowth of vegetation. Her hand shakes as she raises it to a keypad. She looks at me, and I get the message. She might be taking us straight to her doorstep, but she's not giving us the code to get in. I turn away. The keypad beeps.

"Okay," Piper says. We follow her inside, where she turns on the lights, small bell-shaped fixtures that protrude from the walls at the height of the few remaining tables. They don't provide much illumination.

Piper pulls off her wig and runs a trembling hand through her short, dark hair. "Well, this is it."

"Whoa," Zoey breathes. "This is the coolest hideout ever."
Stepping to the right, she traces her fingers along the top of a

bar made from a beautiful natural wood.

"It's a pit of despair," Piper says. "But at least it feels safe."

I marvel at the courage it must've taken, not only to meet us, but also to bring us here. The entire country is after her. She must be terrified. But even so, her pale oval face is set in a look of determination that creates a sudden turbulence inside me.

I do a quick inventory of our surroundings. The building, with its brick walls and hardwood floors, looks like it could easily have been around since the turn of the 20th century. Across from us and to our left is a raised platform with a mattress on top. Maybe a stage of some sort. Piper steps onto it to flip another switch, and more lights, mounted higher on the west wall, begin to glow. They're amber-colored and torch-shaped, no doubt replicas of the tavern's original gas-powered illumination. Like the first set, they don't do much to fight off the darkness.

In the middle of the back wall, beside the stage, there's a door leading into a short hallway, and in the other rear corner, a booth that Piper seems to have claimed as her personal space. A coffee cup, a plate with the remains of a meal, and an HP tablet rest on top. A stack of spiral notepads leans against the wall. The journals she'd said she'd come to the house for?

"Is this your only computer?" Zoey asks, taking a seat at the booth. She's puffing a little, so I suspect the question is as much an excuse to sit down as genuine curiosity. If I were her, I'd be as reluctant to admit my weakness as she is. Still, it pains me to see how much effort she exerts, trying to appear the same as everyone else.

"No. That's my friend Bailey's. I have a laptop. I'm just scared to use it."

Zoey looks up with an expression of genuine puzzlement. "Why?"

"I've heard people can trace you that way."

"Not likely." She shakes her head. "They'd need to have the

MAC address for the specific network interface in your computer. I mean, sure, the guys who tried to kidnap you might've ransacked your house, found the receipt, and subpoenaed the manufacturer for their customer records, but it's doubtful." She glances around. "Where is it? Can I have a look?"

"I guess." Piper walks over to the mattress, reaches behind it, and pulls out a laptop. When she sets it on the table, Zoey fires it up.

"So I don't have to worry about the cops being able to track me?" Piper asks, sliding into the booth across from her.

"Probably not." Zoey's fingers scramble over the keyboard. "But just to be safe, I'm routing you through a VPN. Now if anyone tries to track you, it'll look like you're using this computer from someplace in Australia."

"Huh." Piper folds her arms in front of her on the table. "What if I log into Amazon or Connect Me? You know, one of those places where I've got an account."

"Doesn't matter. They might know it's you, but they won't be able to figure out where you are. Anyway, those are American companies. They're not going to give a rat's right foot about what the cops in a Cascadian city have to say." Zoey types something else and shakes her head. "Sheesh. Don't you ever defrag this thing? It's running like a bloated sloth."

Piper shrugs. "Computers aren't exactly my specialty."

"That's okay," Zoey says, her gaze on the laptop screen. "I'll fix you up."

"Do you think you could get me another one of those Net-Max things, too? My friend Bailey needs one. It's a pain in the butt not being able to communicate with her."

"Sure. I'll bring it next time."

"Thanks." Piper turns to face me. "So why do we have to do this video, anyway? Wouldn't it be easier to track down the people your dad paid to get into Cascadia? I mean, there's got to be evidence somewhere, right?"

"Zoey's already been through his computer. He's wiped out anything that might be incriminating. The best we've been able to do is trace the license plate of the car that's been watching our house. It's registered to Portland Rent-a-Ride."

"And, no," Zoey says before Piper can ask. "I can't bust into their computers to figure out who rented it."

Piper nods. "Okay then. I guess the video's our only option. So how's this plan of yours supposed to work?"

I pull a chair away from one of the tables, flip it around, and sit on it backward. "Are you familiar with the Enigma?"

"Ugh," Zoey groans, rolling her eyes without looking away from the computer. "You'll have to forgive him. He's a history geek."

I shoot my sister a look. "I'll try to keep the boring details to a minimum."

The comment coaxes a smile from Piper. "Never heard of it," she says.

"Well, back in World War II, the Germans had machines called Enigmas that encoded messages. They used them not only when transmitting military information, but also the data gathered from small ships stationed in the North Atlantic that they used as weather stations. When the British figured out that these ships, which were only minimally armed, had Enigma machines and codes, they started going after them. It didn't occur to the Germans to worry when they lost one. They assumed the enemy wouldn't be interested in them since they were only weather stations. But through the capture of a couple of these ships and a U-boat, the British were able to gain information that was helpful to their cause."

Piper's listening, but her bewildered expression shows she has no idea what this has to do with her. "Interesting," she says.

"Logan," Zoey prompts, "get to the point."

"The point is, we need to send a message to the public. Decades ago, it might have been possible to hijack a television or radio broadcast, like Orson Welles did with *War of the Worlds*, but since everything's Net-based now, there's only one access point to the masses: the Emergency Alert System. By law, every computer, phone, and other Net-capable device has to be able to receive EAS messages. And since it's virtually impossible to break through the security features, that means we'll have to take a back door approach. I can just about guarantee the U.S. and Cascadian governments aren't any more worried about securing weather stations than the Germans were. So that's our in." I hope I sound more confident about this than I feel. In theory, it should work. But theories don't always play out the way they're expected to.

"And where are we going to find a weather station?" Piper asks.

I cross my arms over the chair back and lean forward. "There are thousands of them in remote areas all over North America. Mostly, they're used to collect and send data to government agencies, but because they're part of the early warning network for things like tsunamis, floods, and super-storms, they're also tied into the Emergency Alert System. Up until about twenty years ago, meteorologists would interpret the information and determine when to notify the public, but now that forecasting models are so accurate, it's faster and safer to let computers take charge."

Piper slides deeper into the booth until her back is against the wall. "Okay, so we somehow find one of these weather stations—"

"Not a problem," Zoey says. "There are maps on the Net, and we can use a GPS receiver to pinpoint the location."

"Right." Piper glances at her. "So we find the station and broadcast a message. But then what? You think one girl saying her family disappeared will make a difference?"

"Maybe not with the first message," I say. "That'll just make people aware of the issue and direct them to your Connect Me page. But we'll post follow-up videos there and on YouTube. Zoey will also build a website containing static information and a form for collecting data on other disappearances. If we can stir up enough interest, people will tune in and pass along the news. Zoey can help spread the word with her Connect Me personas. She's got three, in addition to herself."

"Six, actually," Zoey says.

Looking skeptical, Piper drums her fingers on the table's surface. "And what's all this public awareness supposed to do? Goad the government into taking action? You really think that'll work?"

"I'm not convinced the government isn't part of it," I say. "The police involvement and the fact that you've been set up as a criminal make it pretty clear whoever's in charge has connections."

Piper scowls. "Yeah, well, that doesn't surprise me. The president's the reason my family was poor enough to be targeted to begin with. Maybe he's trying to get rid of the evidence."

Zoey stiffens, her pale face ominous in the glow of the computer screen, and gives Piper the evil eye. "He wouldn't do that!"

While I'm not naïve enough to believe Cooper doesn't have enemies, I didn't expect any of them to be 17-year-old girls. "It's not necessarily the federal government," I venture, hoping to avert a Zoey meltdown. "It could be state or local. We don't even know whether the disappearances are country-wide or concentrated here in the Portland area. Anyway, I doubt the president is involved. There's no evidence he's done anything remotely criminal in the past, and I don't read it in his character."

Piper blows out an exasperated breath, letting her head fall back against the bricks. "Why does everyone think that guy is such a freakin' saint?"

"Because he's a good person," Zoey says. "He's the only one on the entire continent doing anything about the climate crisis. Even the Canadians are dropping the ball." Her slitted eyes and rigid shoulders somehow render her slight figure formidable. "Logan's right. President Cooper isn't the one responsible for this."

Piper looks from Zoey to me and shakes her head. "Okay, fine. It doesn't matter. I don't care who's responsible. I just—" Her voice catches, and she stops to take a breath, "—want my family back."

Something twinges inside me, though I'm not sure it's empathy so much as guilt over being inadvertently responsible for her loss. "All right then. The first thing we need to do is write a speech. It has to be carefully crafted to appeal to the public psychologically, and I've read a lot of them, so I'll take care of that."

"Good," Piper says, her voice now steady. "'Cause I'd probably just rant and piss everyone off."

A smile pulls at my lips. "We definitely don't want that."

Relieved she's giving us the chance to help, I outline the rest of the plan. "We'll need some decent lights for filming in here, but I can pick those up. Zoey's already got the camera and video editing equipment. It's going to take the better part of a day to do this and get it right, so I suggest we wait until Saturday. Is that okay with you?"

Piper shrugs and pulls her legs up in front of her on the booth seat. "I guess. Maybe my friend Bailey can give us a hand, if she doesn't have a soccer game."

"That's the person you need the NetMax dongle for?"

"Yeah," Piper says. "Her dad owns this place. It's supposed to get torn down so they can build condos, but that's not going to happen till next winter."

"It's a good hideout," I say, taking another look around. "We'll be careful not to let anyone see us as we come and go."

Though I mean to reassure her, Piper responds with only a slight nod, not meeting my eye.

A pang shoots through me. Zoey and I might have lost our mother, but Piper's lost everything—her family, her freedom, even her future. The only thing she had left was the security of this refuge, and I've forced her to give that up. "Bringing us here must've been frightening," I say. "But I promise, we're going to be very discreet about all of this. We won't do anything to put you in danger."

Piper wraps her arms around her raised legs, and her lips twist into a half-hearted smile. "Well, I guess it's too late for second thoughts, so I'll just have to trust you on that."

CHAPTER 5

Piper

Bailey decides to go to the Timbers game after all Friday night, despite the fact that President Cooper will be descending upon the masses with his full Secret Service entourage. Since she has soccer practice after school, that means I don't get to see her at all. It shouldn't matter, but it does.

Logan and Zoey haven't been back since Wednesday, but at least now I'm sure I can trust them. Even though Bailey insists I was twenty kinds of stupid for revealing my hiding place, I'm still here. Besides, I now have full use of my laptop so I can listen to my own music without fear of being mocked. The lonely wail of harmonica and soul-soothing rhythm of walking bass help fill up the big empty space around me.

When I'm done with dinner—the first I've had to cook in a while thanks to my best friend's daily delivery service—I open Grandpa's second journal. In his world, it's now December 2057, a couple of months after Frequent Deadly Lightning released *The Tom McCall Song*. Jefferson Cooper's being bombarded with requests to talk about the climate crisis, and he's become Grandpa's hero.

December 16, 2057 – Cooper held another rally today. Says the states in the Pacific Northwest need to secede, and wants British Columbia to come along for the ride. Canada's almost as bad off as we are, so people are listening.

There's this idea that's been around for over 80 years—a country called Cascadia, with boundaries drawn around the Columbia River basin. Since the Columbia's what everyone wants, either for its water or power, that's what Cooper figures we've gotta protect. He's been giving Goldstein hell, telling him the climate refugees are ruining everything and we can do a better job of managing our own damn resources. Cooper thinks the U.S. should admit it's futile to go on farming the Midwest and put solar panels there instead. He's pissed the government isn't doing crap to build new power infrastructure. But why would they when it's so easy to go on stealing our electricity?

I can't recall the last time I heard anyone talk so much sense. Maybe Cooper should give up his music gig and run for Congress.

I grin. If only Grandpa knew what was coming. As I read the next entry, dated a few weeks later, it's weird to see history I barely remember unfolding through his eyes. One thing's for sure. It's a lot more interesting than learning about it at school.

January 3, 2058 – Seems like this Cascadia deal might actually be going somewhere. Cooper's managed to wrangle Senator Daskalov's attention, which is a good thing, because as much passion as that boy has, he doesn't know squat about politics. They've got an official document drawn up now—The McCall Initiative. I had to laugh when I heard that. McCall was way before my time, but he sure made a name for himself, telling people they should visit Oregon but not stay. Same thing Cooper wants for Cascadia. The land and economy just can't support this huge rush of people.

He says he's gonna take his idea to all the state governments in the region and have them call a special election. Don't ask me how he'll get California, Montana, and Wyoming—let alone British Columbia—to let go of that prime real estate, but if anyone can do it, it'll be him. That young fella's really got it together.

All this Cooper hype shouldn't surprise me. Grandpa never had anything bad to say about the guy, other than that he ought to learn to take a little advice now and then. Whatever *that* was supposed to mean.

I close the journal and set it aside. Grandpa would tear me

one for blaming our financial problems and the kidnappings on the president, but I can't let it go. Someone who cares that much about Cascadia ought to care about the people who live here.

One thing's for sure. I need to be careful about mouthing off in front of Zoey. She's obviously under Cooper's spell, and the last thing I want is to piss off the only ones who might be able to help me.

Amazingly, Bailey doesn't have a soccer game Saturday and shows up at nine.

"Here," she says, handing me a bag. "I brought you some decent clothes. You can't wear that crap to film a video."

"Might I remind you that you're the one who gave me this crap?"

Bailey shrugs. "It was meant as a disguise. Not a rebel uniform."

I dump the clothing onto the bed. Everything is black: tall boots with a broad, angled cuff, stretch jeans so tight and sleek they might have to be surgically removed—*if* I can get into them—a low-cut, long-sleeved shirt that's obviously too short to cover my stomach, and a studded leather vest that laces at the sides.

"Put all that on," Bailey says, "and you'll look like a badass revolutionary."

I groan. She's got to be kidding. "There's no way anyone could fight a revolution in this get-up."

"Then it's a good thing all you have to do is sound tough and look pretty."

Even though the idea of wearing this outfit makes me feel ridiculous, I change because she's right about the unisex jeans and T-shirt I've got on.

The pants are as tight as I expected, and the boots are even worse. "These stupid things are too small," I say. "They're squeezing my toes off."

"They're exactly your size, Piper. You just need to break them in."

I'm wincing my way through a few tentative steps, and Bailey's bragging about how the Timbers thumped the Sounders last night, when there's a knock at the door. She slinks up to it, opens it a crack, and swings it wide. "Get in here before anyone sees you."

Logan, loaded down with an over-stuffed backpack, doesn't flinch at the command as he ushers Zoey inside and shuts the door behind him. "I take it you're Bailey?"

"The one and only."

He offers a hand. "Logan Voigt. And this is my sister, Zoey."

Today, Zoey's wearing purple sneakers and a matching ball cap, but she's still got the Jyunsui jacket on, zipped up to her neck.

"Nice to meet you," Bailey says to Logan, ignoring his sister completely. "*Very* nice to meet you." When she's done smiling at him, she turns to raise an eyebrow at me. Either I've succeeded in convincing her that Logan's legit, or her hormones have finally wiped out the last of her good sense.

Zoey interrupts the flirting by slapping a NetMax dongle into Bailey's palm and explaining how to use it. When she recites the password—Frequent Deadly Lightning rocks—Bailey grins and fist-bumps her. Then the conversation devolves into fan girl bliss as they debate whether *The Tom McCall Song* really was the group's best effort, or some lesser-known work was superior.

"You think President Cooper will go back to the band once he's done running the country?" Zoey asks.

"I dunno. People say he wants to, but it would be a real security nightmare. I feel kind of bad for him, having to give up his passion."

"He didn't give it up," Zoey says. "It's more like he traded it in for a new one. I mean, yeah, he loves music, but he loves Cascadia more."

Great. I'm doomed to spend the day stuck in a Jefferson Cooper smarm-fest. Don't I get enough of the hero-worship in Grandpa's journals?

Fortunately, Logan takes charge of the situation, clearing his throat and turning to focus on me. I cringe as his blue eyes take in every detail of Bailey's fashion nightmare. I've got to look like I belong in some corny adventure movie. But Logan doesn't break into the guffaws I clearly deserve.

"Great outfit," he says. "I wouldn't have thought of that look myself, but it's perfect."

"It's all Bailey. Personally, I feel like an idiot."

"You shouldn't. It's a nice touch. Very revolutionary." Logan shrugs out of his backpack and roots inside for an iPad. "I have your speech ready. Memorizing it would be best, but I've downloaded a teleprompter app, in case you need it."

"I won't," I say, taking the tablet from him. His suggestion doesn't come out of nowhere. He quizzed me relentlessly before he left on Wednesday, scrounging for details that would add emotional punch to my public address. One of the things that came up was how easy it is for me to commit stuff to memory.

I scroll through the speech, impressed by how Logan has turned my sad story into a battle cry.

My name is Piper Hall, and I'm here to tell you the disappearances are real. When I came home the night of May 18th, my house was empty and my family was gone. I narrowly escaped being taken myself. Now I have no idea where my grandpa, mom, and little brother are. I don't even know if they're alive.

The stories the news sites have been spreading about me are nothing but lies. I never threatened anyone's life or stole anything. I've never even touched a gun. Up until two weeks ago, I was a straight-A student, dedicated to winning a scholarship and pursuing a degree in medicine, and in the blink of an eye, my future was snatched away.

I know there are others like me out there. People whose families, friends, or neighbors have disappeared. People who've had to go into hiding or deny what they know about the kidnappings for fear they might be next.

It's time to speak up. To come forward and tell the truth about what's happening. We need to get to the bottom of this before any more Cascadian citizens disappear—before anyone else loses their grandpa, or their mom, or their little brother.

I know you're afraid. I know you think no one will listen. But I'll listen, and I swear to you, I will find out who's behind these crimes. If you don't think I'm capable, take one minute to consider how I've hijacked the Emergency Alert System to deliver this message. The kidnappers made a big mistake when they messed with Piper Hall.

The speech sums up with a note about how people can look me up on Connect Me, or learn more at my website, Piper-hall.com.

"Aren't you laying it on a little thick, here at the end?" I ask.

Logan smiles. "It's all about perception. If you can deliver this speech with the passion and confidence that's packed into the words on that screen, people will buy it. They'll rally around you."

I shake my head. This is so far from how I see myself. I'm no hero.

"Let me have a look," Bailey says, snatching the iPad out of my hand. As she reads, a grin spreads over her face. "Oh yeah. This is gonna be great. Logan, you're a genius."

Clearly, Logan is not used to the likes of my best friend, be-cause he blushes. "We should probably get started. We have a lot of work to do."

While I begin memorizing my speech, Logan and Zoey get things set up, and Bailey sprawls in a booth, quizzing them on various aspects of their lives. She learns they're from Chicago. Zoey's a vegetarian who's way into the green movement, inspired by their environmental reporter mom. Logan has ambitions to serve in the military—something moving to Cascadia has messed up. He also loves history and plays football.

I cringe when I hear this last part. Bailey has taken it as a personal affront that the United States usurped the name of her sacred sport and besmirched it with brutality.

"It's not really football, you know," she says. "There's hardly any kicking involved. It oughta be called throwball. Or catch-it-and-run-like-hell ball."

Logan looks up from the set of lights he's adjusting.

"Ignore her," I say. "She's a soccer snob."

Bailey raises her chin in defiance, oblivious to the fact that she's now got her nose stuck in the air. "It can hardly be considered snobbery when virtually every country in the world plays the sport. How many countries play American football?"

"Why should that matter?" Logan asks. "The games are entirely different, and each has its own appeal. What I like about football, for example, is the strategy."

"There's strategy in soccer," Bailey argues.

"But it's not the same. Football's about developing plays in advance by studying the opponent's strengths and weaknesses, then using those plays to outmaneuver the competition. Soccer puts more emphasis on reading an ever-changing set of circumstances and making split-second decisions."

Zoey's starting to get that fierce look she had when I dissed the president the other day. "Logan kicks butt at football," she says.

"I'm sure he does," Bailey agrees, her eyes sweeping him top-to-bottom. "But you know who's a huge soccer fan? Jefferson. He even plays goalie in a city club. Or at least he used to. He had to back off after the election. It kind of messes up the game for everyone else when you've got Secret Service hanging out everywhere."

"Can you guys keep it down?" I ask before they start making a big deal about Cooper having to give up soccer, too. "I need to get this memorized, or we'll be here all day." Not that I'd totally object. It's kind of nice having people around. I was never much on the whole social scene, but after being stuck here alone for two weeks, I'm desperate for a little human interaction.

"Okay, fine," Bailey says, tossing her long hair. "I can take a hint. No one here is interested in learning about a civilized sport."

Logan looks my direction and raises an eyebrow. Yeah. Bailey has that effect on guys.

When the camera, lights, and computer are set up, Logan and Zoey hang a sheet on the wall to conceal the bricks.

"No need to give anyone a clue about where you're hiding," Logan says, glancing at me with his I've-got-this-under-control expression. He seems to have thought of everything. Well, everything except makeup.

"Wait!" Bailey says as I limp over to stand in front of the backdrop. "You can't film her like that. She's whiter than the sheet. I've seen zombies with more color."

"Gee, thanks." I've always been pale, especially up against her warm Latina complexion, but she doesn't need to act like it's front page news.

"It's the lights," Logan says. "They do that to everyone."

And just how many fugitives has he filmed?

Bailey comes at me with her purse full of makeup. "I can fix it."

She spends the next ten minutes slathering me with foundation and blush, but being the victim of her ministrations is only the beginning of my annoyance. It turns out that even though I've memorized Logan's speech perfectly, he isn't satisfied with anything about my delivery. He makes me repeat it. Over and over.

"Sit up straighter," he says after the first time. Then, "Pause a little before the part about not knowing if your family's still alive." And, "You don't look defiant enough. Put a little more fire into it."

When I try, Bailey cracks up.

"What?" I demand, mowing her down with a glare.

"You look like a porcupine just crawled down your pants."

"Maybe you'd like to try this with the whole world criticizing your every word?"

Zoey peeks out from behind the camera. "*I'm* not criticizing."

"Why can't we just run it the way it is?" I ask. "It's not like I'm trying to win an Oscar."

Logan shakes his head. "No. We've only got one shot at this. It has to be perfect. But I think we could all use a break. Is there a place around here where we could get lunch?"

"I'll go grab something," Bailey says, reaching for her purse. "The fewer of us that are seen coming and going, the better."

When she takes off, Logan suggests I go into the bathroom and practice in front of the mirror. Since I don't have any better ideas, I hobble away to give it a try, my feet complaining with every step.

It irks me to find out Bailey's right. My attempts at defiance make me look like a porcupine crawled down my pants. I experiment with various expressions, but every one of them comes off phony or ridiculous.

There's a noise at the doorway, and Logan appears behind me in the mirror.

"The trouble is, you're not connecting with your emotions," he says, stopping several feet behind me, but in clear view. "This isn't a recitation of the periodic table. You're addressing people who are happy to assume you're a criminal. They're not doing a thing to help you, and all the while, the jerks who took your family and destroyed your future are getting away with it. They're probably out there plotting the next kidnapping as we speak." His eyes pin mine in the reflection, boring into me like the mirror somehow gives him access to my soul. "How does that make you *feel*, Piper?"

His last words are almost a whisper, and the precise emphasis of his tone does exactly what he wants it to. "How the hell do you *think* it makes me feel?" I snap, my fists clenching in a sudden desire to slug him.

Logan smiles and nods at my reflection. "There you go."

Without another word, he steps out of the bathroom, leaving me alone with my smoldering rage.

After that, I have no trouble delivering the speech. I'm going through it a third time when I hear Bailey come in.

She's bought enough food for a small army, and when Logan offers her cash for his and Zoey's share, they get into an argument.

"Look," Bailey finally says. "Buying a few stupid hamburgers doesn't even begin to pay you back for what you're doing for Piper. Just eat the damn food and say thank you, okay?"

"Thank you," Logan says, raising his sandwich to salute her.

Zoey snorts through a mouthful of veggie beef.

While we're eating, Bailey entertains us with stories about the ghosts that supposedly haunt the White Eagle.

"Have you ever seen them, Piper?" Zoey asks, sucked in by the quicksand of Bailey's wild imagination. "Aren't you scared to stay here?"

"Of course not." I've got plenty of reasons to wish I wasn't stuck in this dump, but fear of ghosts isn't one of them.

Zoey shakes her head and stares at me with new respect. "I don't think I'd be able to sleep."

"It's easy," I say. "It's not like there's much else to do around here."

When we're done plowing through the food, we get back to work. This time, I nail the speech on the first try. Passion wells up and rings through my words, making the world blur around the edges, so it isn't till after I'm finished that I notice how everyone is looking at me.

Bailey lets out a long whistle. Zoey whispers, "damn," and Logan grins as if he's the one who just delivered a kickass speech.

"You're a natural at this," he says.

I laugh, amped on the emotion that's still creating eddies in my gut. "Even though it took five million takes to get it right?"

"Definitely." Logan squeezes his sister's shoulder. "Zoey, why don't you play that back so Piper can have a look."

Even though I felt the power of the presentation as I was delivering it, I'm still a little blown away by what I see on the computer screen. I look like a revolutionary—like someone who actually *could* fire up the masses and get to the bottom of the kidnappings. And Bailey's crazy outfit only adds to the effect.

Zoey glances at her brother. "You know who she reminds me of? President Cooper. She's got that same fiery passion."

Great—just who I want to emulate. But I've got to admit, no matter what I might think of the guy personally, he's got charisma. You can't argue with the persuasive power of someone who not only convinced half-a-dozen states to secede, but also made the U.S. government believe it was in their best interest to let them go. If I've got even a quarter of that appeal, maybe there's a chance of finding my family.

"I'll get this edited tonight," Zoey says as she shuts her laptop. "And then Logan can take it to the weather station we've picked out in the Coast Range. We'll set it up to broadcast during the Monday morning rush hour. That way people will see it on their way to work. They'll talk about it all day and go to your Connect Me page to watch it again."

Bailey turns to Logan. "When are you going to the weather station?"

"Probably early afternoon. Why?"

"Because I've got a soccer game in the morning, but if you can wait until after that, I'll ride along and keep you company."

For some reason, Logan glances at me. What—he thinks I'd care? I've seen Bailey work her magic a million times. Why should it bother me?

"Uh . . . sure," he says.

"Great." She gives him a broad grin. "I'll send you my address as soon as I get home and set up that NetMax thing."

I know Bailey's only being Bailey, but I can't help feeling a little smoked. This is my future we're talking about. Would it kill her to put her sex drive in neutral just this once?

CHAPTER 6

Logan

Sunday morning at breakfast, Dad asks Zoey if she'd like to go to the zoo.

"No thanks," she grunts, staring down at the waffles I prepared especially for her.

I bump her knee under the table. She's been prickly toward Dad since she learned the truth, and though I've talked to her about it more than once, she's still having a hard time acting natural. Fortunately, up until today, our differing schedules have kept the two of them mostly apart.

Zoey sighs and lifts her head as if the act requires enormous effort. "Maybe next week. It's going to be too hot to cover up this stupid vest today, and I don't feel like being one of the attractions."

It's the perfect save. We're so accustomed to Zoey's irritability regarding her illness, Dad's unlikely to give her snub a second thought.

"All right then." He glances in my direction. "How about you, Logan? Are you up for a game of chess this afternoon?"

The question catches me off guard, and I have to swallow hard to keep from choking on the bite I just took. Dad taught me the game when I was eight. We used to play all the time, but after I dropped Chess Club in junior high because it conflicted with football practice, he suddenly got too busy.

"Sorry, Dad. I have other plans."

The shallow attempt to win me back should be insulting, but instead, it pulls at something deep inside me.

That afternoon, I'm a little worried about leaving Zoey alone with Dad, but it can't be helped. There's no way I can take her along after she rejected his offer. Besides, I had her with me all day yesterday, and I don't want Dad to start wondering what we've been up to.

Before I leave, I go into her room to impart one final caution. She's at her computer, putting the finishing touches on Piper's website.

"Got a minute, Sparky?"

She shrugs. "Depends. Are you going to lecture me again?"

"Only because it's important." I sit down on her bed. "I understand how difficult all of this is for you, but you've got to try harder with Dad."

She turns away from the laptop. "What if I can't? He did a really bad thing, Logan."

"But he isn't a bad person. He just made one flawed decision, and I'm sure he didn't realize Piper's family was going to be thrown out of Cascadia because of it. You know as well as I do he's too honorable to deliberately be part of something like that." I hate lying to Zoey, but I'm not sure she can get past this otherwise. And as long as she's on the outs with Dad, our whole mission is at risk.

"It's still not right," Zoey says.

"No, it isn't. But he did it with the best of intentions. And he would've done the same thing for me or Mom if we were the ones who were sick."

Zoey's eyes meet mine, a troubled question in them. "Do you think she knows? I mean, maybe Dad lied to her, too."

I nod, composing myself to mislead my sister again. "I'm sure he did. You know how Mom is about uncovering injustice. That's part of her job, right? There's no way Dad would ever tell her about this." The truth is, I still haven't found the courage to broach the subject. Learning of Dad's duplicity was one thing. But he and I have never gotten along, so there wasn't any closeness to lose. Mom, on the other hand, has always been my confidante. She ran interference for me and came to my football games, even when she was overwhelmed by her work and Zoey's health issues. Having Mom stay behind was hard enough. I can't bear losing the *idea* of her, too.

"Look," I say. "I know you're feeling really confused about Dad, but it's okay to forgive him. That's exactly what you should be doing. He's still our father."

"Have you?" Zoey asks.

If I bend the truth here, she won't believe me. "I'm working on it," I say.

She nods, her blue eyes solemn. "Okay, Logan. I'll try."

Before heading over to pick up Bailey in Ladd's Addition, I take the precaution of turning off my phone. It's one of the handheld rectangular models because I don't like the interactive projection field on wrist phones. Zoey's always taunting me about it, but I find a physical screen easier to read.

As I drive, sunlight streams through the SUV's open windows, warm and friendly in comparison to the harsh glare I know from home. We've only had a few nice days since I've been here, and this one is spectacular. I think of Piper, holed up in that dark building. I'd hate to be shut away from a day like this.

The diagonal layout of Bailey's neighborhood—at odds with the surrounding street grid and shaped somewhat like the spokes of a wagon wheel—would make it a challenge to navigate if not for the Toyota's GPS. The area has a sort of charm to it. A sense of community pride that emanates from the numerous people walking or biking the tree-lined streets and from the well-kept yards that smell of fresh-cut grass.

When I reach the address, I park at the curb and go up to knock on the door. Bailey opens it within seconds and steps out onto the porch wearing skintight jeans, hiking boots, and a T-shirt that's definitely made for a girl. "Water and snacks," she says, smiling as she holds up a small daypack. "You said we'd have to hoof it, so I thought I should be prepared."

"Good idea."

I find it hard to hold up my end of the conversation as we get underway, the SUV self-navigating to Powell Boulevard then across the Willamette—which I've learned is pronounced Will-*am*-et. It's not that I feel all that awkward with the opposite sex. I've had a few girlfriends and usually didn't have much difficulty talking to them. But I'm not sure what Bailey wants. Is she simply the flirty type, or was she trying to start something yesterday?

The thought swirls inside me, stirring up the murk of uneasiness I'm already feeling about Dad and Zoey. Bailey's a nice enough girl, but we have important business to take care of. Her advances could make things awkward for Piper, and if she pushes to the point where I have to say something, it could compromise the mission. I can only hope she's got enough sense not to take it that far.

We merge onto Sunset Highway heading west, occasional potholes jarring us. They're nothing compared to those we encountered on the drive across the Midwest and Great Plains, but still big enough that the smart suspension can't compensate. While I'm now used to them, they were a surprise when we first got here. I suppose on some level I was expecting Cascadia to be perfect.

Bailey, who's taken off her boots and rested her feet on the dash, has been chatting about the soccer game she played that morning. This segues into a recap of Friday night's match between the Timbers and the Sounders, which put Portland in the lead for taking the Cascadia Cup this season.

"You'd think the Cup's something that started after the secession," Bailey says, sliding me an engaging sideways look. "But it's been around since '04, and it doesn't even include all the teams in the country, just Portland, New Seattle, and Vancouver. Some people say Jefferson got the idea for Cascadia from being a soccer fan, but it's not like we invented the concept. It's been around forever."

"I know," I say. "The school made me watch the promotional propaganda."

Bailey grins. "Brainwashing, eh?"

Before I can answer, she flicks the reins of the conversation, sending it charging back to the topic of her own soccer team.

My mind drifts to the plan I've gone over countless times already. Zoey has emphatically stated that it's flawless, but there are so many ways things could go wrong. This weather station might be off-line. I could run into trouble uploading, despite my belief that the computer won't be protected. Even if the video broadcasts, people might ignore it, unconvinced it's in their best interest to get involved. I'd feel terrible if I couldn't follow through, now that I've assured Piper we can help.

We've been driving for about thirty minutes when the city gives way to farmland in an almost instantaneous shift. Above us, the sky stretches out, a vibrant, piercing blue. Such a contrast to Chicago, where it's a washed-out, whitish color this time of year, despite the relentless sun.

"I don't suppose we could talk about football for a while," I say when I can squeeze a word past Bailey's monologue.

She turns to face me, twirling her auburn hair around a finger. "You mean because of what I said yesterday? I was just messing with ya. I used to get into it with Piper's grandpa, too—he's a big football fan. Of course he was pretty good at slinging it back." Bailey shakes her head, a sad smile drifting across her lips.

"So you knew her family pretty well."

"I spent nearly as much time at her place as I did at home."

The SUV makes a left onto Highway 6—the route to the Oregon Coast. That's something I'd love to see, but for today, we're just going to a remote location in the mountains that separate the Willamette Valley from the ocean.

"I guess Piper's little brother isn't much younger than Zoey," I say. That's the part of all this I can most easily relate to.

"Nick?" She nods. "Yeah, he's nine. Typical little brother. Snakes in your sleeping bag and all that."

I laugh, glad Bailey's providing these insights. When I interviewed Piper for her speech, she offered ample details about her family, but delivered them in a guarded, clinical sort of way. Nothing personal, nothing with any emotion to it. Yet her efforts to keep me at a distance said as much about how she was feeling as if she'd bared her soul.

"She really misses him—all of them." Bailey brushes her long bangs back behind her ear. "I'm glad you're helping. I promised I'd do something, but about all I'm good for is stashing people away in abandoned buildings."

"At least you're not the cause of her problems," I say as the Toyota climbs into the Coast Range and the forest closes in, straight, tall evergreens guarding the highway like sentinels.

Bailey tilts her head slightly, her expression softening. Her fingertips brush my arm. "It's not your fault, Logan. That is, unless you're the only teenager in the world who can actually make his parents do something."

"Not hardly." We come up on an older model Ford, the type you have to steer yourself, and I wonder what it would be like to drive one on a twisty road like this. The idea seems thrilling, but also a little dangerous. How did people manage to hold a conversation back before cars could self-navigate?

"Have you talked to the authorities about Piper's family?" I ask. "There must have been other disappearances. I can't believe nobody's reported them."

"We reported it, all right," Bailey says as we turn onto a winding secondary road, and the trees swoop even closer. "The cops told my parents everything's legit. They said Piper's mom moved the family to southern California when she got a job offer there. Piper stayed behind to finish her junior year, and then she flipped out and pulled a gun on some doctor at OHSU."

It's the same story I read on the Net a few days ago. "And your parents bought that?"

"Well, they're not best buddies with her family or anything. I mean, they can't believe Piper would do something like that, but they're not gonna rattle anyone's cage about it." She takes her feet off the dash and wiggles them into her boots as the SUV makes a left, continuing up the densely wooded grade. "What gets me is this one-on-one exchange you think they're doing. I mean, why bother? Your dad already paid, right? So why not let your mom in?"

"My guess is it's a power play. Whoever's behind the kidnappings is trying to create an illusion of scarcity. The harder it is to get into Cascadia, the higher a price people will be willing to pay."

"Hmm," Bailey says as she pulls her laces tight. "I guess that makes sense."

I reach into the center console for my hand-held navigation system. There's an app on my phone that would work just as well, but I don't want to risk being connected to this location. Even though there's no reason for anyone to be looking for us, it's best to establish the habit of not leaving a trail. I'm a little worried about someone retroactively tracing the path of our vehicle, but I reassure myself that there must be hundreds of others pinging off the nearest locator at this specific time. Besides, I have a cute girl along as cover—a role Bailey seems more than willing to fill.

"The thing I'm curious about is what the police told people who'd be likely to push harder than your parents," I say. "Family friends and coworkers, for example. I don't see how they could buy the story you were given."

Bailey shrugs. "I dunno. I could try to find out."

126

I shake my head. "It doesn't matter. Asking that sort of question isn't going to get us any real answers, and it might attract attention. We need to lie as low as possible if we want to keep Piper safe."

It's strange, just how strongly I feel about protecting Piper. I barely know the girl, and she doesn't seem the type who'd normally need looking out for. But after witnessing the defiant conviction in her speech yesterday, I feel compelled to fend off anyone who might try to take another shot at her.

The Toyota pulls onto a narrow gravel road, brush scraping both sides, and after a few hundred feet, comes to a stop. When we get out, the forest envelops me in a cool breath laced with the tangy scent of evergreen. For a few seconds I stand with my eyes closed, soaking it in. Then an errant thought disrupts my moment of reverie. *What if this doesn't work?*

"Where to now, Cap'n?" Bailey asks.

I open my eyes. She's leaning toward me with a quirky grin on her face, arms resting on the hood of the SUV. A good leader wouldn't let her know about his worries. "Up to the top of this mountain," I say, unlatching the back door to grab my pack.

After switching on the nav unit, I study the readout, and then the woods around us. "I have to say, I'm impressed by how efficient the authorities have been at hushing everything up. Have you talked to any of Piper's other friends about it?"

Bailey slings her pack over her shoulder. "What other friends? She's got me, and that's about it. Don't get me wrong." She holds up a hand as if to stave off potential protests. "I love Piper like a sister—but she's not exactly the social type. Her idea of a smokin' Friday night is to sit at home memorizing the names of bones."

I can recall similar evenings, engrossed in history books, though I've never put them before real people. I start off to the west, following the remains of a path. "What about her boy-friend?"

Bailey snorts as she falls into step beside me, so close her shoulder bumps against mine. "Piper wouldn't know what to do with a boy if somebody left one gift-wrapped on her doorstep. That girl's had only one thing on her mind since fifth grade— earning a scholarship so she can go to med school." She cuts me a sideways glance, her chin angled toward me. "Guys don't get that, you know?"

"*I* get it. There's nothing wrong with realizing what you want out of life."

"Well, the position's open if you're interested," Bailey quips.

So *that's* what this is all about. Relief ripples through me. I can't say that under normal circumstances I wouldn't be tempted. But pursuing the idea now hardly seems appropriate. "With all that's happened, do you really think Piper's in the market for a boyfriend?"

"Well ... maybe not." Bailey slaps the branch of an evergreen with tiny, flat needles out of her way.

The path narrows, and she falls in behind me as we let the forest take over the conversation. Wind murmurs through the tops of the huge firs, birds call out in a chorus of competing songs, and in the clearings, bees hum from flower to flower. Though I've read that bees make a buzzing sound, up until now, I've never heard it. It's pleasant and tranquil. Full of warmth, like the sun.

As we hike to the top of the mountain, I take occasional bearings from the navigation system, but mostly just let myself get lost in the pure pleasure of Oregon. There's so much to look at. Hundreds of different kinds of plants. At first, they're all just a mass of green, but after a while I begin to recognize the repetition of various trees. One, which Bailey informs me is a big leaf maple, has huge lobed leaves, twice the size of my hand.

After half an hour, we break out of the sweet coolness of the forest into another clearing. The mountaintop looms before us, a small structure rising from its peak. When we reach it, Bailey stops, resting hands on hips as she tips her head back to study the assortment of meteorological instruments mounted on a sturdy metal pole.

"Not much to it, is there?"

"There doesn't need to be." I pull a pair of gloves from my pack and step closer to examine the lock on the box that protects the computer components. It's a simple padlock, easily dispatched with bolt cutters.

The door squeals open on rusty hinges to reveal a console draped in spider webs. I brush them aside and pull off the protective plastic. After inserting the flash drive, I type the command Zoey said will upload the video and modify something called crontab to make it play at 7:30 tomorrow morning. I hope she's right. And that I remembered everything correctly. Though I'm used to being in a position of leadership, I've never had a team depending on me for anything so critical before.

"That's it?" Bailey asks as I pull the plastic back over the computer.

"According to Zoey, and she's the expert."

"Okay then." Bailey strolls over to a huge boulder and sits down, opening her pack to take out a Nitrous bar. "As long as I lugged my sorry butt all the way up here, I might as well give the poor deprived Midwesterner a chance to enjoy the view."

I close the box, peel off my gloves, and go over to take a seat beside her. "The poor deprived Midwesterner appreciates that," I say.

Heat from the sun-soaked rock seeps through my jeans as I look out over the expanse of blue-green hills. The air smells so fresh, feels so dry and light compared to the clinging humidity of Illinois. As wrong as my father was in bringing us here, I can't help feeling grateful for the chance to experience this.

Bailey unwraps her energy bar, takes a bite, and then works a second one out of her pack to hand to me. We snack without speaking, the whisper of wind the only thing interrupting the silence.

"You were right, you know," Bailey finally says.

"What?"

"About Piper. She's not looking for a boyfriend. I was out of line, saying that stuff." She stops speaking, her eyes focused on her fingers as they fold the Nitrous wrapper into a tiny cube. "I guess I don't want to think about her life getting tanked, you know? I'd like to believe there's nothing more important to worry about than fixing her up with the next scorching guy who comes along." Bailey's fist closes around the wrapper, and she looks up, staring out over the valley.

"I can't imagine how hard it must be, watching your best friend go through something like this," I say. It's been difficult enough, leaving people like my buddy Paulo behind. At least I know he's okay.

"She's always known exactly what she wants," Bailey says, shaking her head. "I'm changing my mind practically every two minutes about what I plan to be—ballerina, elephant trainer, arctic explorer, center midfield for the Portland Thorns—but Piper's been on the same track forever." She stuffs the wrapper into her pocket before stretching down to pick up a rock, which she lobs at a tree thirty feet from us. The thud of it connecting echoes off the surrounding hills. "We met in Ms. Monahan's kindergarten class, and even back *then* she knew she wanted to be a doctor. You know what I wanted to be when I was five?" Her eyes catch mine. "A guinea pig."

A laugh escapes, despite my effort to respect the seriousness of what she's sharing.

"I can't stand to think of her losing everything," Bailey says, drawing her legs up onto the boulder and hugging them to her chest. "What if this plan doesn't work?"

"Don't worry about that. We'll sort everything out, and once we do, you can go back to setting Piper up with the most scorching guy in Cascadia."

It's amazing how convincing my words sound, considering I don't fully believe them myself.

CHAPTER 7

Logan

Monday morning, I get up early to talk to Dad before he leaves for work. I need him to sign a permission form that will allow me to participate in my new school's JROTC program. I've had it since Friday, but I haven't been able to work up the nerve to approach him about it, and all the activity with Piper and Bailey has given me sufficient excuse to put it off.

As I approach him at the breakfast table with the electronic form pulled up on my phone, my stomach folds in on itself. "Dad?" I say.

He looks up from his breakfast. "What's got you out of bed so early?"

"I need to have you sign a permission form."

His gaze meets mine for only a moment before dropping back to his iPad, which is logged into *The Oregonian*'s news site. The thought of what tomorrow's front page headline might be makes my stomach clench tighter.

"What's it for?" he asks.

"JROTC."

His sigh fills the kitchen. "Isn't school about to get out?"

"I'd like to meet the people in the program before next year. You wanted me to make friends. This is my chance." I hold my breath, knowing his approval is a long shot.

Dad leans back in his chair. "Logan, when are you going to start thinking seriously about your future?"

"I *am* thinking seriously. I've been thinking seriously for years." My leg muscles tense and I itch to look away, but I force myself to stand straight and meet my father's gaze.

"You don't even live in the United States. The Army isn't an option."

"Where I live doesn't matter. I was born there. I have citizenship."

"So you're going to up and leave your little sister when you know what's coming?" Dad shakes his head.

A cold wave pulses through me, and I stare at him. As often as he's expressed his disappointment, he's never gone this far. But then, things are different now.

"She's losing ground, you know," he says, gaze hardening. "We can't count on this Doernbecher study to give us a miracle."

How can he think I'm not every bit as aware of what's happening with Zoey as he is? "You want me to go to college, don't you? I'll be doing that regardless. To become a commissioned officer, I'll need a degree." Though I'd rather go the enlisted route, which would allow me a more hands-on approach to being a leader, as an officer, there's a chance I might one day earn Dad's respect.

"You're asking me to pay for a college education so you can squander it by going into the Army?"

Another first. He's never so much as hinted that he wouldn't cover my tuition.

"JROTC isn't just for kids who want to go into the military," I say, hoping to talk him down. "It's about learning leadership skills. I could use those in any career."

Dad sears me with a look of contempt. "Don't try to snow me. Everyone knows that program is just a backhanded way of recruiting high schoolers. If you want to learn leadership skills, join the Boy Scouts."

It's clear I'm not going to get anywhere with him. I should've sent the form to Mom. Doing so might have felt underhanded, but it would have been a way around this mess.

There are so many things I'd like to say to Dad. So many ways I could defend my choices. I want him to know I can, and will, achieve my goals regardless of his support. But talking back has never come easy, and doing so now will only lead to a confrontation that might hurt my efforts to help Piper.

Without saying another word, I turn and walk out of the kitchen.

Back in my room, I'm tempted to forge my father's name on the permission slip. But I can't do it. Just because he's dishonest doesn't mean I should be. I'll call Mom tonight and talk to her about it. Maybe she can convince him to reconsider. It will be good to have something relatively normal to discuss. Since I learned about how we got here, our conversations have been stilted. I just can't open up, knowing she might be part of Dad's plan.

As seven-thirty draws near, I go across the hall to Zoey's room and knock on the door. Her recent MB episode gives her the ultimate free pass as far as school is concerned, but she's up anyway, waiting for the broadcast.

"This is going to be so cool, Logan," she says, grinning at me from her desk where she's sitting at her computer wearing frog pajamas. "We're going to make history."

"Don't you think it's a little early in the morning to be that ambitious?"

"Oh—right." She gives me a nod. "World-changing activities should be reserved for after eight o'clock." The excitement in her voice is so encouraging, I'd hack the Emergency Alert System a hundred times over to go on hearing it. For her sake, and for Piper's, I hope this works.

I close the door and take a seat on the unmade bed while Zoey turns back to the OLED wall screen that's wirelessly connected to her laptop. It's large enough to display a half-dozen windows at once. In addition to Piper's website, she's monitoring her Connect Me and YouTube accounts, where the video is uploaded but sitting dormant because no one knows about it yet. She's also got KPTV, "Portland's First and Foremost

News Station," fired up in anticipation of the breaking story.

At exactly 7:30, an emergency alert pop-up fills the screen. The familiar sound shrills, not just from the laptop, but also from my phone and Denise's computer down in the basement. The noise jolts me like the shock from a live wire, and it's only now that I realize how deeply I've been doubting my ability to make this happen.

Zoey turns to slap my palm, her face a riot of excitement. I know she's dying to let out a war whoop, but neither of us dares with her nurse so close by. After the "Important News Bulletin" graphic fades away, Piper's image fills the screen, strong and deadly serious.

I can't explain exactly what happens within me as I'm watching the speech. Part of it is a solid feeling of satisfaction. Pride in putting all this together—leading a team that pulled off something so professional and revolutionary. But part of it has nothing to do with our efforts.

As Piper reveals the truth about the kidnappings and implores Cascadians to take a stand, her eyes drilling into mine, I feel as though she's talking directly to me. Once again, the compulsion to protect her rises up, a fierce, powerful conviction. I remember my conversation with Bailey and wonder if I was being entirely honest with her or myself.

Despite my confliction on that account, one thing is clear. I've got to see Piper through this, no matter what it takes.

CHAPTER 8

Piper

I get up early to catch the broadcast as it goes live, even though I'm not sure I believe Logan's plan will work. When the emergency alert signal goes off, a weird tingle shoots through me. A thrill of hope follows close behind. This is actually happening. There's a real chance of finding my family.

As the black screen fades into an image of me, I'm suddenly self-conscious. Everyone in Cascadia is watching this, passing judgment on my stupid outfit, the way I'm holding myself, the words spilling out of my mouth. But then the power of Logan's speech makes me forget all that. Even though I know it's me on the screen, it seems like someone else. Someone powerful.

I watch without breathing, and when it's over, I sit staring at the screen. I'm dying to jump around and holler and pound everyone I know on the back, but there's no one here to celebrate with. I'm neck-deep in revved up emotions, and I've got no way to get rid of them.

Before I can figure out what to do, the Carrier Pigeon window pops up.

GreenGirl007: *How awesome was that? You're a total rock star.*

Grateful as I am to have someone to talk to, I can't put my excitement into words. What flows out of my fingers is my lingering doubt.

Futuresuture: *You think it'll work?*

GreenGirl007: *Duh!*

I grin at Zoey's attitude, imagining what would happen if I put her in a room with my little brother. The idea seems like a *when* now, instead of an *if*.

Futuresuture: *You guys are coming later, right?*

There's no way I can wait till after Bailey's soccer practice to talk to someone about all this.

GreenGirl007: *Of course. We'll be there at 3:30.*

When Zoey signs off, I try to read the book I downloaded last night, but I can't concentrate. I keep stopping to look online to see if anything's happening. All the major news websites already have stories posted, but they don't say much. I check my email and find twenty-seven messages, all fielded through the website and Connect Me. Every one of them is from somebody who's on my side. Somebody who lost a friend or neighbor, or just heard the rumors and believed them. I don't know how to answer, and I'm afraid of screwing up Logan's plan, so I decide to wait until he gets here before doing anything.

Bailey shows up right after school, blowing off soccer practice for maybe the third time in her life. Since she didn't stop by last night, and Logan only sent a cryptic message that said, "mission accomplished," I'm eager to hear how things went at the weather station.

"Did you see the broadcast?" Bailey asks before the door even slaps shut behind her.

I'm sitting at the table with my computer, reading email number seventy-nine and wondering how many hours it'll take to answer them. No one so far has any real leads on my family. Mostly, they're offering sympathy or saying they also know someone who's been taken. "Yup. I can't believe it worked."

"Everyone at school's talking about it." Bailey drops down across from me in the booth. "You're the biggest thing since the secession. People are acting like they were your best friend or something."

Right. Because everyone at Cleveland High was a huge Piper Hall fan. "I'm sure you're setting them straight."

"Well, it wouldn't be smart to draw suspicion by changing my M.O. now, would it?" Bailey grins and does a little drum roll on the table with her hands.

My brain is crammed full of the news clips I've been reading all day, and I'm still so amped I can hardly think. I want to talk about the video, but Logan and Zoey will be here soon, and there's no sense repeating myself. Besides, there's something I won't be able to mention once they get here.

"So what happened on the hike with Logan? Did you wind up breaking Simon's heart?" I'm trying to sound nonchalant, but my voice comes out razor-sharp. If Bailey blows my one chance at finding my family because she can't resist going after every guy she sees, I'll probably have to kill her.

"Simon has nothing to worry about," Bailey says with a smirk. "Logan's not interested."

I snort. "Of course he's interested. They're *all* interested."

"Not when they've got their eye on someone else." The smarmy look she's giving me can only mean one thing. But she can't be serious.

"Bailey, that's ridiculous."

"Oh?" She raises an eyebrow. "Then why did he give you that look on Saturday when I suggested going to the weather station with him? You know—like he was asking for your permission."

She noticed that? "Don't be a dimwad," I say, turning my attention back to the computer screen. I really should do something about these—now eighty-one—emails.

"I don't see why you think it's such a crazy idea. You're cute and smart and kind of sassy. Guys like that."

"Which is why they've been lining up at my door since puberty, right?" Even *she* can't argue with the facts.

Bailey sighs. "The problem is, you're too fierce. You scare them off. They probably think you're going to cut out their appendix or something."

"Ha! Well, no worries there. I was planning on waiting until after med school to try my hand at surgery, and it looks like that's not an option anymore."

Bailey's smug grin twists into a frown. "Damn it, Piper, you need to stop talking like that. We're going to get you out of this. Maybe I couldn't do it on my own, but we have Logan and Zoey now. Didn't they get that broadcast to work, just like they promised? We're going to find your family and restore your reputation. And then you'll win a scholarship, become a doctor, and live happily ever after." The grin returns as she leans forward, elbows on the table. "*Maybe* even with Logan. Because you know what? He's not the type who gets scared off. In fact, I think he likes it that you're so fierce."

The feeling of annoyance that's been nagging at me evaporates. I should've known Bailey would have my back. I shake my head and smile. "You're crazy, y'know."

"Well, sure I am," she says with a laugh. "But just because I'm crazy doesn't mean I'm not right."

Someone knocks at the door and I jump. Crap. Now I'm not going to be able to look at Logan without wondering if Bailey's onto something. And knowing her romantic super-senses, she is.

I get up to let him and his sister in.

"Hey," Zoey says, bouncing on her toes. "What did you think of that broadcast?" She holds out her palm for me to slap.

"Totally prime," I say, following the gesture with the requisite fist-bump. "It worked just like you said it would."

"Of course. I purposely fed the story to every conspiracy theorist I know. Trying to cover it up now would be like trying to un-pee in a pool."

Bailey laughs, and Logan lays a hand on Zoey's shoulder. From the annoyed sideways look she gives him, I gather it's his "take it easy" signal.

But his expression is serious enough that I know he's worried about something bigger than Zoey wearing herself out.

"What's wrong?"

Our eyes meet, and I will myself not to flinch. Is he checking me out? Damn it, why can't Bailey keep her stupid opinions to herself?

"Nothing, yet," Logan says. "But it was a challenge to sneak in here without the construction workers across the street seeing us. We might have to limit our visits to evenings and weekends. And our dad will get suspicious of that pretty quickly."

Bailey turns around in the booth, draping her arm across the back of it. "There might be another way in."

"Oh?"

"Yeah. Have you heard of the Shanghai tunnels?"

Logan shakes his head.

"All right then," Bailey says, settling into story-telling mode. "At the turn of the twentieth century, there were all these ships coming into Portland that needed crew members. Nobody wanted to work on them, so these dudes called 'crimps' would go around town getting guys drunk, kidnapping them, and selling them to the ships' captains. According to legend, they'd drop them down these trapdoors in the floors of bars and drag them through tunnels that ran under the streets of Portland. But the so-called experts say that's a myth. Since it was perfectly legal to shanghai people, the crimps most likely took the easy way out and lugged them through the streets."

"Then what were the tunnels for?" Zoey asks.

"Probably transporting alcohol."

"You're a history buff?" Logan looks as shocked as I'd be to find out Bailey's been secretly harboring an intellectual hobby.

Zoey laughs as she seats herself at one of the tables. "In your dreams." The way she's smirking at her brother, it's clear she doesn't think it's me he's pining for.

"I don't give a rat's right foot about history," Bailey says. "My dad just has some interesting properties. I've done a little research on them."

"So one of these tunnels connects to the White Eagle?" Logan asks.

"That's what the stories say."

"And where does it lead to?"

"The waterfront, about a quarter mile from here."

"But *where* on the waterfront?" Zoey asks. "I mean, the tunnel's been around nearly a hundred and sixty years, right? How come no one's found it?"

Bailey's shoulders hunch into a shrug. "Don't ask me. I'm just telling you what I've read."

"Okay. So let's find out what's there." Zoey hits a button on her wrist phone, and the interactive field pops up, hovering a couple of inches above her arm. She types something into the virtual screen. "Looks like there's a strip of vegetation under the Fremont Bridge, from River Street to the water. It's about a block wide, and it goes all the way south to where the train tracks curve out to the shoreline." She flicks her fingers to zoom out. "If you project a straight line from the White Eagle— I'm guessing the tunnel builders would've taken the most direct route—that puts the exit somewhere in that area."

"First we've got to find the entrance," Bailey says, sliding out of the booth. "C'mon, I'll show you where I think it is." She leads us through the small kitchen and into the basement. When she squats to lift the big wooden step at the bottom of the staircase, Logan hurries forward to help. They heave it up, and Bailey gestures with one hand at the damp, mismatched concrete.

"According to what I've heard, it's under here."

"Well," Logan says, staring at the basement floor, "this obviously isn't part of the original concrete."

Bailey kicks aside some trash to reveal a small grate. "See? There's a drain. That has to go somewhere."

"Yeah," I say, standing behind them with my arms across my chest. "Into the sewer."

Bailey turns to give me a withering glare. "Oh, ye of little faith. . . . I say we get some sledgehammers and crowbars and bust this sucker open. What do you think, Logan?" She waylays him with those big, hazel eyes that have the power to hypnotize anyone possessing a Y chromosome.

"It's worth a try. I'll bring some tools tomorrow." He starts to lower the platform, and Bailey helps put it back in place. I notice she actually keeps hold of it the whole way to the floor instead of dropping it, like she did with me.

"According to this," says Zoey, who's at my elbow, still studying her phone, "that area by the river was a Superfund site. It was going to cost too much to dig up all the contaminated soil, so they capped it and planted vegetation on top that's supposed to help break down PCBs."

"Which means that if the tunnel exists, they most likely discovered the end of it during construction and back-filled it," Logan says. "But on the positive side, at least it will be in a remote location."

"*If* you can manage to dig through all that contaminated soil," I say.

Zoey squeezes past her brother to get to the staircase. "Okay, now that that's settled, let's get back to business." She heads up the steps, Bailey darting after her in a strategic effort to leave Logan and me alone together.

When Zoey gets to the top, she's out of breath—more so than the last two times she's been here—but she keeps plodding until she reaches the table where I left my laptop.

I hesitate outside the kitchen, glancing from her to Logan and wondering if this is something to be worried about.

"She's fine," he says. "Believe me, the one question you do *not* want to ask her right now is how she's feeling."

"You should try to get her into that study at Doernbecher," I say, keeping my voice low.

"You know about that?" Logan's tone is just as quiet.

"Sure. I was supposed to be helping out with it this summer, but..."

Logan's eyes go sympathetic, and I instantly feel like crap. I mean, sure, my future's tanked and my family is gone, but at least there's a chance we can change all that. What hope does he have? No one's ever survived Magnusson-Bell. Logan's doomed to see his sister die a slow death.

"Anyway," I say, watching Zoey hunch over my laptop, "it's cutting-edge research—the best anywhere in the U.S. and Cascadia."

"I know. That's one of the reasons Dad wanted to move here. Zoey's first appointment is Wednesday."

The mention of his father makes me flinch. Even though I never held what happened to my family against Logan and Zoey, I *have* blamed their dad. But if he did it to give his kid a chance at beating a terminal illness, how can I hate him? I'd probably have done the same thing for Nick.

"Hey," Zoey calls, glancing up from the computer. "What are you guys standing around for? We've got work to do."

Bailey glances over her shoulder with a sly grin. "*Yeah,* Piper."

I hurry across the room and pull a chair up to the table. Logan grabs another one and hauls it over beside mine. Out of the corner of my eye, I scrutinize the distance between us. He's not far enough away to make me question the staying power of my deodorant, but he's also not close enough to confirm Bailey's lame-ass theory. If he was as interested as she claims, wouldn't he take advantage of this opportunity?

"Lots of comments on your Connect Me wall," Zoey says. "Why haven't you responded?"

"I figured I should wait to get Logan's input. There's a bunch of emails, too. You can look at them if you want."

Zoey launches the program, and as twenty-three new messages download to my inbox, my stomach contorts like someone's

143

trying to fold it into an origami swan.

"Aw, man. Not more. How am I supposed to answer these?" It's a worry that's been smoldering in me all day. As much as I like hearing from people who believe me—as exciting as each potential connection to my family is—I feel like I'm being sucked downstream by a flash flood.

"I'll help," Logan says. "Don't worry. It won't be as daunting as it seems. We'll put together a form letter, and you can tweak it to fit your individual responses."

I turn in my chair. "You want me to tweak a hundred and four separate emails? What if they don't stop coming?"

"Piper, it's not going to be that bad." His calm eyes catch hold of mine, trying to still the angst that's about to choke off my air supply. "If it gets to be too overwhelming, we'll post a message on Connect Me saying that even though you appreciate everyone's support, you can't respond to individual emails."

"But—"

The emergency alert signal cuts me off before I can say more. As Zoey swivels the computer so Logan and Bailey can see it, President Cooper's image fills the screen. He's sitting at his desk in Pittock Mansion's oval office, and he hasn't looked this serious since the secession.

"My fellow Cascadians," he says. "This morning, I watched with all of you as Piper Hall alleged that the rumored disappearances are real. I've spoken with the Portland Police, and they have assured me this young woman is, in fact, guilty of the crimes she's been charged with."

Of course he's going to believe the cops. He's probably the one who put them up to it. I want to reach through the computer screen and punch him right in his scorching face.

"However," Cooper continues, "I cannot, in good conscience, simply write off Ms. Hall's claims. If there's even a remote chance Cascadian citizens are at risk, I want to know about it. No one should have to fear for his or her safety.

"Vice President Sarto is as concerned as I am and will work in conjunction with the Cascadian Security Administration to look into the matter. Rest assured that we will conduct a thorough investigation and get to the bottom of this issue."

The broadcast ends, and Zoey lets out a whoop. "How cool is that? We got a direct response from the president!"

"And we're supposed to buy that BS?" As smooth as Cooper sounds, I can see right through his feel-good politics. "If he's that concerned, why's he buying this story about how I'm guilty? It's a load of crap."

"But he doesn't necessarily know that, Piper." Logan's patient look, which I'm sure he intends to be soothing, only manages to smoke me.

"Sure—unless he's trying to cover his ass. Maybe he's the one who gave the order to have my family taken, and now he's scared of getting caught." I know even hinting at this is going to make Zoey go nuclear, but I can't hold back. Cooper's obviously piling on the bull to boost his ratings for the election.

"Jeez, Piper," Bailey says, "where do you come up with this stuff? I know you don't like the guy, but—"

"Okay, so say he isn't responsible. It's still his job to be on top of this kind of thing. If someone's got enough control over the police to make a story like this stick, how did they get it past Cooper? What kind of president is that clueless?"

"Give him a break," Logan says. "Even if he dropped the ball, he's trying to rectify the situation now. You have to remember, Cascadia's a brand new country, and Cooper's not really a politician. He never intended to be president. He just accepted the job because that's what the public wanted."

"Yeah!" Zoey looks like she's a second away from poking me in the eye with the nearest sharp object. "It's not fair to blame him for this."

Why is everyone trying to tear me one? Don't I have a right to an opinion? "What's not fair is a president who sits around spouting idealism and watching soccer games while people like me get shafted."

"Stop talking about him that way!" Zoey says. "Why do you hate him so much? What did he ever do to you?"

Logan nods. "Zoey's right. I know you're frustrated, but slandering the president won't change your situation. If you don't respect the man, at least try to respect the office."

This is bullshit. There's no reason I should have to respect anyone, and I can't see why it's such a big deal. Zoey and Bailey need to face the fact that not everyone worships Jefferson Cooper.

"She thinks it's his fault her family's poor," Bailey butts in.

And it's also nobody's business. I give her the evil eye. "Shut up, Bailey."

But shutting up has never been her strong suit. "Her dad was in a car accident right after the secession," she says. "The NHS had already bailed, and the Cascadian Health Service hadn't kicked in yet, so lots of people got stuck with huge medical bills."

"Shut *up*, Bailey!" It's bad enough everyone knows about the things that happened a couple of weeks ago. I don't need her dredging up my ancient history.

Dodging my glare, Bailey focuses on Logan. "Piper thinks Jefferson should've done something about it. That's why she's always gunning for him."

And there it is—the explanation that makes total sense in my head, but sounds stupid when someone says it out loud. "Damn it, Bailey," I growl. "Why can't you keep your mouth shut?"

"But your dad wasn't one of the people kidnapped, right?" Zoey asks, latching onto the one detail I was hoping to avoid. "Because that would have been four—"

"He died, okay?" I say it before she can ask. "And I don't want to talk about it, so maybe you and Logan can learn from my supposed-best friend's mistake and just drop it."

Zoey stares at me for several seconds, her mouth hanging open, before she glances at Logan for help.

I turn to fry him with a look. Whatever he might be thinking about saying, I don't want to hear it.

His eyes deflect every bit of my rage. "I'm sorry, Piper," he says, sounding like he actually means it. "I can see why you wouldn't want to talk about that—and why you might resent the president. But the important issue now is finding your family. You can't let your anger get in the way of that."

Silence fills the room. Everyone stares at me. Damn it, why does Logan always have to know the exact right thing to say?

I drop my gaze and take a deep breath to still my quaking innards.

"Fine," I grunt. "I don't know why everyone's making such a big deal about it, anyway. Shouldn't we be working on those emails?"

CHAPTER 9

Logan

Tuesday afternoon, I wait until nearly five o'clock to leave for the White Eagle. Denise is watching her soaps, so it's easy to sneak the tools we'll need into the back of Dad's Toyota. After making some sandwiches and packing them into a thermo bag, I tell Denise I'm taking Zoey for a drive through the Gorge and we won't be back for several hours.

When we arrive at the tavern, the construction workers have already gone home. This section of town, right beside a busy freeway interchange, looks like it used to be largely industrial, but it's undergoing a transformation. Several condos are in various stages of construction, and other buildings lie derelict, slated for demolition, according to Bailey. A few customers sit at tables outside the Widmer Brewery at the end of the next block, enjoying the warm afternoon. Beyond that, there aren't many people around.

I drive right into the White Eagle parking lot so Zoey won't have to walk and I won't have to lug a pick, shovel, and sledge-hammer conspicuously up the street. When I've unloaded the Toyota, I instruct it to park itself a few blocks away.

Piper holds the door open while I carry everything inside. Neither of us mention yesterday's outburst, but the things Bailey said have been weighing on my mind. Piper's had so much taken from her these past couple of weeks. To have lost her father as well . . .

I'm trying not to think of what I'll be feeling for my sister in a few years, when I realize my sympathy is exactly what Piper was hoping to avoid. I can't blame her for that. Who wants to be pitied? The kindest thing to do is follow her lead and pretend the confrontation never happened.

We carry the tools downstairs. Zoey follows as far as the top step before sitting down to rest.

"Where's Bailey?" she asks.

"Soccer practice." Piper helps me drag the platform away from the base of the stairs.

I'm glad Zoey's not giving her the cold shoulder. We had a discussion on the way home last night, and I made it clear I expect her to show some compassion, regardless of what she thinks of Piper's anti-Cooper stance. It's not that I don't trust my sister to do the right thing. It's just that she's so young, she still sees everything as black and white.

I pull on my gloves and safety glasses and grab the pick. Piper reaches tentatively for the long-handled sledgehammer.

"It'll probably be safest for one of us to tackle this at a time," I say. "Let me go first, and you can take over when I get tired."

Piper might be tough and smart, but she's got about as much muscle-tone as my little sister. The only thing she's likely to tear up with that sledgehammer is herself.

She steps back, and I set to work slamming the pick into the rough-textured concrete. It chips easily, chunks flying in every direction.

The floor here is only a couple of inches thick, and it's not long before my pick wedges into something soft. I get down on my hands and knees to pull away the rubble. Underneath, I find a patch of wood. I'm about to attack it with the pick when Piper stops me.

"If Bailey's right, that could be a door. You'll probably want to keep it in one piece."

"Good thinking." I concentrate my efforts on the surrounding concrete, chipping away at everything that looks different than the original flooring. When I stop to rest, and Piper offers to take over, it's evident from her tone that she'd really rather not.

"That's okay," I say. "I'm almost finished. How about if you clear away this junk instead?"

After an hour's work, we've exposed a row of heavy wooden planks about three feet square with a small grate in the center. The board closest to the wall is hinged, and the nail heads placed at regular intervals suggest supports underneath that hold everything together. While there isn't a handle, a patch of concrete embedded in the board closest to me might have filled what was once a handhold. Piper gives me the crowbar before I can ask for it. I force it between the wood and concrete to pry. Nothing happens.

"Maybe it's not a door after all," Piper says.

"Or maybe the cement flowed into the cracks and sealed it shut. See the hinges?" I point them out before rapping at the center of the boards. A hollow thud tells me there's nothing underneath. With the aid of the hammer, I drive the crowbar, inch by inch, into the crevices surrounding the door. When I'm finished, I wedge it into the original spot and heave. Still nothing. I throw all my weight against the tool, and with a sudden crack, the door pops loose.

"Bonus!" shouts Zoey.

As she comes down to join us, I work my fingers under the door and pry it upward. The ancient hinges groan, rust flaking away.

Piper crouches beside me, and we peer down a staircase so steep it could almost be considered a ladder. The basement's poor lighting makes it difficult to see to the bottom.

"Hey, Zoey," Piper says. "There's a light tube on the table by my computer. You want to get it for me?"

"Sure." She plods back upstairs and disappears through the doorway.

"Well, that will earn you some points," I say, shucking off my gloves and safety glasses.

"Huh?" Piper gives me a quizzical look.

"Putting her to work instead of treating her like an invalid."

"Oh." Piper laughs and waves off the comment with a flip of her hand. "It wasn't that calculated. I just didn't feel like going up there myself."

"Even better. She'll appreciate the fact that you forgot she's not like everyone else."

When Zoey comes back, she hands the light tube to Piper, who twists it on and hunkers down, leaning into the hole in the floor.

"This thing's useless," she says. "What we need is a flashlight."

I take the glowing plastic from her. "It'll be fine once we get down there."

"Once *you* get down there," Zoey says, crossing her arms over her chest. "Let me know when you've killed all the spiders, and I might consider following."

Piper lets out a shaky laugh.

"I can scout ahead, if you want," I suggest.

"No, that's okay." She glances back into the hole. "It's not like it's going to be full of monsters. Or even drug dealers, for that matter. I mean, the other end's been blocked off for years, right?"

"So that just leaves rats, bugs, and maybe an occasional bat," Zoey says.

Ignoring her, I begin down the steps, sweeping spider webs out of the way with my hand.

"Logan," Piper says.

I turn, and she holds out the crowbar.

"Don't use your hand for that. They're rare, but we've got black widows."

"Now I'm definitely not going down there," Zoey says.

The cool, musty air closes around me as I descend the staircase. At the bottom, I find a moist dirt floor flanked by brick walls maybe five feet apart. The ceiling of the tunnel—also brick—is arched to support the weight of the earth above. Even when I stand in the center, I have to stoop slightly to avoid hitting my head. I hold the light out at arm's length. It's impossible to see more than a few yards.

The steps creak, and I glance over my shoulder at Piper.

"Right behind you," she says, her voice tight.

Zoey hands the tools down to her. "Here, you're going to need these at the other end. And do me a favor. If something gets you, scream really loud so I'll know to call for help."

I share a grin with Piper as I trade her the light tube and crowbar for the heavier tools. "Will do, Sparky."

"You think there's enough oxygen in here?" Piper asks.

"I guess we'll find out." With the shovel raised to lay waste to spider webs, I turn and start down the tunnel. The dirt path is damp, but not muddy, and flatter than I was expecting, though that should be no surprise if Bailey's right about what these passageways were used for.

I expect the tunnel to end at any moment, cut off by the wall of some building that's gone up in the past century-and-a-half, but every step just reveals more of the dank, clammy darkness. At least we're still breathing easily enough.

Piper follows close at my heels, not saying a word until a rat skitters in front of us and she gasps.

"Still with me?" I ask, stopping to look back.

"Of course." She tosses her head, narrowing her eyes at me. "I just prefer to see those things belly-up and pinned to a dissection tray."

I laugh. "Don't let Zoey hear you say that."

"Not likely," Piper grunts. "We've got to be almost to the end of this thing by now."

"I think we're about halfway. We've gone two hundred and sixty-three steps. A quarter mile's about five hundred."

"You're counting our steps?" Piper's tone pitches upward in appreciation. "Damn. I never would've thought of that."

"And *I* never would have thought of backing off with the

pick before I tore a hole in the trapdoor."

Piper's mouth twists at one corner. "We're a regular couple of geniuses."

As we continue toward the river, the silence wells back up around us. The soft glow of the light tube bounces off the ground and walls, revealing small crevices and an occasional fallen brick, but no doorways or intersecting tunnels.

At step four-forty-seven, dust-covered cans and bottles begin to appear, along with other trash that indicates this was once a high school hangout. A few yards later, the path ends in a cinderblock wall.

"Interesting," I say as I run my fingers over the rough surface.

Piper comes to a stop behind me, raising the light. "Why do you say that?"

"I would have expected concrete. Maybe even for this whole end of the tunnel to be filled with it. But it might have been walled off and buried before the government ever got involved."

"So now what?" Piper asks.

"Now you hand me that sledgehammer, and I take it down."

Piper passes the tool to me, along with a skeptical look. "You really think it's worth the trouble?"

"That depends on how much trouble it turns out to be. But the more we come and go, the greater the risk of someone getting suspicious. And if we want to find your family, it's probably going to take a lot of coming and going."

Piper bites her lip as she studies the wall. "I guess there's no way around that, huh?"

"Not if you're going to stay at the White Eagle. And that seems like the safest place for you at the moment. Now stand back. There's going to be a lot of debris."

She edges away. "What if this is part of a building?"

"It's not. We've come nearly a quarter mile. We have to be

right down by the river."

The wall is easier to break through than the floor was, though it takes longer due to its size. I start at the top, letting gravity help. The noise reverberates through the narrow passage. While the safety glasses protect my eyes, bits of flying cinderblock graze my face and arms, and I cough as the dust scratches my throat. I remembered to bring clothes to change into so as not to arouse Dad or Denise's suspicion, but I didn't think to bring any kind of mask.

At last, the wall is lying in rubble at my feet, the soil behind it fully exposed. It's solidly packed, an impression of the blocks imbedded in its face. I stand panting like I've just run a marathon. Sweat burns the dozens of cuts left by flying fragments. My arms look like I've done battle with an army of cats, and by the feel of it, my face must be just as bad. There's no way my dad will fail to notice.

Piper steps up, pick in hand. "How many PCBs do you think are lurking in that dirt?"

"According to Zoey, not enough to hurt us. She did some research last night. Apparently, the plants they used to cover this area, combined with the nanotechnology they introduced later, are pretty good at breaking them down. And it's been almost forty years."

"Okay then." Piper raises the pick to tackle the soil barricade.

After I've caught my breath, I grab the shovel and begin slinging dirt and broken cinderblocks back into the depths of the tunnel. I try to pile everything close to the walls to keep the center clear.

It's not long before Piper hollers, "Roots! I hit roots!"

We trade jobs, and I battle my way through the tangle, grit coating my arms and face. Finally, the pick catches. When I wrestle it free, more soil falls away, revealing a tiny bit of light. I attack with a vengeance, the pinprick of brightness growing.

Soon, I've hacked my way through to daylight.

"Well, what do you know," Piper says. "Bailey was right. Guess I better prepare myself for the mother of all I-told-you-so's."

Roots block the path, but after pushing them away, I'm able to wiggle through the hole I've excavated. I shove aside a partially upended shrub to emerge onto a sloping bank that's shrouded in trees and brush. An island of vegetation, surrounded by inner city.

"What do you see?" Piper calls.

"I'm only about twenty feet from the river, but it's not very visible from here. The area's pretty heavily wooded. I think we can make this work."

An hour later, we have a person-sized hole carved out of the hillside. I stand on the bank of the river, feet planted to keep from sliding down the slope, but Piper won't leave the mouth of the tunnel.

"You should come out here," I say. "It's a beautiful evening. How long has it been since you've had any fresh air?"

"Someone might see me." She waves a hand at the Fremont Bridge. It's nearly obscured by trees, and the cars zipping along it are close to two-hundred feet above us. "You'd better get back in here yourself. We don't need anyone spotting the entrance."

"I'm not particularly worried. As thick as these bushes are, it would be difficult for anyone to see it until they were right on top of it. And none of the other vegetation looks like it's been trampled. I doubt anyone ever comes here."

Piper chews her bottom lip. "Let's go back. Zoey's going to be worried."

She carries both the sledgehammer and pick, saying I did all the hard work. By the time we get to the White Eagle, I'm so tired and sore I feel like I've been through a week-long football practice. Zoey pesters us with questions as I lower the trapdoor, and I'm happy to let Piper do the explaining.

She insists on dragging the wooden platform back into place.

"But how will Zoey and I get in?" I ask as I give her a hand with it.

"Send a message before you leave home. I'll pull it off then."

"You can't handle this by yourself."

"Oh yes I can." She gives the step a final shove with her foot. "I'm not leaving it open. What if someone sneaks in during the night?"

That's hardly likely, but I'm not going to argue with a girl who has to sleep alone in an abandoned tavern.

We trudge upstairs, where I drop into the nearest chair.

"Jeez, Logan, you look like you've been through a war," Zoey says.

I glance down at myself. I'm covered in dirt. Dark streaks and splotches mark the spots where blood congealed on my arms as the dust caked it.

Piper studies me with a frown. "You should clean up those scratches. I'll get some water."

While she's in the kitchen, Bailey, wearing her soccer uniform, lets herself in. Zoey updates her with second-hand knowledge, as proudly as if she'd done all the work herself.

"We got lucky," I say. "The tunnel came out right at the slope going down to the river, so we only had to dig through a few feet of soil."

"It only takes one to three feet to cap a Superfund site," Zoey informs us. "Depending on the contaminants, of course."

Piper returns from the kitchen with a dented pot of water. She sets it on the table beside me and pulls out a small towel, wringing it until it stops dripping. Her own hands and face are clean, now, though her clothes are nearly as dirty as mine.

I'm surprised when she lifts my arm and begins wiping away the grime, her gentle touch a contrast to the curt toughness I've seen from her so far. Up until now, she's kept a wall of personal space between us. And yesterday, the looks she gave me were downright skittish. But maybe her healing instincts run deeper than her need to hide.

"None of these are too bad," she says, examining one of the deeper abrasions on my left arm. "But you should put some antiseptic on them when you get home. There's no telling what's in that Superfund dirt. And Bailey," she tosses a glance at her friend, "if we're going to lead a revolution, it might be nice to have a first aid kit."

Zoey's smirking at me. She has been since Piper began. "Antiseptic's not going to help him now," she says in a voice of doom. "PCBs are absorbed through the skin—whether it's broken or not."

I give her a look. "I thought you said PCBs wouldn't be a problem any more."

"You *ne-ver* know," she sing-songs.

I'm exhausted and need to get her home before Dad sends out a search party, so I tell Piper and Bailey we have to be going. After changing into the spare T-shirt and jeans I brought, I rake the worst of the grit out of my hair. I'm still not sure what to do about the cuts.

"Tell him you had a run-in with some blackberries," Bailey suggests. "They're all over the Gorge. All over the whole damn state."

I check to be sure no one's watching then call the Toyota to the parking lot. It's getting dark, but the air is still warm as Bailey and I load up the tools.

It's not until we're buckled in and on our way that I realize Zoey's grinning at me.

"What?" I say.

"You totally loved that. You were just like Grandma's cat when she rubs his belly and he gets that slitty-eyed look."

The SUV's air-conditioning can't compensate for the heat that flushes across my cheeks. "What are you talking about?"

"You." She laughs. "And Piper. *You* know, when she was *tending to your wounds.*"

The heat migrates down my neck. "You're seeing things. And anyway, you sound like you swallowed a romance novel."

Zoey strokes her chin, regarding me with a sly smile. "I figured you were hot for Bailey, but now I see you're playing the field. Bold move, Logan. Bold move."

"I'm not hot for anyone."

"Uh huh." She tilts her head to the side, her lips curling at the corners in wicked satisfaction. "You know, if you'd worked that right, you probably could've gotten a back rub out of it."

I turn to focus on the street ahead. "Shut up, Sparky."

CHAPTER 10

Piper

As soon as Logan and Zoey take off, Bailey starts in. "It's nice to see you finally taking my advice."

"Advice? What advice?"

She motions toward the pan of muddy water. "Brilliant approach. I'm proud of you."

"He was hurt, Bailey. You saw how beat up he was with all that blood and dirt on him."

"Mm hmm." Her lips purse and her face goes all smug. "Life-threatening injuries, for sure.... Or maybe instinct just got the better of you."

I narrow my eyes. "That's right—my instinct to help people who are hurt. There's no ulterior motive in that."

"Whatever you say," Bailey chirps, shaking her head. "If you wanna play doctor with Logan, it's no business of mine."

I open my mouth to argue, but realize it's useless. Why can't Bailey lay off the matchmaking? I don't need my every action analyzed. There's little enough I can do as it is. Logan's a mastermind, Zoey's a computer genius, and Bailey herself gave me this place to hide. All I am is a poster child. Taking care of people is the one thing I can give back.

I'm on my own Wednesday afternoon because of Zoey's appointment at Doernbecher. Logan messages me, saying he feels obligated to go with her, since it's the first time she's been there. Even though it's so like him to look out for his little sister, I can't help obsessing. What if Bailey was right? What if I sent the wrong message yesterday, and now Logan's avoiding me because he thinks I'm after him? Every time the thought pops into my head, I tell myself not to be stupid. Bailey's just got me paranoid with her meddling.

While I was big news Monday and Tuesday, and the media said police were seeing a huge jump in kidnapping reports, I've now been upstaged by Jefferson Cooper's pending deal with the Japanese. They've developed a new generator that's powered by ocean waves, but they're so overpopulated, they don't have the space to build factories. Cooper's hoping to trade land for all the generators Cascadia needs, along with a maintenance program. Naturally, it's a big snarling mess, with half the country loving the idea, and the other half thinking Cooper's selling out. And it's totally stolen my thunder.

But even though the news sites have forgotten about me, the people haven't. The emails are still coming, and I'm constantly fielding comments on Connect Me and YouTube. After the first hundred or so responses, I started to get the hang of it. Now, the more I tackle, the more I feel like the mythical revolutionary Logan fabricated.

Thursday afternoon, he and Zoey come in the regular way. His face and arms are just as beat up as I remember.

"What did your dad say about the cuts?" I ask.

"Fortunately, he bought the blackberry story."

"Good." I don't even want to think about what would happen if his dad got suspicious. I turn to Zoey. "How was your appointment? Did they start you on Tri-Inhibitase yet?"

She rolls her eyes and groans. "Do we have to talk about that?"

"Just trying to be polite." And maybe get a peek into the study I'm missing out on.

"Well, stop."

Logan interrupts, holding up a camouflage tarp. "It'll probably be hard to find the tunnel from the road," he says, "so it's best to start from this end the first time. I figured we could work on concealing the entrance today. I'll tie this to the roots of the shrubs above it. If I fasten enough branches to it, anyone who finds it will think it's a pile of brush."

He doesn't seem nervous, and he hasn't looked at me funny, so I figure I can forget about the worries Bailey planted in my head.

"Have fun," Zoey says, taking a seat at the laptop. "I'll mess around with my spreadsheet. Tons of people have been filling out the response form on the website."

She's been collecting information on the disappearances and charting all the data: location, economic status, number of victims, and any clues that were left behind. Lots of people are claiming they're in the same position as I am and want to talk to me in person, but even Logan, who seems to be on top of everything, isn't sure how to safely make that happen. He's worried about the kidnappers setting me up.

"That reminds me," he says. "I started looking at the data yesterday, and I'm definitely seeing a pattern. All the people who ask about a kidnapped family are being told they've left the country. After that, there's no trace of them. But the interesting thing is that several people have reported one identical detail: a Shipshape Moving van coming in to take out all the belongings after the family disappears. I asked our neighbors if they'd seen one, and it turns out they had. So I called the company and pretended I'd hired them. They have no record of being at that address."

"Interesting," I say.

"Yes. It confirms that the disappearances are connected, and it also shows that whoever's behind the kidnappings is going to great lengths to make this moving story look legitimate. Zoey's going to follow up about it with the people who are filling out the web form. You should ask everyone who emails you, too."

"Sure. No problem."

We're heading for the staircase when the squeal of an emergency alert stops us short. Zoey turns up the volume on the computer as Logan and I rush back to the table. Vice President Sarto's voice catches us and reels us in.

"Citizens of Cascadia: as you know, I've been conducting an investigation of the alleged disappearances. I'm relieved to inform you that I've found no evidence to support Piper Hall's claims. I realize it's frightening to hear conspiracy theories like the one delivered Monday morning. I want to reassure you that your safety is not an issue. Pay no attention to this 'Pied Piper.' Her objective is clearly to undermine the stability of our country by leading Cascadians down a dark pathway of fear and dissent."

"Oooh!" Zoey says when the broadcast ends. "Pied Piper. I like that."

Logan shakes his head. "Whether Sarto knows it or not, he made a huge blunder by giving you a nickname."

"But it's a lie!" I say, not realizing I'm clenching my fists until my fingernails dig into my palms. "None of that's true. He knows it's not true! I told you the government was behind it!"

"Or they had nothing to do with it," Logan says, "but they feel it's in their best interest to ignore the issue."

I turn on him with fury. "Why are you always defending Cooper?"

"I'm not defending him, Piper. I'm trying to remind you that there are other possibilities. If we jump to conclusions, we might overlook clues that will lead us to your family."

"What clues?" I demand, my hands sweeping upward in disgust. "Sarto just said the disappearances never happened. We're at a dead end."

"No, we're not." Logan's voice is a deep river of calm. "Zoey's sitting on top of a truckload of information, and this isn't the end of it with the government. I'll write you another speech. We can tape it on Saturday."

Zoey's eyes go from Logan to me, full of fight. I know she's waiting for me to go nuclear on Cooper again.

But there's no point. It won't change anything.

Logan rests a steadying hand on my shoulder to steer me toward the basement steps. "Let's conceal that tunnel entrance. We can talk about this on the way."

I don't resist. Talking won't change it either, but being in Logan's still, steady presence will eventually leech away my outrage.

Saturday morning, Logan shows up early with a new speech. He's using the tunnel now, piggybacking Zoey because she can't handle the quarter-mile walk. I don't know how he manages to carry her that far, hunched over so they don't brain themselves on the low ceiling. But he's an athlete, and if my relationship with Bailey has proven anything, it's that athletes are a little bit crazy.

As soon as Logan's upstairs, he hands me his iPad. The speech begins all right, stating that the disappearances are real and I believe someone in the government might be covering them up. But when I read the ending, anger burbles inside me like hot water in a geyser. I'm supposed to say I believe someone might be trying to deceive the president and call on him to look into the matter himself.

"You've got to be kidding, Logan. Maybe you can keep me from voicing my *totally legitimate* opinion about Cooper, but I'm not going to suck up to him."

"It's not sucking up. It's politics. If Cooper's not responsible, this gives him an out while still calling the government on the carpet. And if he is responsible," he says, glancing at his sister, "it lets him know you're on to him and are willing to say so publicly."

The argument makes sense, but I still don't like it. "I can't do it, Logan. Not with a straight face."

He shakes his head and smiles. "Of course you can. I have complete confidence you'll be willing to do whatever it takes to get your family back, no matter how reprehensible you might find it."

Damn it, why does he have to be right?

"Fine," I say. "But don't expect me to look good this time. Bailey has a soccer game and she won't be here until one."

Despite my threat, I do a decent job with my own makeup. I still feel like a freak in Bailey's get-up, and the boots haven't stopped rubbing my feet, but the second filming goes easier than the first.

When we're done, I change into normal clothes and offer to fix lunch, but Logan asks if he can do it. Amazingly, he whips the boring stuff in the kitchen into something delicious.

"My brother's a pretty good cook, huh?" Zoey says through a mouthful of noodles and sautéed vegetables smothered in cheese.

"I think this is the best food I've had since I got here."

Logan ducks his head, his cheeks going a little pink. "Our parents both have pretty intense jobs, so I just sort of stepped into it."

"Well, if your military career doesn't work out, you can always become a chef."

We're just getting finished when Bailey shows up.

"You won't believe what I saw today," she says as she takes a seat beside me.

"What?" Zoey asks, licking cheese off the back of her fork.

"Graffiti on the side of a building down on Burnside."

"Oh, there's a surprise," I say.

Bailey slugs my arm. "I wasn't finished."

I pull away, laughing, then bow to her with my hands in the prayer position. "Oh please, honorable Bailey-san, forgive me for my transgression."

"Okay, I'll bite," Logan interrupts. "What did the graffiti say?"

Bailey grins broadly and straightens up in her chair. "It said . . ." she pauses, going for full drama, ". . . 'Piper Hall doesn't lie' followed by a bunch of exclamation points."

Zoey lets out a shriek and pounds her fists on the table. "It's working!"

"The presidential address and ten thousand Connect Me comments didn't clue you in?" I ask.

"Well, sure," Zoey says with an eye roll that rivals the best one my little brother could deliver. "But when people start spraying your name on a wall, you know you've arrived."

"Face it, Piper," Bailey says. "You're a hero. You're becoming the stuff of legends. One day, people will sing songs about you."

Even though I know she's kidding, there's a layer of truth behind her words. The emails have proven that. Those people whose families have disappeared aren't just trying to support me. They're looking to me for help.

"I don't want to be a hero," I say, getting up to stack the lunch plates. "I just want my family."

I hype the upcoming broadcast all weekend on Connect Me, announcing that it will air at 7:30 Monday morning. Even though I'm bombarded with a constant stream of questions about Sarto's statement, I don't address his announcement in any other way. Logan says there's a tactical advantage to making people wait for answers.

By Sunday afternoon, I'm sick of playing revolutionary. I pull out one of Grandpa's journals and escape into the past, where Cascadia was a new idea and everyone was still hopeful about it.

January 6, 2059 – The Cascadian Congress met for the first time today. Right here in Portland at the Benson Hotel. This is the damnedest thing. Like the start of the U.S., with George Washington and the Continental Congress all over again. Hard to believe I'm getting a chance to witness it first-hand.

I never thought about it like that. To me, it's just regular life. I wonder if George Washington felt the same way—or if he knew he was making history the whole time.

I've been successfully limiting myself to a couple of journal entries a day to make them last, but tonight it feels so good to have Grandpa right here in the room with me that I keep going. He talks about how Cooper negotiated with the U.S. and Canadian governments, and how it was BC that caused the worst problems. Canada didn't want to give up its western ports, so eventually they worked out a deal where only the southern half joined Cascadia.

I find myself getting caught up in Grandpa's excitement, especially since I know what's coming. And then, there it is. His own personal account of the most important day in Cascadian history.

April 23, 2059 – The secession went through today. We're officially a new nation. The hoopla is unbelievable. People shooting off guns, honking horns, and partying in the streets. Cascadia's gonna start its second day with one hell of a hangover.

We're already working on ways to close the border. The U.S. isn't too happy about that, but what are they gonna do? Their government's got Cooper's guarantee for five years of water and electricity. They aren't likely to rock the boat just to keep a few citizens from griping.

Here at home, Cooper's got about a ninety percent approval rating on this border deal. He spoke some damn fine words about it on the news last night: "Do I want to slam the door on people who are just looking to provide for their families? People who are suffering through no fault of their own? Of course not. And maybe in the future, we can revisit this issue. But at this time, we need to build up Cascadia. Nature has decreed us the new breadbasket of North America, not just in terms of food, but water and power as well. We can't squander these re-sources. We must take on the unfortunate responsibility of saying 'no' today so we can build a strong nation that will be able to come to the aid of her neighbors in the future. If we don't first see to the needs of our own citizens, there's no way we can look out for the rest of the world."

A ripple of sadness starts in my gut and spreads through me. I shut the journal and stick it back with the others.

Grandpa was proud enough of Cooper's idea to quote him. And now, because of that idea, he's gone.

Right on time Monday morning, Zoey uploads the video to YouTube. Naturally, all the weather stations were secured after our first broadcast, but that's okay because we've got half of Cascadia following us. Within minutes, I'm buried in an onslaught of emails and Connect Me comments. Of course, by now I'm an expert and know how to deal with them.

Zoey sends me updates throughout the day.

Greengirl007: *You wouldn't believe the number of shares we're getting on Connect Me.*

Greengirl007: *Did you see? All the news stations posted the video. And not just here in Portland.*

Greengirl007: *You should check out the talk on the political forums. People all over North America are speculating about what's going to happen to the Cascadian government. Some guys from Australia and Brazil even weighed in.*

When she and Logan show up at 3:30, we spend a few minutes basking in our collective glory before getting down to the business of going through the feedback and making plans. It takes most of the afternoon to sort things out.

When our stomachs start growling, Logan passes around some sandwiches he brought with him.

"Do you think we'll hear directly from Cooper?" I ask.

Logan unwraps his faux-tuna on rye. "I'd be surprised if we didn't."

"It seems kind of extreme that they're using the Emergency

Alert System," I say. "Why not just give the story directly to the press?"

"Because not everybody pays attention to the news. They obviously want to get the word out to the entire populace. And there's only one way to be sure of that."

At exactly six o'clock, the emergency alert signal goes off. Just as predicted, Cooper himself delivers the address. It's short and to the point. He assures the public he has complete faith in Sarto's abilities, but he'll ask him to look into the matter further.

I stand glaring at the computer screen, even after Cooper's gone. I don't care how genuine he sounds. This is just a stall tactic to keep people on his side while he figures out how to cover his ass.

"Hey, he didn't call you the Pied Piper," Zoey says, glancing at me.

"That's because he's smarter than Sarto," Logan notes.

I don't say a word, don't bother to voice my opinion. I just get up, furious, and walk away.

CHAPTER 11

Logan

The Wednesday following our second broadcast is the last day of school. It comes as a great relief. While the hallways have been less intimidating since I met Bailey, she has her own crowd, and I don't want to be a nuisance. But it's time management, rather than loneliness, that's the real issue. It's not easy to go to school full time and run a revolution.

By now, everyone at home is used to me taking Zoey out regularly to "experience Portland." Since she's still using her PVAD, Denise doesn't approve, but I've assured her I don't allow Zoey to overexert herself, and I've convinced Dad her recent upbeat attitude is due to our excursions. It's not exactly a lie.

I've been alternating our approach to the White Eagle, depending on the day and time, so we won't establish a recognizable pattern. On Friday, we arrive after lunch by the regular entrance. Zoey's happy about that. She hates the tunnel, though not nearly as much as she hates the idea of being left behind.

After sending the Toyota off to park itself, I let myself in using the code for the keypad Piper gave me over a week ago. "More emails?" I ask, seeing her at her laptop, intently typing.

"Not from the person who should be emailing me."

She's been angry since the last presidential statement. I'm not sure if it's stubbornness or frustration, but Bailey didn't help by pointing out how interesting it is that nobody in the government has personally contacted Piper. Now, she can't seem to think of anything else.

"His lack of response isn't personal," I say.

"I know, I know." She waves a hand in the air. "It's *politics*.

'Cooper can't give power to dissidents by addressing them directly.'"

At least I know she's listening.

I take off my backpack.

"More food?" Piper asks.

"Yeah." After seeing how impressed she was by the lunch I cooked for her, I realized how limited her meals must be. Since then, I've been bringing fresh fruits and vegetables to supplement her supply, along with spices, so I can get creative on the nights we're here at dinnertime.

"You don't have to do that, Logan. Bailey's taking care of it."

"I want to be sure you have a good stockpile in case something happens and we can't get here for a while. Besides, Zoey and I have been eating here a lot."

My sister smirks at me, one eyebrow arching upward, but fortunately, Piper doesn't seem to notice.

"Well, you know where to put it," she says, shaking her head as she turns back to her computer.

We spend the day reading emails, studying data, and brainstorming ideas for our next steps. These are all things we could do independently, connecting through Carrier Pigeon to get each other's feedback, but I prefer to come to the White Eagle. It isn't like I have other social obligations. Besides, I feel bad for Piper, being stuck here by herself.

It's clear the containment is eating at her. It would do her good to spend some time in the garden area outside the door, but she refuses. Her fear only reaffirms how much courage it must have taken to meet us at Coffee Madness. More and more often, I find myself wanting to put an arm around her and tell her everything will be okay. But she's likely to interpret that as a threat, rather than a comfort, so I don't.

At four o'clock, we're startled by the shrill of an incoming emergency alert. We huddle around the laptop to watch, Piper and me standing beside the table that serves as her desk, and

Zoey sitting behind it. Sarto's face appears on the screen.

"After an intensive investigation, we've uncovered disturbing evidence that points to vigilante squads kidnapping Cascadian citizens. Apparently, wealthy Americans are seeking entrance to our country, and these criminals are selling the identities of displaced Cascadians to them."

"Bullshit!" Piper yells, drowning him out. "How can he possibly think anyone will believe it's vigilantes?"

I put my hand on her arm, and her muscles tremble under my fingers. "Easy. We need to hear this."

She tenses, her jaw knotting, as if clamping her mouth shut is the only way to cut off the outburst.

Sarto's announcement continues: "I regret my earlier statement regarding the disappearances. The influence of these vigilantes has penetrated our police force and local government, and I was misled. There is one thing that hasn't changed, however. Piper Hall is still a dangerous criminal, and any evidence of her whereabouts should be reported immediately."

Beside me, Piper flinches.

"I want to assure you that now that we've learned the truth, the kidnappers will no longer be a threat. Every effort will be made to track down these vigilantes and bring them to justice."

The broadcast ends and Piper slaps the laptop shut. "Somebody needs to bring *you* to justice, asshole!" Slumping into the booth, she sinks her elbows onto the table and buries her face in her hands.

My fingers hover at my side, reaching out, but I pull them back. What Piper needs from me now is action. "It's obvious he's stalling," I say. "The story he's constructed won't stand up for long, and he's got to know it."

Piper doesn't answer. Zoey slips her a worried look. While she hasn't said as much, I know she feels as responsible as I do for Piper's situation.

"One of two things is going on," I say. "Either Sarto is so

desperate he's throwing any excuse he can think of at the public, or he's working on a plan and hoping to placate everyone long enough to pull it off."

"So what do we do now?" Zoey's eyes dart from me to Piper and back again.

"We publicly point out the holes in his story. The people who have been directly affected by the kidnappings can already see them, but everyone else will need us to connect the dots. A hard push now will force Sarto to play his hand before he's ready. Or, if we're lucky, it might make him crack."

"*Niiice.*" Zoey nods, drawing out the word before punctuating it with a grin. "How fast can you put a speech like that together?"

"I'll have it done by morning. We can film it tomorrow and upload in the evening."

Piper pulls her hands away from her face and looks up at me. "What if it doesn't work?"

"It will."

But even as I say the words, doubt worms its way into my resolve. There are so many things that could go wrong. And I don't want to see what it will do to her when we finally run out of options.

Saturday morning, Zoey and I show up at the White Eagle with the latest speech. Piper memorizes it in fifteen minutes. While she had trouble connecting with her feelings for the first broadcast, she can barely rein them in this time.

"Google my mother or grandfather's name and see what you find," she says, glaring at the camera and infusing every word with venom. "There's no trace of them in California, where the police claim they've gone. If you research other people who've disappeared, you'll get the same result. What vigilante has the authority to convince a person's employer or school they've left the country without having said a word about it in advance? What vigilante can deceive the police into believing that innocent people such as myself have committed crimes? What vigilante has control over the media and government?"

Bailey shakes her head. "Jeez, Piper, you look like you're ready to kill someone. Can't you dial it back from genocidal maniac to merely smoked?"

"Cut," I say. "Let's start over from the beginning."

Piper turns on her friend, her face a twist of bitterness. "That bastard *lied* about me, Bailey. He undid all the work we've put in, convincing the public to trust us. Why shouldn't I be pissed?"

"You should be," I say. "You have every right to be furious. But if your audience sees that fury controlling you, it will only reinforce what Sarto said."

Piper scorches me with a look. "You're being too easy on him. All this hinting around is going to drag things out forever. We need to bust him and Cooper."

It's something we've been over before. I steady myself with a breath so my dwindling patience won't escalate the situation. "Allowing the public to draw their own conclusions gives them ownership of the idea. There's a psychological advantage to that. Besides, if Cooper were involved, he wouldn't have asked Sarto to take a closer look. He'd have insisted the kidnappings never happened."

"Right." Piper flicks her short, dark hair off her forehead. "You've always got an answer."

We do another take, and then another. All the while, I'm thinking about her argument. As good as my defense of Cooper sounded, I'm no longer entirely convinced of his innocence. Piper had a point when she said he had an obligation to be on top of the problem, and recent experience with my father proves I'm not the judge of character I once thought I was. Maybe the president really is involved.

After an hour, Piper finally manages a good performance. "Okay," I say. "I think that will cover it."

She turns abruptly and storms off toward the basement without even changing out of her rebel attire. My gaze fixes on the doorway she disappeared through as I sink down onto the nearest chair. Maybe I should be put off by her meanness, but all it tells me is how desperate she's become.

"You should go down and comfort her," Bailey says.

I glance over to see her pulling the white backdrop off the wall. "I'm not sure she wants comforting."

Bailey laughs as she rolls up the sheet and tosses it onto Piper's bed. "Every girl wants comforting. With her, you just have to finesse it a little."

It's the pull inside me, more than Bailey's words, that persuades me.

I go downstairs.

Piper's huddled in the far corner of the basement with her back against the wall and her feet pulled up in front of her, arms clasped around her knees. She doesn't move as I approach.

"I'm surprised you're sitting like that," I say. "The rats in this basement aren't likely to be belly-up and pinned to a dissection tray."

Piper stares past my legs with disturbing emptiness. "I don't give a rat's right foot about the stupid rats."

It's clear from her expression she has no idea she made a joke. I lower myself to the ground beside her, close enough that our arms almost touch. "Me either."

She draws a deep breath and lets it out in a whoosh. "Bailey sent you down here, didn't she?"

"She's worried about you."

Piper snorts. "Bailey's something, but worried isn't it."

Since I don't know how to respond to that, I sit and wait. The chill from the concrete seeps through my T-shirt and jeans.

Piper sighs again, fidgeting with the buckle on her boot. "You really think this broadcast is going to make a difference?"

"Yes."

Her head falls back against the wall. "I don't know why it would. Nothing's worked so far."

The defeat echoing through her words is even more unsettling than her anger. "It might feel that way," I say, "but look at all the responses we've been getting. Look at the graffiti, and the fact that the government is taking us seriously. We actually got Sarto to contradict himself."

Piper closes her eyes, her forehead wrinkling. "But none of that is getting us any closer."

"Of course it is. You can't expect results overnight. Things like this take time."

She tenses. "They wouldn't, if anyone bothered to speak up for me. Where are all the people who know me, Logan? The kids at school and my teachers and the doctors in the JSA program?" Her fingers clench over the boot buckle, knuckles straining against the skin. "How can they let Sarto call me a criminal? How can Bailey's parents, who've known me since I was *five*, let him get away with that?" Her words end in a whimper.

Never in my life have I wanted to hurt anyone as badly as I want to hurt the people who've betrayed this girl. "Because they're cowards," I say. "It isn't fair and it isn't right. But not everyone's as brave as you."

Piper lets out a grunt of a laugh. "Yeah. I'm *so* brave. Sniveling away down here in the basement."

"Being brave isn't the same as not being scared."

She shakes her head and hunches forward, hugging her knees. "I just miss them so much, Logan." Her voice cracks. "Why does this stuff always happen to me? Wasn't the thing with my dad bad enough?"

The question makes my throat clench. "Yeah," I say. "It was."

Piper draws a deep breath, her fingers pressing into the flesh of her upper arms. For a long time, she doesn't say anything.

I ache to pull her close. To offer one small bit of comfort against all this loss. Nobody should have to go through the things that have happened to her.

"It's worst at night," she finally says. "That's when it's hardest to be here alone. I just can't stop thinking about Mom and Grandpa and Nick. I try to tell myself it's different than with Dad—that I'm going to see them again—but then this little voice says, 'how do you know?'"

As much as I'd like to tell her that voice is a liar, I keep the thought to myself. I can't guarantee our efforts will work. I can't even be sure her family is still alive.

I picture her lying alone in this cold, dark tavern and realize just how powerless I am. All my plans, all my strategies, are useless in helping her then.

Piper's grip on her legs relaxes, her hand sliding down to rest against her wrist. "When my dad died, it felt like my whole life was over. Like that horrible empty feeling was never going to go away." She hesitates, her eyes shutting and her face drawing tight. "I can't handle going through that again, Logan. I just can't."

The urge to hold her wells back up. She's so close, and it could be so easy, yet it's impossibly complicated. "I'd be scared of that, too," I say. "I've only been apart from my mom for a month, and it seems like forever. I don't know what I'd do if I found out I'd never get to see her again."

My words seem to float right past Piper.

"Dad was the one who got me interested in medicine," she says. "He was a paramedic. He'd come home from work, and I'd want to know all about the things he'd had to deal with on his shift. He was always teaching me stuff. He even bought me pigs' feet so I could practice sutures." Piper's lips pull into a shadow of a smile, and her eyes focus somewhere in the distance. "Mom would say, 'She's eleven years old, Adam. What on earth does she need to practice sutures for? Meat costs too much to be wasting that way.' Then Dad would say 'How can it be a waste? It's educational. Our daughter has a passion, and it's our responsibility to nurture it.'"

This is the first time Piper's shared anything intimate about her family. She didn't even mention her father the day I interviewed her, and I'd assumed her parents were divorced until Bailey brought up the accident. "He sounds like a great dad," I say.

She nods. "Yeah. He believed I could do anything. He didn't want me to grow up like him, too scared to go after the things I wanted. He always dreamed about being a doctor, but he was so afraid he wouldn't make it into med school that he never tried."

That kind of insecurity is so un-Piper, I have to smile. "I can't see you ever giving up that easily."

She laughs. "Neither could my dad. He liked to tell people I was so ambitious I busted out of the womb two weeks early." She shakes her head, another faint smile darting across her lips. "He had this great sense of humor. If Nick would get going with some story about how his teacher was an alien, Dad would ask, 'What planet is she from?' And when Nick told him, he'd say, 'Oh, I hear they have great pastrami there.' He'd do it with such a straight face, it always cracked Mom up. She'd try to play the heavy and lecture the two of them to settle down, but she could never pull it off."

Piper's words seem to catch in her throat. She shuts her eyes, her lips quivering until her head falls forward and her dark hair hides them from view.

The silent tremble that goes through her is too much. I give in to instinct, my hand cupping the smooth, pale skin at the back of her neck.

A tiny sound escapes her and she freezes. "Logan . . . don't."

I pull my hand away. How could I be so foolish? I told Bailey this wasn't a good idea. Why didn't I listen to my own advice?

"I'm sorry," I say. The last thing she needs is to worry about some guy putting a move on her. There's few enough people she can trust. "It won't happen again. I promise."

Piper leans back, her head resting against the wall. "It's okay. I know you were just trying to help."

"I hate seeing you so sad. I wasn't trying to take advantage."

"I know." She sighs, blowing a few strands of hair out of her face as she turns to look at me. "It isn't that I don't like you, Logan. I could see thinking about you that way if things were different. But my head's a mess right now."

"Yeah."

"And . . ." She hesitates, her teeth working her lower lip. "Well . . . I've never had a boyfriend." Her cheeks flush with color.

"I know," I say.

Piper's eyes widen and then immediately narrow. "Bailey?"

I nod. "Bailey."

Her mouth hitches up at one corner, and she shakes her head. "I guess I should've seen that coming."

"She just wants you to be happy. And I do too. So from now on, things will be strictly professional between us. I'd like you to be able to trust me."

Piper smiles. "I do trust you. And I hope you won't be too professional. I kind of like having you as a friend."

It's not quite the way I wish she'd think of me, but it's a start.

Zoey spends the rest of the afternoon editing the video. She uploads it to Connect Me and YouTube as soon as she's finished.

"How long do you think it'll take Sarto to respond?" Piper asks.

"That depends on what he's up to. Judging by how sloppy he was with that last broadcast, I wouldn't be surprised if we heard from him tomorrow."

But Sunday passes with no word from him or Cooper. After forty-eight hours, we're still waiting.

Piper's managed to keep a handle on her temper since our talk, but as she paces the worn hardwood floor Monday afternoon, fists balled at her sides, it's clear her veil of calm is fraying.

"What's taking so long?" she demands.

"I don't know." This is something I've been wondering myself. But on one level, it makes sense. "When you're backed into a corner, sometimes the best response is no response at all."

Piper stops mid-stride and whips around to face me. "But you said poking holes in Sarto's story would make him crack."

"I said that *might* happen. The other possibility is he's got a plan in the works and was hoping to buy time with his last broadcast. If that's the case, you can bet we've put pressure on him. Now we just need to be patient."

Piper comes at me, back straight and eyes full of fire. "I'm tired of being patient! I've been patient for a month. We need to do something other than just make these stupid broadcasts. Something that will *work*."

"Hey!" Zoey says, bristling in her seat. "Stop yelling at my brother. He's doing everything he can. It's not like we can send in a spy to follow Sarto around."

Her statement fires a spark through my brain. "Spying isn't the only way to get a look inside his day-to-day activities," I say.

Bailey glances up from Piper's bed, where she's stretched out like a cat. "So what do you think we should do? Bug his house?"

Zoey laughs. "Like that's even possible."

"There are other ways to get an idea of what Sarto's doing." I glance around at all of them, excitement bolstering my confidence. "What about the man who's watching our house? He's got to be in touch with his superiors, and I'll bet he's contacting them through a laptop or tablet. That would keep him from being overheard, and it would allow for a written record of his orders to prevent mistakes."

My words melt something in Piper. She eases back, anger ebbing.

Zoey grunts, and her skeptical expression morphs into a devilish smile. "So that's our in," she says, nodding. "All we have to do is figure out a way to bug that device."

THE
McCALL
INITIATIVE
EPISODE 1.3: CONSPIRACY

LISA NOWAK

CHAPTER 1

Piper

As I stand beside Logan, my outrage drains away and my clenched fists go limp. I want to believe his plan can work, but how are we going to bug a computer? How will we even get close enough? It's not like we can sneak up on people whose sole purpose is to watch my old house for suspicious activity.

"You really think it's possible?" I ask. "I mean, which one of them would you go after?" Logan's told me there are several different cars, depending on what day and time it is.

"My guess is the one who's there on weekdays is likely to be in charge. It's the most desirable shift, so that's the one he'd take himself. I'll follow his car and see what I can learn."

Right. Even if this guy really is the leader, it's not like he's going to conveniently leave his computer lying around where anyone can get at it.

"I can write a trojan that will send any emails to us before they're encrypted," Zoey says. "I'll just need to know what operating system he's running."

Bailey, who's sprawled on my bed, props herself up on one elbow. "What if he's using his phone to text his boss?"

My thoughts exactly. Logan and Zoey are making an awful lot of assumptions.

"That's possible," Logan says, "But it wouldn't be very secure. Phone records can be subpoenaed. Encryption technology would ensure that any emails falling into the wrong hands couldn't be read."

I glance at Zoey, afraid to get my hopes up, but she nods. "He's right."

"So how are you gonna follow him?" Bailey asks, twirling her hair around her index finger. "To program your navigation computer, you'd have to know where he's going."

"I can deal with that," Zoey says. "Every car has an override for mechanics. It's pretty easy to access if you know what you're doing."

Logan nails her with a big brother look. "You're not coming. It's too dangerous."

"Especially if you're following this dude in your dad's Toyota," Bailey adds. "He'd recognize that thing in a heartbeat. We should take my Mustang."

"We?" Logan says, turning to face her. "There is no 'we.' I'm doing this alone. It's pointless for all of us to put ourselves at risk."

Bailey snorts. "Oh come on, Logan. Do you really think it's smart, following him in a vehicle he sees sitting in your driveway every day?"

"If he can't override the navigation system, it doesn't matter." Zoey's lips curl into a smirk. "He's not going to get far winging it."

Logan glances from one of them to the other. "You could lend me your car, Bailey. And Zoey, you could show me how to override the system."

"No way," Bailey says, shaking her head. "My car, my rules."

"Yeah," Zoey adds. "And that's not something I can teach you in five minutes. If you don't know what you're doing, this guy will get away from you."

"What about soccer practice?" Logan asks.

"Right—like that's more important than my best friend's life."

Sighing, Logan turns to me. "Please don't tell me you want to come, too."

"Nope. I'm perfectly happy to stay right here." I'm not particularly amped about the three of them taking this risk for me, but it's not like I'd be any help.

"All right then," Bailey says, hoisting herself up off the bed. "Logan, you and Zoey come meet me at my place tomorrow afternoon, and we'll go from there."

Hope sparks inside me. This is the best I've felt all week.

But my optimism can't choke out my worries. It's one thing to broadcast messages that challenge the government. It's another for the only people I have left to tail the thugs who made my family disappear.

CHAPTER 2

Logan

The moment Bailey steps onto her front porch, Zoey snatches the key from her hand. "I'm driving, remember?"

"How could I forget?" Bailey raises an eyebrow at me, her quirky smile going unnoticed by my sister, who's already rushing toward the car.

It's not as if there's any reason Zoey shouldn't drive, but it isn't something that normally happens when she and I are in a vehicle together. Still, neither Bailey nor I can argue the fact that she knows what she's doing.

Bailey insists on riding shotgun, so I sit in back as Zoey directs the Mustang to our neighborhood. Since the silver Ford that watches our house always leaves around five o'clock, we park up the street and wait.

"Are you sure this guy's going to lead us to someone important?" Bailey asks, lowering her sunglasses to peer at me between them and the bill of her Portland Timbers hat. Apparently, this is her idea of a disguise.

"No. But we have to start somewhere."

She pushes her glasses into place. "You know Piper's gonna lose it if this doesn't work."

That's my fear too, but a good leader doesn't confess such things to his troops. And he certainly doesn't admit his best strategy is a long shot. "You should give her a little more credit. She's doing as well as anyone could under the circumstances."

Zoey giggles, her face pulling into a grin. "Logan and Piper, sitting in a tree—"

I smack her shoulder, and she yelps. "Hey!"

Half a block down the street, the silver Ford pulls away from the curb. Instantly, Zoey forgets her annoyance and types something into the navigation console. The Mustang's engine hums to life. After a moment's hesitation, we're following the Ford at a respectable distance.

We turn onto 21st and go north a few blocks until we reach Division, where we make a right. Just east of 30th, the Ford pulls into Hal's, a small, run-down restaurant with only a few cars out front. Zoey directs the Mustang into the lot of a coffee shop a couple of doors down.

"Now what?" she asks.

Bailey reaches for the door handle. "I'll go scope things out. Whoever that guy is, he knows you two, but he's not gonna recognize me."

"I can't argue with that," I say. "But be careful."

Bailey's face is a mask of mock seriousness as she pops open the door. "Careful is my middle name."

While we sit and wait, Zoey browses the Mustang's navigation computer and I re-read *The Art of War* on my iPad. Even though the book is technically about warfare, at its core it's about strategy for overcoming opposition, regardless of the arena. The precepts are simple: all battle is about deception; to be successful, you need to know your enemy and yourself; good strategy is based on current circumstances, not past victories. Reminding myself of these things always centers me.

After fifteen minutes, my sister lets out a sigh. "What's taking so long?"

"Give her a chance."

Ten more minutes pass. Zoey shifts in her seat. "You should go see if she's okay."

"She's fine, Sparky. Just be patient."

Five minutes later, as Zoey's restlessness is simmering to a full boil, Bailey saunters down the sidewalk and gets into the front seat.

"Jeez," Zoey says. "What did you do? Order a ten-course dinner?"

"No, just a piece of pie and some coffee."

My sister's mouth drops open. "And you didn't bring us any?"

"Sure—that would've been inconspicuous."

I lean between the seats. "So what did you learn?"

"Well, for one thing, they've got one heck of a good cherry pie."

"I wouldn't know," Zoey says, turning away with her arms crossed over the front of her PVAD vest.

"Can you two be serious?"

"Sure." Bailey shifts to face me, her expression sobering. "Our guy's name is Eric. I know that because the waitress was super chatty. She asked if he wanted his usual, so I'm guessing he goes there a lot. She was kind of teasing him, like she knows him pretty well and wanted to get a smile out of him, but he was being a total Mr. Grumpypants."

"Anything else?" I ask.

"Yeah, his laptop's a Toshiba. He had it open and was working on something, but he was sitting in a booth with his back against the wall, so I couldn't see what he was doing."

"That's not going to do me any good," Zoey says. "To write the trojan, I need to know what operating system he's running."

"Sorry, I tried walking past him to the bathroom, but I couldn't get a look at the screen."

Zoey sighs. "I guess we'll just have to hope he bought the thing from a regular store and hasn't installed a different operating system."

"How likely is that?" I ask.

"Pretty likely, if he's just an average guy. But we could be in big trouble if he's a closet geek."

"He definitely looked more henchman-y than geeky," Bailey says. She turns to me. "So what now, Cap'n?"

"I'll come back later this evening to get a look at the layout of the place and let you know."

"Heck, I can give you the layout."

"In detail? I'm going to need specifics."

Bailey treats me to a dramatic eye roll as she reaches over the seat. "Gimme that tablet."

When I hand it to her, she opens the sketch program and uses her finger to draw a map of the restaurant's floor plan.

"Okay, so it's one of those seat yourself places, and it's shaped like an 'L' inside. Eric was sitting in the shorter leg of it, right here in back." She taps the line that represents the rear wall. "That part's really narrow and has booths on both sides, with an aisle down the middle that leads to the bathrooms." She scribbles a few more lines. "The entrance and front counter are in the main section, along with most of the seating. Right now it's pretty dead in there. Just a couple people up front, probably because it's a dark, nasty little dive, even if it *does* have rockin' pie. I'm guessing our dude likes it in back because he's got more privacy."

I take the tablet from her and study the diagram. "So you sat near him?"

Bailey nods. "Of course. How else was I gonna eavesdrop?"

"Then he'd recognize you if he saw you again."

"Not necessarily." She takes off her hat and sunglasses and releases her ponytail, allowing her long auburn hair to cascade down her back. "If I lose the disguise and put on a slinky top and shorts, *voila!* I'm a totally different girl."

"A girl he's more likely to notice."

Bailey bats her eyelashes. "What does it matter, if he didn't look closely enough today to remember me?"

"Point taken."

She flashes a triumphant smile. "So what's next?"

"I'm not sure. I'll need time to think about it. Do you have soccer practice tomorrow?"

"Yup. But it gets over at five, and I can skip if you need me."

Despite the nonchalant hair flip that accompanies this statement, I know missing practice is a sacrifice for her.

"Give me tonight to think it over," I say. "I'll be in touch first thing tomorrow."

CHAPTER 3

Logan

I consider our situation from every angle, but by morning, I still don't have a concrete plan. There are just too many variables. Does Eric have dinner at this restaurant on a regular basis? Will we be able to get him away from his laptop long enough to upload the trojan? What will we do about the other customers? And most critical of all, what if he's not running the operating system Zoey wrote the program for? Short of taking the time to follow Eric for several days, the only logical approach is to improvise. I don't like the idea, but Bailey's right about Piper. She needs to see progress.

After breakfast, I message Bailey through Carrier Pigeon.

Blitzkrieg1: *Zoey and I will have dinner at Hal's tonight at five. If Eric shows up, we'll be ready for him, and if not, we can try again. I'd like you to be there. Bring a computer to communicate with us, but keep your phone off. Get your own table in the front section and let me know when you're there. Depending on how things play out, we may need you to upload the trojan. I'll have Zoey get in touch with instructions. I can drop a flash drive off at your convenience.*

With Bailey so gung-ho about adventure, my hope is she'll step up. But I'm not as certain as I'd like to be. This is different from any of the other things she's done to help Piper. She could get into real trouble.

After only a few minutes, I receive a response.

Soccerocker: *Will do, Cap'n. Come on over. I'll be here till noon.*

I take the flash drive to her then come home and start a chat with Piper on Carrier Pigeon. I'd rather be at the White Eagle, but there's a limit to how often I can leave the house without drawing suspicion. Besides, Zoey has a Doernbecher appointment at 10:30, and though she hasn't wanted me there after the first one, she can't stand the idea of me going off without her.

Last night, I told Piper what we discovered. While she was surprised at our good luck, she was also cynical about our prospects for success. That's not the sort of energy I want to surround myself with right now, so instead of bringing up the mission, I direct our conversation to more casual things: cat videos we've seen on Connect Me, the books Piper's been reading, and how Portland compares to Chicago. We've been doing a lot of this sort of chatting lately. It seems to ease Piper's loneliness, and it's provided a non-threatening way for me to get closer to her.

At 9:45, Zoey comes in without knocking and falls dramatically backward onto my bed.

I glance away from the computer. "Shouldn't you be getting ready for your appointment?"

"I *am* ready. We aren't leaving for fifteen minutes." She spreads out her arms and sighs. "I wish Mom could take me."

I wish that, too. Mom has always been Zoey's staunchest advocate, making sure she gets the best possible care even when it means standing up to condescending doctors. As much as Dad dotes on Zoey, he's never been good at that sort of thing, which is why he lets her nurse handle the medical appointments.

"I could give you a ride," I say. Even though I'm no substitute for Mom, I've been trying to fill the void where I can.

Zoey's down-turned hands clasp fistfuls of blanket. "Forget it. That would be worse than Denise taking me."

"Why?"

"It just would."

How can I argue with a statement like that? I swivel around to give her my full attention.

Rather than explain, she tucks her hands behind her head, bony elbows poking out, and stares at the ceiling. "Do you think we'll ever see Mom again?"

"I don't know." Zoey and I rarely talk about our mother's absence. I'm not exactly sure why, but I suspect it has something to do with Piper. When I compare our loss to hers, it doesn't seem fair to complain.

Zoey sighs. "I miss her, Logan."

"So do I." Neither of us has told Mom what we know about Dad, and that only adds to the feeling of separation. Along with the enormous physical gulf, there's an emotional one that's even more intimidating.

Zoey swings her feet, thudding her Birkenstocks against the end of my bed. "Do you think they'll ever open the border?"

"Cooper says he wants to, eventually."

"'Eventually' is a long time."

"Yeah."

Denise hollers from the living room, and Zoey releases a long breath before rolling off the bed and getting to her feet. "See you in a couple of hours. . . . *If* I survive."

"I thought the new treatment wasn't painful."

"It's not. But I still hate it. They keep me hooked up to an IV for *hours*. And they ask the same stupid questions about side effects every week."

I smile. "Be sure to mention the excessive crankiness." It's not entirely a joke. Zoey *has* been moodier since she started treatment. While this is difficult to put up with, the silver lining is that it provides an excuse for the distance that's grown between her and Dad. Despite the efforts she's been making since I spoke to her about it, their relationship still isn't what it used to be.

Zoey scowls over her shoulder as she strides toward the door, but she doesn't trouble herself by answering.

The next six hours drag out, my doubts growing with every

passing minute. An attempt to distract myself by reading fails because I can't keep my mind on the words. There are too many possibilities to worry about. Too many ways things could go wrong tonight. I review the various ideas I've come up with, hoping to reassure myself, but the effort only makes me feel worse.

At four o'clock, I hear Zoey coming in, grumbling to Denise, who responds in a soothing tone. How Denise remains so patient in the face of my sister's surliness, I have no idea.

I wait half an hour before crossing the hall to Zoey's room. She's in her desk chair, her face a pucker of concentration as she practices chords on the guitar she got for her birthday a few months ago. Dad has yet to find her a teacher here in Portland, so she's making do with tutorials she's found on the Net.

"Hey," I say. "Are you ready to head out?"

She looks up. "Yeah. What's the plan?"

"I'm not sure yet." While this isn't entirely true, my best idea is bound to meet with resistance. I'm waiting until the last minute to reveal it.

"You're not *sure*?"

"That's right. We're going to wing it."

Zoey purses her lips and gives me a squint-eyed look. "Since when do you 'wing' anything?"

"In this case, we don't have much choice. I could spend days, even weeks, watching Eric, and that might establish a pattern, but it's not going to tell us how to get that trojan onto his laptop."

"True enough." Zoey stands up to set her guitar back in its case. "But you've got to have *some* idea."

"Of course I have ideas. I just won't know which one's the most viable until I see what we have to work with."

I can't blame my sister for the skeptical look she gives me. I feel just as uncertain. Even if Eric is a regular at this restaurant, that doesn't mean he's going to show up tonight. And if he does, the place could be so crowded it would be impossible to get close to his computer. Uploading the first broadcast to the weather station made me nervous enough, but at least that plan had limited variables and no repercussions for failure. In this case, one misstep could tip off Eric and whoever he's working for. It could even get us deported, should someone connect us to Piper.

We leave the house before the silver Ford does, so we can be seated at Hal's when our mark arrives.

Zoey trails me through the main part of the restaurant as I take note of the other customers. There's an older couple, a man sitting by himself, and a young woman with two little kids. The place is dimly lit and looks worn-out. I'm not sure if it's that or the early hour that accounts for the lack of customers.

I head for the back section, which is empty, and find a place a few tables from the one Eric sat at yesterday. Zoey tries to take the seat that would face him, but I shoo her to the other side.

"What if he doesn't show up?" she asks as she activates her iPad.

"*Shhh.* We don't need to tell everyone what we're up to."

"Oh yeah, *everyone's* sure to hear." She motions toward the empty booths.

"We can't be too careful," I say, waking my own tablet. "Now fire up Carrier Pigeon and we'll talk through that. But be sure to mute the sound. We—"

"I know, I know," she swipes a hand through the air, as if I'm a pesky fly. "We don't need to tell everyone what we're up to."

The waitress arrives a moment later with menus. She's taking our drink order when I receive a message from Bailey.

Soccerocker: *Okay, I'm here. What's the plan?*

I glance at the time display on my iPad. 5:21. It should only take a few minutes to get here from the house, and Eric usually leaves right at five.

Blitzkrieg1: *Just sit tight for now.*

Soccerocker: *Are you sure it's safe to chat? What if this Eric dude has some super high tech spy software?*

Greengirl007: *Impossible. The NetMax dongle scrambles everything. The only way he could eavesdrop is if he knew our passphrase, and he'd never figure it out in a million years. Diffie-Hellman still hasn't been cracked in an observational fashion after all this time.*

Soccerocker: *Uh … okay. If you say so.*

Greengirl007: *Anyway, he's got to show up for that to be an issue.*

Blitzkrieg1: *Just relax. If he doesn't show, we'll enjoy our dinner and come up with a new plan. No harm done.*

Greengirl007: *I better get some pie out of this.*

Soccerocker: *He's here!*

Zoey looks up and I kick her under the table. Gently, of course. She catches herself and drops her attention to her iPad. I tap my screen to minimize the chat box.

A few moments later, Eric walks past. Out of the corner of my eye, I see him do a double-take, but I keep my attention on my tablet. As soon as he's at his table in the corner, I open Carrier Pigeon and type a new message.

Blitzkrieg1: *He recognizes Zoey and me, but I'm sure he doesn't know we recognize him. He's got no reason to suspect we didn't walk in completely by chance. Just act natural.*

The waitress comes back with our drinks. "Look at you two," she says, shaking her head. "Out for a nice dinner together, and you're all wrapped up in your toys."

"He's my brother," Zoey says. "How 'nice' can it be?"

I give the waitress a longsuffering look. "Babysitting," I say.

"Yeah, and all he wants to do is chat with his *girlfriend*." Zoey pats her iPad. "If I didn't have this, I'd be reading the back of the ketchup bottle."

The waitress laughs. "You're as bad as me and my little brother." She takes our order and moves on to Eric.

Something flickers on my tablet, drawing my attention.

Greengirl007: *Was that natural enough for you?*

Soccerocker: *What did I miss?*

Greengirl007: *Only an award-winning performance. Now what's next?*

Blitzkrieg1: *Bailey, when I give the word, you'll get up and head for the bathroom. Zoey, I want you to fake a seizure. I'll stand up to help, and then call on Eric to give me a hand getting you off the floor. When I squeeze your arm, 'come to' and act groggy. Bailey, after Eric leaves his seat, slip out and upload the trojan. I'll keep him distracted.*

Greengirl007: *No way! I'm not doing that!!!!!!*

She glares at me across the table.

Blitzkrieg1: *It's the best idea I have. And back off with the attitude. Do you want Eric to notice?*

Greengirl007: *It's a STUPID idea. MB doesn't give you seizures, Logan.*

Blitzkrieg1: *Eric doesn't know that. He probably doesn't even know you have MB.*

Greengirl007: *He might! I've been wearing this stupid PVAD vest for over three weeks. And I have no idea how to fake a seizure.*

Blitzkrieg1: *After that last performance, I'm convinced you'll figure it out.*

Soccerocker: *I know it sucks, Zoey, but you need to take one for the team. Piper's counting on you.*

Her comment is tactically brilliant, and yet thirty seconds go by with no response. I glance at my sister. She's got an eye-lock on her tablet and won't acknowledge me. After another fifteen seconds, her fingers begin moving.

Greengirl007: *Fine. But you owe me. I want a pie. A WHOLE pie.*

Soccerocker: *LOL. You've got it, girlfriend. I'll buy you two.*

The waitress arrives with our food. I'd like to let Zoey eat, but the longer I wait, the more chance there is of someone sitting in our section or the waitress returning with Eric's dinner.

As if sensing her limited opportunity, Zoey begins swiping French fries through a lake of ketchup, three at a time, and stuffing them into her mouth. At this rate, she might choke and eliminate the need for faking.

I send Bailey the signal. After a moment, she comes around the corner, heading for the bathroom behind Eric's booth. She's kept her word about looking like a completely different girl today. Her hair flows in waves past her shoulders, short shorts hug her rear end, and her tank top, which sports the Portland Thorns logo, reads "Feeling Thorny." Eric glances up from his laptop and doesn't look back down until she's passed.

Blitzkrieg1: *Okay, Zoey. Do your thing.*

My sister licks salt off her fingers, wipes them on her shirt, and shuts down Carrier Pigeon. A second later, she stiffens in her seat. Her eyes roll back in her head and she begins to shake. Slumping sideways, she flops to the ground to twitch like a fish.

"Zoey!" I holler, scrambling out of the booth and kneeling beside her. I pull her into my arms, cradling her, and glance desperately at Eric. He's watching with the look of a man who doesn't want to get involved.

"Hey mister, can you help me?"

He sighs, stands up, and comes over to squat beside us. I can't believe this is working. It's been too easy.

Behind Eric, Bailey slips out and sits down at his booth. She needs less than twenty seconds to upload the trojan, but if anyone comes around the corner to use the bathroom during that time, we're sunk.

"What do you want me to do?" Eric asks.

I surreptitiously squeeze my sister's arm. She stops shaking and goes limp, her eyes fluttering. "Wha-what happened?"

"You had a seizure. It's okay. You're going to be all right."

"Maybe I should call an ambulance." Eric reaches for his wrist phone.

"No!"

His eyes pin me.

"It's just that my sister hates being a spectacle," I say, looking past him toward Bailey, whose gaze is riveted on the computer screen. "She'll be fine now. This happens all the time. Just help me get her off the floor."

Even though I could clearly manage Zoey's weight on my own, Eric scoots forward, taking one of her arms while I begin hoisting her to her feet.

As we help her up, she subtly shifts her position, forcing Eric to keep his back to the bathrooms. I can barely make out Bailey in my peripheral vision as she gets up from the table.

"Everything all right here?"

I whip around to see the waitress coming toward us with Eric's order, and my heart leaps to full alert. Something small clatters to the floor behind me.

"Yeah, fine," I say, searching the waitress's face for any sign she noticed Bailey at Eric's table. "My little sister just had an episode."

"But I'm okay now," Zoey says, her voice shaking.

I sneak a glance toward the bathrooms. Bailey's frozen in the doorway, staring at the flash drive, which lies on the floor near Eric's booth. Neither picking it up nor leaving it seems like a good idea, but either would be better than her deer-in-the-headlights impression.

Zoey pulls away from Eric and me, easing into her seat. All sad-eyed and frail, she peers up into his face. "Thank you."

"Sure," Eric grunts. He shoots me a glance I can't quite read before turning to head for his table. When he gets to the flash drive, he stops.

My heart pumps a shot of pure ice through my veins as he bends down to grab it.

"This yours?" he asks, straightening up and looking at Bailey.

I can't breathe as I wait for her response.

"Uh . . . yeah." The terrified expression flickers away as she smiles, stepping forward to take it. "I guess I dropped it. Thanks."

As she walks by, ignoring us, I sit down across from my sister. Eric seems preoccupied with his dinner now, but I'd like to get out of here before he realizes that if Zoey has seizures all the time, they wouldn't disturb me enough to ask strangers for help.

"If you want," I say, motioning toward Zoey's plate, "we can box that up and take it home."

She gives me a this-better-not-cost-me-my-pie look. "I think I can manage."

The waitress stops at our table on her way back from delivering Eric's food. "You poor thing. Do you think a scoop of ice cream would help?"

"Maybe," Zoey says in a trembling voice. "If it had a slice of pie under it."

"I think we'd better make that to go," I add. "Our dad will never let me hear the end of it if I don't get her back home."

"I'll bring you a couple of boxes."

The waitress pats Zoey's shoulder, and as she hustles away, a new message appears on my iPad.

Soccerocker: *Oh crap. I thought I was gonna pee myself. Does he look suspicious?*

Blitzkrieg1: *A little. But I don't think he's realized the three of us are together. Was he running the stock operating system?*

Soccerocker: *Yup. We're good.*

Greengirl007: *Unless he figures out what that flash drive was for.*

That's my worry, too. But the sooner we're gone, the less reason he'll have to keep thinking about us. When the waitress comes back, we box up our food and leave as quickly as possible.

CHAPTER 4

Piper

As I stew over how things are going with the trojan upload, I wish I hadn't been so stubborn about staying at the White Eagle. It doesn't seem right, letting everyone else take the risks for me. If Logan and Zoey get caught, they could be sent back to Chicago. And who knows what would happen to Bailey. Just because she's an adrenaline junkie doesn't mean I need to take advantage of her lack of good sense.

I open my laptop and think about logging into Carrier Pigeon to lurk on their conversation. But I don't want to distract them, and if something goes wrong, it would freak me out to watch it going down. Instead I check the weather again, so I'll know what I'm missing. The 7-day forecast comes up, a row of little yellow suns. It's been dry and in the eighties for over a week. Even in my dark dungeon, I can feel it. The air used to be constantly chilly, but now it's warm enough that a T-shirt feels comfortable.

Of course, being outside would be even better. Not that *that* will ever happen. Except for going down in the tunnel a couple of times, I haven't left this building since I met Logan and Zoey at Coffee Madness twenty-one days ago. Sometimes I think I'll never go out again.

I glance at my laptop's clock. Five nineteen. Only four minutes since the last time I looked. I've got to do something to distract myself so I won't think about what Logan, Zoey, and Bailey are trying to do for me. Why didn't I tell them not to? Sure, Sarto's got me totally smoked, but that's no excuse for letting my friends do something this insane. What the hell is wrong with me?

I pick up Bailey's tablet to open the book I've been reading and immediately change my mind. Maybe I should get back to Grandpa's journals instead. I've been so busy fielding emails and Connect Me comments, I haven't touched his notebooks in over a week. Or at least that's what I tell myself every time I think about them. Somehow, it's just been easier to read the stuff I've been buying through Bailey's Amazon account. It lets me get lost in another world instead of reminding me of how craptastic mine is.

But as hard as it is to think about my family, I miss being inside Grandpa's head, so I pull journal #3 from the top of the pile and open it.

May 3, 2059 – Portland's busting its backside to help out as Cascadia's capitol. They gave Congress the old downtown library and donated Pittock Mansion to be the "White House of the West." Of course, considering how much work that place needs, the city might be getting the better end of the deal. They're also digging tunnels to tie the government buildings together: Congress, Pittock Mansion, the Treasury, the Federal Building, and the Benson Hotel, where they plan on hosting all the foreign dignitaries. Kind of funny to think about that, but the prime minister of Japan is already talking about forming an alliance.

Everyone's tossing their hat into the ring to be our first president. The Republicans and Democrats seem to think they've got things locked up, just like in the U.S., but the Libertarians and Greens hope they'll have a better shot now. I'd like to see Cooper run. He's young, sure, but there's nothing in Cascadia's Constitution to hold him back.

That's true. Daskalov made sure there was no age restriction on the office of president. According to the rumors, he had plans for Cooper all along, even though Cooper, and apparently Grandpa, didn't know it.

I close my eyes for a second, wondering what's going on at Hal's. Maybe this Eric guy won't even show up. Is that what I want? If he doesn't, my friends will be safe, but then nothing will change. And if I don't see some progress soon, I think I'm going to lose it.

I catch my thoughts tanking and open my eyes.

May 7, 2059 – By God, Daskalov did it. Cooper was determined to return to his rock star life, but Daskalov convinced him to give the people what they want. Everyone's been speculating over whether Cooper would run on a Republican or Democratic ticket, seeing as he seems to march to the beat of a different political drummer, but he sure threw them for a loop. Said he was creating his own party—the Cascadian Party. It's based on something called the Third Force. I guess Tom McCall came up with it when he was governor. It's supposed to be this common sense, middle-of-the-road deal, where politicians vote on each issue, instead of along party lines. Cooper says partisan politics tore the U.S. apart, and he doesn't want that for Cascadia. He calls the Cascadian party "a place where people can reach across the political void to do what's right for the country." I've gotta say, I like the sound of that.

When I get to the end of the entry, I glance over to check my laptop, in case I missed an incoming message. Not that I possibly could, sitting this close and having the sound cranked up.

Nada. Of course, it's only five thirty. There's no way they could be done already. *Relax, Piper. You can't help them.* I turn back to Grandpa's hand-scribbled words.

May 13, 2059 – The more I hear about Cooper's platform, the more hope I have for this new nation. Yesterday he announced he's donating the proceeds from The Tom McCall Song *to start something called the Cascadia Fund. He's bent on building wind farms, geothermal plants, and desalinization facilities so we'll have plenty of electricity and water, not just for ourselves, but to sell to America. And since Cascadia doesn't have much money in her coffers yet, he's willing to grease the wheels on all this. He's asking others to add to the fund—sort of a voluntary tax—and the members of his band were the first to get on board. It's a damn fine strategy, if you ask me. Bound to win him a few votes, and even if he doesn't get elected, he's still got money earmarked for his goals. Whoever takes office can't spend it any other way.*

I'm not sure how much more of Grandpa's hero worship I can take. Maybe he's got an excuse, since he couldn't have any idea we'd wind up here, but I still don't want to read it. And yet, I keep going.

May 22, 2059 – Senator Daskalov is dead. The whole country's in shock. Everyone knows what a mentor he was to Cooper, and it's like we're all holding our breath, waiting to see what will happen. My heart sure goes out to that poor kid. He'd have been lost this past year and a half without Daskalov, and any fool can see the man was like a father to him. I'm crossing my fingers this doesn't break him. I'd like to think he's stronger than that, but the truth is, I'm flat-out worried. Cascadia needs Cooper.

My laptop beeps, startling me out of the past, and I look up to see Logan's message.

Blitzkrieg1: *We did it. I'll give you the details when I see you in the morning, but I wanted to let you know everything's okay.*

I start to type a response that says how worried I've been, but halfway through, I delete it.

Futuresuture: *Good to hear. I'll see you tomorrow.*

I swear, this is the last time I'm letting them take a risk like this for me.

Thursday morning, I can't drum up the energy to reply to my new emails and Connect Me comments, even though I know last night's mission was a success and Logan will be here soon.

It seems like so much work. All those people want me to help them, but I can't even help myself.

We still haven't heard anything from Sarto, and it's been almost a week. What if he never responds? I know the public's still behind me because I can see the evidence online. But once again, I've lost the media. This time, to the mess out at Hanford. I guess the temporary measures the U.S. took in the '20s were a little *too* temporary, and everyone's worried nuclear waste will start leaking into the Columbia. Like that's anything new. Grandpa said they had this same problem when he was a kid.

While I wait for Logan, I distract myself by going a few rounds with the diagnostic feature of the Sim Medical Suite. I don't kick butt with it like I do with Sim Surgery, but since I haven't got the equipment for the virtual reality part of the program, I'm out of luck.

Just before nine, Logan sends a message to let me know he's on his way. I go downstairs and slide the platform back from the door.

Almost every day, either he or Bailey stop by at some point, but yesterday I was on my own. I know they've got better things to do than hang with me. I shouldn't expect it. But the more time I spend alone here, the jumpier I get.

The basement's even more depressing than the rest of the tavern, so I go back upstairs and open the side door a few inches to let the green-smelling tangle of vines, branches, and flowers mesmerize me. Sometimes I just stand like this, wishing I had the guts to go out. Maybe Logan and Bailey are right about it being safe to sit on the patio, but the whole point of doing that is to relax. How can I relax if I'm constantly psyching about people spotting me?

It's a perfect day. Little spots of sunlight fight their way through the branches to dance over the pavers, and a breeze stirs the leaves. Bailey's probably headed to the river right now. She didn't want to say anything when I talked to her on Carrier

Pigeon yesterday, but I finally got her to admit she was going to Carver with some friends. Last year, she always went with me.

I hate being stuck in here where I can't see the sky or spend my afternoons baking in the sun. I hate missing summer. With everything else that's happened, that should be the least of my worries, but sometimes it feels so huge.

I'm still standing in the doorway when I hear Logan's voice downstairs. By the time I get to the kitchen entrance, he's at the top of the steps, his face darkened by a brooding look that sends my gut plunging.

"What's wrong?"

The sharp note in my voice startles him, and he focuses on me like he just now realized I'm here. "Oh. Sorry, Piper. It's nothing serious. Zoey's ready to tear me one." He shakes his head, glancing back down the staircase. "She insisted on walking the whole way."

"And you let her?"

"I tried to pick her up, but it was like wrestling a bag of cats." He squeezes past me into the main part of the tavern.

"Is she okay?" I ask, following him over to the table in the back corner.

"Yeah. She just needs to catch her breath. She'll be up in a minute. Unless she's trying to make a point about not wanting to be in the same room with me." He attempts a smile, but it falls flat.

"Why's she mad?"

Logan sits down, running a hand through his hair as he takes his time to answer. "I made her fake a seizure to distract our mark."

"Oh." No wonder she's smoked.

"She's been grumpy a lot lately."

I nod. "From the early reports, it looks like that's going to be a common side-effect of Tri-Inhibitase. Yesterday was her third treatment, right?"

"Yeah, but I think it's more than just that. She's been using her PVAD for over three weeks now, and there's no improvement. Usually her heart starts recovering sooner than this."

I'm itching to hear about what happened at the restaurant last night, but Logan obviously needs someone to talk to. "So it's time for an implanted device."

"Yeah." He sighs and slumps back, his arms out in front of him on the table. "And she's terrified of surgery. When she got her port four years ago, she had a bad reaction to the anesthetic and almost died."

I slide into the seat across from him. "They weren't expecting it? Anyone treating MB should know that's a possibility. I'm surprised they weren't taking precautions."

"They were. She's just particularly sensitive, I guess." Logan goes quiet, staring at his hands. "She really needs that surgery, but she's going to fight it as long as she can. Not that I blame her. I don't like thinking about it either. It just means she's one step closer, you know?" He looks up, and something in his eyes stabs me deep.

"Yeah." It's the first time I've seen behind Logan's sure steadiness. Now I understand why he felt such a need to comfort me in the basement the other day. Part of me—a crazy part—wants to reach across the table and put my hand over his.

"She tries to act like there's nothing wrong," Logan says, his eyes cutting away, "but underneath, I can see she's scared. It doesn't take a degree in psychology to know all those Connect Me personalities are more than just a way of bucking authority."

When it comes to Magnusson-Bell, there's only so much that can be done, but Logan's been here for me all these weeks, taking charge and offering hope. I want to do the same for him. "This new drug is showing real promise," I say. "There's a good chance it will buy Zoey a couple of years, and by then, we'll have more options."

Logan's sigh makes it clear he's not convinced.

"You know about the problem with anti-rejection drugs, right?" I ask.

"Yeah."

"Well, we're not far from getting past that. If you start with a person's own DNA, rejection isn't an issue. And we're probably only five or six years away from lab-grown hearts. They're already doing preliminary studies with kidneys in Great Britain."

I'm hoping this will melt a little of Logan's sadness, but he just shakes his head. "She isn't going to last that long if she won't have the surgery. We'll force her if we have to, but I hate to think of her going into something like that so upset."

"It's definitely not the best way to do it." I glance toward the kitchen. Zoey still hasn't come upstairs. I'd be worried if I didn't have a little brother who's just as stubborn. "You know, I've done a lot of reading about MB. There are ways of dealing with those reactions."

"That's what her nurse said. But Zoey doesn't believe it."

"You want me to try talking to her?"

Logan looks up. "Would you? I'd really appreciate it. Zoey respects you, you know."

"Even though I'm a dirty Cooper-hater?"

A smile breaks through the gloom on Logan's face. "She might not be too fond of that aspect of your personality, but your strong points outweigh it."

I laugh as I push away from the table. "Well, that's something, I guess."

When I poke my head through the basement doorway, Zoey's hunched on the bottom step.

"Hey," I say as I plod down to join her. "Isn't it boring sitting here by yourself?"

"Maybe. But it's better than the company upstairs."

I squeeze in beside her, forcing her to scoot. "Does that include me?"

"Of course not. *Duh*."

"Good." We're both quiet for a while because it's not like I can go in with my guns blazing. "Your brother told me what he made you do at the restaurant," I finally say. "That must've been humiliating."

Zoey buries her face in her hands, bony arms propped against her knees. "He's such a dimwad. I'm never going to forgive him."

"I don't blame you. Some things should be off-limits."

"*Exactly.* And it wasn't even medically accurate. I mean, passing out, maybe, but a seizure?" She pulls her hands away from her face so I can get the full effect of her scorn. "If it wasn't for you, I would've told Logan where he could stuff his stupid seizure."

I laugh. "Well, I appreciate it. I really do." Of all the things Bailey, Logan, and Zoey have done for me, this makes me feel guiltiest. The risks they've taken might have been more dangerous, but nothing stings like public humiliation.

Zoey's eyes bore into me. "It's not funny," she says. "I owe you big time. I could fake a million seizures and it wouldn't be enough."

"What? That's whacked. I'm the one who owes *you*."

"Right. Like you'd be in this mess if it wasn't for me." She leans back, a scrawny, bristly bundle of fierceness. "My dad brought us here because I'm sick. It's *my* fault your family's gone."

If Logan's sadness tugged at my heart, this rips it right in half. "That's not true."

"Yes it is!"

"Zoey, even if my family hadn't been kicked out to make room for yours, they'd still be gone. There'd just be someone else living in my house."

Her eyes narrow and her lips press together, then slowly, the skepticism fades. "Really?"

"Yeah. There's got to be a ton of people wanting to buy their way in. We were targeted because we're poor. It has nothing to do with you."

She looks away. "That doesn't make what my dad did okay."

"True. But there's no reason you should feel guilty about it."

"If you say so." Zoey yanks at her PVAD vest, straightening it before reaching underneath to smooth out her tank top.

"I'll bet that thing gets to be a real pain," I say, seeing my chance. "Especially when it's hot."

"I *hate* it."

She's playing right into my hand, but the slightest wrong word will tip her off. Which doesn't leave me many options. "Not much you can do about it," I say.

"Don't give me that."

I fake an innocent look. "Don't give you *what*?"

"Logan talked to you. I know he did. He told you all about the surgery and what happened last time."

It's pointless to deny it. "Yeah," I say. "So what?"

"So I bet he sent you down here to brainwash me."

I stick my hand in front of her, palm up. When she pushes it away, I shove it back.

"Stop that!"

"No. You bet wrong and you need to pay up. Logan didn't send me, I volunteered."

"Great." Zoey crosses her arms. "Now *you'll* be nagging me, too. Well, you can save your breath. I'm on Tri-Inhibitase, so I don't need an implant."

She's too smart to believe that, which means she's got to be hoping I won't know any better. "Tri-Inhibitase only lengthens the periods of remission. It's not going to cure you or repair the damage that's already been done to your heart."

"So?" She gives me a stubborn look.

"So stop trying to snow me. I was supposed to help with that study this summer. I know all about it."

"And now you're going to use your cutting-edge knowledge to convince me to get that surgery?"

I snort. "Like I could convince you of anything."

Her scowl melts away, leaving her lips fighting off a smile.

"There are ways around that reaction you had last time, though," I say. "Yours might've been worse than most people's, but it happens to everyone with MB. That's why they're constantly working on new anesthetics. They came up with one just a few months ago, and another about a year before that. Even if those are too risky, there are other options. Like they could do the surgery without putting you under."

Zoey's eyes go wide. "You mean I'd be *awake*?"

"Yeah, but you wouldn't feel anything. They'd block the pain and give you something to help you stay calm."

Her face crumples like she just caught a whiff of week-old road kill. "Ewwww!"

"Oh, come on." I bump my shoulder against hers. "I've seen how curious you are. You're always looking things up. Don't you think it would be interesting to learn first-hand what happens during surgery?"

"Uh—*no*." She rolls her eyes. "That's disgusting, Piper."

"I don't think it is."

"Well, you're weird."

"And you aren't?" I give her another shoulder bump. "How many eleven-year-old girls do you think spend their time chatting with conspiracy theorists and writing computer code?"

She pulls back, twisting her upper body to get a direct line for a glare. "I'm *not* having that surgery."

"Fine with me." I shrug. "I'm not the one who has to walk around wearing a PVAD vest. But you might want to think about your family. They'll be the people who suffer when you're gone. If I were you, I'd try to put that off as long as possible, no matter how scared I was."

Zoey turns away and sits quietly for a few seconds, wrapping a string from her cut-offs around one finger.

"Well, I'm going upstairs to ask Logan about what happened at the restaurant yesterday," I say, getting to my feet. "You can go on sitting here as long as you want."

I only make it halfway up the stairs before I hear her footsteps behind me.

CHAPTER 5

Logan

Friday morning, Dad's voice rouses me from a sound sleep. "Logan, we need to talk."

I open my eyes to see him standing at the foot of my bed. Along with his work clothes, he's wearing his don't-question-me expression. It's a look that had more impact before I learned of his dishonesty.

"What's going on?" I ask, rubbing a hand across my face.

"Denise is concerned about how much time your sister's spending away from the house. She can't do her job if Zoey's not here for her to look after."

The words are an instant reveille, but I manage not to let my alarm show. "Dad, we've talked about this. Zoey likes getting out and seeing things. All that fresh air has to be good for her."

"If it's so good for her," Dad says, his eyes challenging me, "then why isn't she showing any signs of improvement?"

"She likes seeing all the trees and flowers. They make her happy. That's worth something, don't you think?" I'm at a disadvantage with him towering over me, but it wouldn't be much better to stand up wearing only my boxers.

"It's not worth as much as keeping her healthy." Dad folds his arms over his chest, a sure sign he won't tolerate further discussion. "There's no need for her to be constantly traipsing all over town. If you want to take her out for an hour or two, that's one thing. But no more of these all-day excursions."

If I tell Zoey she has to cut back on her visits to the White Eagle, there will be hell to pay. She's still barely speaking to me. But pushing Dad any harder can only result in me being confined to the house. I don't want to think about the effect it might have on Piper to be locked up in that tavern with no one but Bailey for company.

"Okay," I say. "I'll talk to her."

On my morning jog, I realize the silver Ford isn't parked down the street. I'm not sure what to make of that. Does it mean the kidnappers are no longer watching the house? We've learned nothing about them through the emails Zoey's intercepted, beyond that Eric's last name is DeBrassie, so it's hard to say.

At least we're receiving the emails. Until the first one arrived, I worried DeBrassie might have put our presence at Hal's together with the flash drive to figure out what we'd done. Even now, I have the occasional paranoid thought that he knows and hasn't taken preventive measures because he's trying to trap us.

When I'm on my second lap, I notice a blue Nissan that's new to the neighborhood. A closer look through the tinted windows reveals a man in the driver's seat. I'm careful not to make eye contact as I jog by.

So where is DeBrassie? Has he been reassigned, or does he realize his position has been compromised?

When I get back to the house, I sign onto Carrier Pigeon to let Piper know we won't be there until later this afternoon. I've just clicked "post" when a message from Bailey appears.

Soccerocker: *Hey, when are you going to see Piper?*

Blitzkrieg1: *Not until this evening. My dad's worried about Zoey being away from the house so much.*

Soccerocker: *Piper's not going to like that.*

Blitzkrieg1: *I know.*

Soccerocker: *I'm getting kind of worried about her. It was bad enough when she was just pissed off all the time, but now she's totally whupped.*

Blitzkrieg1: *I've noticed. I'll still spend time with her as often as I can. I just won't be able to bring Zoey as much.*

Soccerocker: *Maybe that's a good thing. You've kind of got this mellowing mojo when it comes to Piper. Being alone with you will probably be good for her.*

Blitzkrieg1: *If you're rethinking that boyfriend idea, you can stop right now. Piper and I had a talk. She's not ready for that.*

Soccerocker: *You did?????*

Blitzkrieg1: *Yes. And I'm not going to push her. She's got enough on her mind without having to worry about my intentions.*

Soccerocker: *Who said anything about pushing her? I just think you're a good influence as a friend.*

Blitzkrieg1: *Right.*

Soccerocker: *And if things happen to go beyond that later, well, so be it.*

"Hey, Logan," Zoey interrupts from my open doorway. "When are we leaving?"

"Just a second," I say, and type a final message.

Blitzkrieg1: *I've got to go. Time to break the news to Zoey.*

Soccerocker: *Good luck.*

I log out of Carrier Pigeon and swivel around in my seat. "We'll head over there around seven o'clock."

Zoey slumps against the door frame with a sigh so heavy it blows her bangs off her forehead. "Why can't we go *now*?"

"Because Dad doesn't think it's good for you to be out so much."

Her face darkens like the sky before a superstorm. "What's that supposed to mean?"

"He wants you here where Denise can keep a closer eye on you."

"But what about Piper?"

I put a finger to my lips.

Scowling, Zoey steps inside and closes the door behind her. "We can't just leave her by herself all the time," she says in a hiss of a whisper. "She's *lonely*."

If it's obvious to Zoey, it's a bigger problem than I thought. "I know. That's why I'll go on seeing her. But you won't be able to come along every day, and we'll have to make your visits shorter."

The storm breaks loose in a flash as quick as lightning. "That's not fair! I'm part of this too."

"I know you are, Sparky. I don't like it any more than you do. But I can tell Dad's not going to budge. You can talk to Piper all you like through Carrier Pigeon."

"I don't want to talk to her through Carrier Pigeon!" Zoey stomps her foot, barely making a thump against the carpet.

"Then I suggest you take it up with Dad," I say. "But as long as you're using that PVAD, don't expect him to change his mind."

CHAPTER 6

Logan

I stay home with Zoey all afternoon, not wanting to cross Denise and risk being reported on the first day of Dad's new restrictions. But the conversation with Bailey has left me uneasy. More and more lately, it seems that when Piper's on her own, the fight drains out of her. And yesterday, instead of being sensitive to this and offering a distraction, I wallowed in my own problems. I can't let that happen again.

I launch Carrier Pigeon and attempt a conversation with Piper, but even though I can sense that she doesn't want me to sign off, her comments are brief and stilted, making my apprehension swell. Tomorrow, regardless of Zoey, Denise, and everything else, I'll go spend the day at the White Eagle. Even if Piper and I do nothing but sit and stare at each other, it will be better than leaving her by herself.

At dinner, Zoey tries to convince Dad it's unhealthy for her to be locked up in the house all day.

"And it's better to have you coming home exhausted the way you did last night?"

Zoey glares at her plate, stabbing a stray green bean. It has to frost her to know she's got no one to blame but herself.

"She's been resting all day," I say. "And I've been looking for things we can do that won't be too taxing. Portland has a program where they show movies in the parks during the summer. There's one tonight. That might be a good way for Zoey to get some fresh air without having to walk too much."

Dad nods, thinking it over. "Sounds like fun. I've got half a mind to join you."

Zoey stiffens so visibly there's no way he could miss it, and I glance in his direction, expecting a barrage of questions.

He only laughs. "Already too cool for your old dad, huh? Well, that's all right. I have work to do anyway."

Melting into her normal posture, Zoey finishes her dinner in record time.

By six thirty, we're ready to leave. As we walk out onto the front porch, I notice the colorful bursts of flowers in the raised beds.

"Maybe you should take some of those to Piper," I suggest. "It must be hard to be stuck inside when you're used to having so much green around you."

Zoey snickers and gives me a sidelong glance. "Sure. She's probably sitting in the White Eagle right now, her heart breaking because she misses a bunch of stupid flowers."

Normally, Zoey's snark ricochets off of me without doing any damage, but for some reason, this comment achieves a direct hit. "Just for once, could you drop the attitude?"

"I dunno," she sasses, riveting me with a look. "Just for once, could you admit you like Piper?"

I glance away. "Zoey..."

"Well, you do, don't you?" Her hands go to her hips, and her chin rises in challenge.

"How *I* feel doesn't matter."

A grin swaggers across my sister's face. "Ha! I knew it."

It's futile to go on denying it, and by trying, I run the risk of her mentioning it in front of Piper.

"Okay. You're right," I say. "I *do* like her. But she lost her whole family. She's living in an abandoned tavern. Would you want some boy pressuring you if you were in that situation?"

The grin falters, and a sense of understanding dawns in Zoey's eyes. Her shoulders sag. "Wow.... I never thought about it that way." She shakes her head. "That must make you really sad, Logan."

This unexpected compassion catches me off guard. I've never thought of confiding in my little sister, but at this moment, I realize it's exactly what I need to do. "Yeah," I admit. "It's hard, seeing Piper so upset and not being able to make her feel better. I'm really worried. You were right about her being lonely. That's why it's so important for me to spend time with her, even if I have to leave you behind."

Zoey nods just once, her thin face resolute. "Okay," she says. "I won't give you a hard time anymore. And I'll take some flowers to Piper."

Since the construction workers won't be around this late, I decide it's safe to go in through the regular entrance. But a few blocks from the White Eagle, I notice a cluster of people loitering out front on the sidewalk.

"What's all that?" Zoey asks, leaning forward and nearly crushing the flowers she's holding.

"I'm not sure."

The sound of mingled voices grows as we get closer, and that, along with the signs the crowd is carrying, makes it obvious: a protest. I type a quick re-routing command into the Toyota's console as Zoey reads one of the placards.

"'Save the White Eagle.' Oh great. Like we didn't have enough problems."

"It's okay," I say. "We still have the tunnel."

To be honest, I prefer to avoid it, and not just because it means carrying Zoey. I have to let her out of the Toyota as close to the entrance as possible, which means I often have to choose between letting someone see us or circling the block several times to avoid it. Either way, it's stressful.

When we reach the edge of the Superfund site, I send the SUV to find a parking spot. Each time I do this, I'm careful to give it slightly different directions so it's never seen in the same place twice.

Zoey's conversation with Dad must have made an impression, because she doesn't put up a fuss about me piggybacking her tonight. It's tiring, carrying her a quarter mile through the tunnel, especially when I can't stand fully upright, but I tell myself it's a good way to stay in shape for football.

When we get to the staircase that leads to the White Eagle, Zoey climbs up first then reaches back down for the jar of flowers. I step into the basement to see Piper sitting on one of the lower steps, lost in a fog.

"Hey," she mumbles.

"Rough day?"

Piper shrugs. "Bailey had to run a bunch of errands for her dad. It kept her busy until soccer practice. I guess I can't complain. I mean, if I was her, I sure as hell wouldn't come here every day." She hoists herself to her feet, moving as if the act requires every bit of energy she has.

"I brought you some flowers," Zoey says, holding them out. Up until now, I don't think Piper even noticed them.

"Are those from Grandpa's garden?"

"Yeah. Since you can't go outside, I figured I'd bring a little of the outside in here to you."

Piper's chin trembles. "Aw, Zoey." Her voice breaks, and she steps forward to pull my sister close. "That was really sweet of you," she says when she finally lets go.

Zoey glances in my direction with a sad little look that tells me she knows this hug was rightfully mine.

When we get upstairs, the low murmur of the protestors is audible even through the brick walls. "I didn't think you'd be able to hear that in here," I say, glancing toward the front of the building. At least I'd hoped she wouldn't.

"Yeah. It's been going on all day," she says. "What is it?"

"Some sort of protest. I'm assuming it has something to do with the demolition." I describe the scene outside.

"Well, that's just prime. Absolutely prime." Piper sets the flowers on a table in the middle of the room and sinks into the nearest chair.

"I don't think it will be much of a problem. Other than for Bailey. She might have to start using the tunnel."

"Yeah, she'll love that. She might talk big about playing revolutionary, but she hates spiders even worse than Zoey does."

This doesn't seem like the best time to mention Dad's new restrictions, so I tell Piper about the blue Nissan. Zoey follows with an update on the DeBrassie emails.

"There hasn't been anything useful. Since last night, all he's gotten are an invitation to his twentieth high school reunion and a date request from some lady at e-smoochery.com who calls herself Lotz2Love."

"E-smoochery?" Piper's forehead wrinkles.

"Kidding! It was 'A Match Made in Cascadia.' Like that's any better." She treats us to one of her trademark eye rolls. "The only emails he's sent are to some guy he can't go out for beers with tomorrow, and his neighbor, who wants the phone number for the kid who mows his lawn."

Piper shakes her head. "You'd think if this DeBrassie guy was anyone important, we'd have gotten something incriminating by now."

"Not necessarily," I say. "It's only been two days."

Zoey slides into the booth where Piper left her computer. "I'll log into my email and see if there's anything new."

There's a sound on the stairwell, and Piper startles. It's something I haven't seen her do in weeks.

Bailey comes through the kitchen, carrying a laundry bag as if it were a Santa sack.

"I hope my pies are in there," Zoey says.

"You think I can manage all this and pies, too? I'll bring them tomorrow." She lugs the bag across the room, sweeps it over her shoulder, and thumps it on Piper's bed. "Did you know there's a protest going on out there? Crazy. I had to schlep this stuff a quarter mile through that nasty tunnel. I swear, one of these days I'm gonna bring you your own washer and dryer."

A shadow of guilt flits across Piper's face, and then she forces a smile. "If you think you can fit them in that bag."

"Aw, hell," Bailey says, wincing. "I didn't mean it like that. I'm happy to do your laundry. It's an honor to wash the socks of Cascadia's greatest hero."

"No it isn't. You hate it."

"Piper—"

She shakes her head. "I'm nothing but trouble to all of you. What kind of life can you have, hanging out here every day?"

"A helluva lot better one than you've got," Bailey counters. "At least we're not locked up all the time."

I step toward Piper, wishing she'd let me put my arms around her. "You're *not* a problem. Helping you is the least Zoey and I can do after we got you into this situation."

She gives me a tortured look. "When are you going to stop blaming yourself for that? You're risking *everything*, and one of these days you're going to get caught."

It's not myself I blame, it's my father. But still, I have to make this right.

The shriek of an emergency alert fills the room, interrupting the argument that's about to leave my lips.

Piper rushes over, her outburst derailed, and Bailey and I follow. As we cluster around the computer, Sarto's face fills the screen. His right cheek is bruised, his forehead bandaged, and he looks as if he's just learned of a death in his family.

"Citizens of Cascadia, after Piper Hall's last video, I was alarmed enough to take another look into the kidnappings. Sadly, it appears the story about the vigilantes was fabricated by members of our own government. In my investigation, I uncovered disturbing evidence that seemed to implicate President Cooper. As you can imagine, I was shocked and wanted to believe there might be some mistake.

"This afternoon, I went to Pittock Mansion to walk the

grounds with the president so I might speak privately with him. I was hoping to learn I was wrong. Instead, he attacked me and knocked me unconscious. When I came to, he was gone. His Secret Service agents had disappeared as well, and the guard at the back gate was drugged. Upon investigation, a gap was discovered in security camera footage, leading us to conclude he had help in his escape.

"I'm deeply saddened to deliver this news about our president, a man I considered a close friend. Truly, this will be a day of mourning for Cascadia. Unfortunately, Cooper's behavior only confirms his guilt, so I have no choice but to step into the role of Commander in Chief.

"I'm left in a difficult position regarding Cooper's administration and the Pittock Mansion staff. While I'd like to believe none of them had any part in the kidnappings, evidence suggests otherwise. At this point, I don't know just how far this conspiracy might extend. Therefore, in the coming weeks, I will be making changes, both for my safety and the safety of all of you. Please bear with me and the members of Congress in this difficult time."

"I knew it!" Piper says as Sarto's image fades away. "You see? I told you Cooper was behind this. Now we've got proof."

"I don't believe it," Zoey says, her face setting up in a stubborn look. "He didn't do it. Sarto's lying."

"Oh come on! You saw the evidence. I know he's your hero, but it's time to face the facts."

"Let me see that," I say, turning the laptop away from my sister so I can check the news sites.

"Jefferson's innocent!" Zoey insists. "I know it."

"I believe you. Now hush." I type in the URL for KPTV.com, my earlier doubts about Cooper evaporating. This new development makes it clear who the responsible party is.

"What about Sarto's face?" Piper demands. "Who did that to him if it wasn't Cooper?"

"It could be make-up."

Piper steps up behind me. "Damn it, Logan, all this time you've been telling me Cooper didn't do it—that I have to respect the president. You guys have been making me feel like some kind of freak because I wouldn't give him a chance. Now it turns out you're wrong. Why can't you admit it?"

I look at her over my shoulder. "Because there's something that doesn't sit right about that broadcast. If Sarto truly believed Cooper was guilty, why didn't he get the CBI involved? Why did he confront him on his own?"

"You heard him." Piper brandishes a hand at the computer. "Cooper's his friend. He wanted to give him the benefit of the doubt."

Zoey starts to protest, and I silence her with a look. "That's what he's hoping you'll believe, but anyone with a modicum of intelligence would have delivered his evidence to the proper authority. And Sarto's story doesn't make sense. Why would Cooper's agents be in on the kidnappings? If he really was responsible, he'd want to play it as close to the vest as possible. Some members of his administration might be involved, but not his Secret Service." I keep my eyes on the computer screen as I speak, looking for a story about the incident at Pittock, but apparently it isn't up yet. "Besides, why would that guard be drugged? If Cooper had his agents with him, the guard would have no reason to suspect anything. It would be pointless to take him out."

Even though I'm not looking at her, I can feel the fury radiating from Piper.

"I don't care about all that!" she hollers. "I don't give a rat's right foot if it doesn't make sense to you. Sarto gave us the answer. They'll have to clear my name now. I can leave this dump. Maybe he's even got some leads that will help me find my family."

I could kick myself for not realizing the true reason behind her tirade. I turn away from the computer to look at her.

Bailey's looking, too, with wariness in her eyes. "I don't think so," she says, her voice soft.

Piper swings around to face her. "What's that supposed to mean?"

"Well ... if you're right about Cooper then sure, you're probably off the hook. But what if Logan's right? You've gotta admit, all Sarto's arguments sound pretty sketchy. And he never took back what he said earlier, about you being a criminal. Now that he's got someone to pin the kidnappings on, you could blow everything. My guess is he'll want to make you disappear."

Piper's face knots, her cheeks flushing red. "Why are all of you so stubborn? I don't *care* if Sarto's lying. I don't *care* if he makes me disappear. I'm tired of being locked up in this stinking tavern. I'm tired of being a revolutionary. I'm just *so ...damned ... tired.*"

She's shaking now, fighting to hold back tears. Her whole body trembles with the effort, and still they break loose.

Bailey steps close and pulls her into a hug. "Hey, now. It's gonna be okay. You'll see. We'll fix this."

Piper sobs in her embrace, arms stiff at her sides, until Bailey leads her to the bed where they sit down. I wish I could be the one holding her. The one stroking her hair and murmuring soothing things. It makes me feel so helpless to see her this hurt and angry.

I slide into the booth across from Zoey, who's somehow managed to contain her indignation throughout the exchange. She glances from Piper to me, her face frozen in shock, and I shake my head.

For once, my little sister seems to get the message. She reaches for the laptop and keeps her mouth shut.

CHAPTER 7

Piper

After Logan and Zoey leave, I take a seat at the table with my laptop. Bailey plops down across from me. My eyes are still hot and swollen, and I know I've got to look like hell. At least everyone had the decency to pretend my humiliating outburst never happened. I just wish Logan hadn't seen it. It's one thing to get pissed and rant, but that crying-in-Bailey's-arms deal was flat-out mortifying. Logan must think I'm a complete baby.

"Sorry about the meltdown," I grunt.

Bailey waves a dismissive hand at me. "Not a problem. If anyone deserves to bitch, it's you. I think I'd have offed myself by now if I was stuck in here." A look of horror rushes across her face. "Not that there's any reason to. Or you're even thinking that way. Or—"

"Relax, Bailey. I'm not going to kill myself."

She stops babbling, her eyes still round, like she's not quite sure she should believe me. "Well, that was twenty kinds of stupid."

"Don't worry about it. I'd have said the same thing."

"You would not."

I shrug. "So? I guess if I can nuke out, you can put your foot in your mouth." I slide my mouse in little circles over the table. Zoey always gives me crap for using it, but in my opinion, navigating the touchpad on a laptop is like trying to eat with chopsticks.

"You know . . ." Bailey says, "you might not be so emotional if you had something to take your mind off all this." She motions around her at the empty tavern. "Logan really likes you. It was slaughtering him to see you so upset. What would it hurt to let him in a little?"

I raise an eyebrow. "You know that thing about putting your foot in your mouth?"

"I'm serious, Piper. I mean, you like him, don't you?"

"Well, sure. He's a great guy—"

"And scorching," Bailey adds, waggling her eyebrows.

"Yeah, that too. But this isn't the time for that kind of thing. Where could it even go, with me trapped in here?"

"What do you mean, 'not the time'? It's the perfect time. You need a distraction. You need someone to care about you and hold your hand and give you hugs."

I fold my arms on the table in front of me. "If I want a hug, I'll get one from you."

"But—"

"Drop it, Bailey."

She sighs. "Fine. I need to get going anyway. I have an early soccer game tomorrow."

She leaves through the tunnel, and I'm left in the White Eagle's never-ending dimness, with nothing to do but obsess about our conversation and listen to the protestors.

The sad truth is, I kind of wish I *could* let Logan in. Somehow, he always makes me feel solid. Even when I know he can't fix a problem, it seems like he can, and that's about the only thing that cuts through the crap in my head these days.

Maybe I shouldn't have pulled away from him last week. It's not like it would kill me to let him be more than just a friend. He hasn't touched me once since I told him to back off, and it wasn't until he stopped that I realized how often he was putting a hand on my arm or squeezing my shoulder to calm me down. Now I miss it. But I don't know how to get it back without opening up a big can of crazy.

Thinking about all this can't lead anywhere good, so I check the news sites for an update on Sarto's address. There's no shortage of commentators speculating about what it means, but I don't find much real information. On Monday, Congress will decide what to do if Cooper isn't found. For now, Sarto's running the country. The doctor who treated him says he's got a mild concussion and a laceration that required five stitches. Logan's argument made sense, but how could anyone fake an injury like that?

I click over to check my email. People are already contacting me about Sarto's latest announcement. Some are horrified and some wonder what I think about it, but none seem to doubt that the VP was telling the truth. I open another contact form, sent through the website, and instantly forget how to breathe.

> *Dear Piper Hall,*
>
> *By now you have undoubtedly seen my announcement regarding the kidnappings. While this news is devastating to the country, it proves you have been innocent all along. I realize you have been deeply wronged, and I would like to meet with you to begin the process of clearing your name. I ask only that you stay silent about this issue until we've had a chance to discuss it in person. As you can surely understand, this new development has left the country in turmoil, and as acting president, I must do everything possible to minimize the impact. Any public statements on your part right now would only cause pain to other families who have lost loved ones. Please contact me immediately to set up a meeting. I need to hear back from you by noon tomorrow.*
>
> *With my deepest apologies,*
>
> *President Rick Sarto*

A rush of heat sweeps my body, followed by a wave of giddiness. I'm free! After all these weeks, I'm finally free! I can leave this rat hole, get my life back, maybe even find my family.

With my heart pounding and hands shaking, I hit "reply" and type a response.

Dear President Sarto,

Yes, of course I'll keep quiet until we've spoken.
Just tell me where and when you'd like to meet.

Piper Hall

I'm about to click "send" when Bailey's voice sneaks into my head. *My guess is he'll want to make you disappear.* She'd kill me if she found out I responded. And Logan—well, I've never seen him lose his temper, but he'd be disappointed, and that would be just as bad. He'd say Sarto's request is suspicious. He'd tell me to wait. But I'm sick of waiting. I don't want to delay this even long enough to give Logan a chance to read the email. I've been stuck here for over a month, and the sooner I can get moving on a solution, the better. Besides, Logan's got an unrealistic bias toward Cooper. All of them do. How can they *not* suspect Sarto's motives?

The pointer hovers over the "send" button. What could it hurt to try? It's not like I'm giving away my position or telling Sarto anything he doesn't already know. In fact, answering might help us learn more about him.

I've got myself convinced to do it, and still, something holds me back. What the hell is wrong with me? Am I such a wimp I need Logan's permission for everything? Can't I make even one stupid decision for myself?

Apparently not.

With a sigh, I delete my response, shut the laptop, and go to bed.

CHAPTER 8

Piper

I can't sleep worth a crap. My brain's a total mess, obsessing over Sarto's message and the possibility he might have a lead on the people who've been kidnapped. This is all so sudden, so crazy. Can I really be this close to seeing Mom and Nick and Grandpa again?

The thought of Grandpa makes my insides shrink. What was it he'd said about Sarto in that first journal? It wasn't flattering, but I can't remember the words well enough to judge whether it was a rational opinion or one of his conspiracy theories.

Once I start wondering about it, I can't stop. I get up, turn on my light tube, and go to the table. The noise outside has died away, but that only makes me feel more alone. I pull the first journal out of the pile and flip through until I find the entry.

Once a snake, always a snake, no matter how good you are at putting a nice shine on things for the public.

Well, *that* doesn't help. I need details. I don't remember Grandpa mentioning Sarto a second time, but when Logan interrupted me yesterday, Cooper had just decided to run for president and Daskalov had died. I know Sarto got involved right after that. I grab the third journal, and within seconds, find what I'm looking for.

June 2, 2059 – The damnedest thing happened today. Cooper picked Sarto as his running mate. Seems like those two hardly ever agree on anything, and up till now, Sarto was planning on making his own bid for the presidency.

I don't understand it. Amanda Cheng from BC was fa-vored, and there's a half-dozen other people who would've made a decent choice. But then, if you ask me, a damned ape would've been an improvement.

It's disgusting how Sarto's been sucking up to Cooper since Daskalov died. It's like he's trying to be his new best buddy, which makes me wonder whether that heart attack really was a heart attack. No one gave it a second thought, but it seems pretty suspicious to me. In this day and age, how can a man who's in a hospital, expected to make a complete recovery, suddenly have a second heart attack and die?

It's not like Sarto's afraid of taking out someone who gets in his way. I saw it with my own eyes in Colombia back in '33. But I couldn't prove he fragged that officer anymore than I'd be able to prove any of the other shady crap that's followed him wherever he goes. He's too good at covering his ass.

In all the years I've been hearing Grandpa's wild stories, he's never once said he actually saw the things he talked about. I want to pretend it doesn't make a difference, but I can't. With my hopes tanking, I read on.

June 8, 2059 – Adam had us over for a barbeque last night. When I told him I thought there might be something fishy about Daskalov's death, he laughed. But I can't stop thinking about what he said. "Come on, Dad. How could this be foul play? You think someone snuck into his hospital room and shot potassium into his IV?"

Turns out, if that had happened, it would've sent Daskalov into ventricular fibrillation just like the news articles said. As far as I'm concerned, that proves his death could've been intentional. I don't know why Adam thinks the idea is so farfetched.

A chill pulses through me. Grandpa's right. It would totally be possible to put someone into cardiac arrest that way. I'd like to go on thinking this might still be part of his hopped-up imagination, but I can't shake the creepy feeling that's slunk over me.

I force my eyes to refocus on the words. The only useful

232

thing I find in weeks of entries is an account of how Grandpa warned Cooper about Sarto while shaking hands with him at a political rally and got the brush-off. When I get to the election, I stop. I know what's coming, and I don't need to read Grandpa's memories about it. I have enough of my own.

It's way too easy to remember those first weeks after the accident. Nick wasn't even five, and he couldn't wrap his head around the idea that Dad wasn't coming home. His babysitter gave him the standard line you tell little kids, about how his Daddy went to heaven to live with the angels. That only made it worse.

"I don't want him to live with the angels! They don't need him. We need Daddy *here*."

Mom had been trying not to cry in front of us, but of course that destroyed her.

I shake off the memory and shove the journal aside. It's after eleven, but there's no way I'll be able to sleep. What's going on now isn't any easier than what happened three-and-a-half years ago. It's just so wrong to finally get a little hope and immediately have it ripped away. I guess there's a chance Sarto isn't responsible for the kidnappings, but that's probably as likely as snow in Portland—something no one's seen in over twenty years.

Maybe I should try to follow up on what Grandpa said. I open my computer to look up "frag" then change my mind and launch Carrier Pigeon. Logan's avatar has a little green dot beside it. A surge of warmth flows over me.

Futuresuture: *I've got a question for you. What does "frag" mean?*

For a second, I worry he's already asleep and just forgot to log out. I hold my breath until the screen displays a message that says, "Blitzkreig1 is typing."

Blitzkreig1: *It's a term they use in the military for intentionally killing one of your own. Where did you hear that?*

Futuresuture: *Grandpa's journal. He says Sarto fragged*

an officer. *I guess they were in the Army together. He also thinks he had Daskalov killed.*

Blitzkreig1: *Did he give specifics?*

Futuresuture: *He thinks Sarto had someone inject potassium into his IV after his heart attack.*

Blitzkreig1: *Would that work?*

Futuresuture: *Yeah. And an elevated potassium level wouldn't have made anyone suspicious if they did an autopsy. But they probably wouldn't have bothered, since Daskalov had a history of heart problems.*

Blitzkreig1: *This is huge, Piper. If your Grandpa's right, it means we're not just looking at kidnappings, we're looking at a coup. I hate to consider what this might mean for the president.*

I'm startled by an unexpected twinge of sympathy for Cooper.

Futuresuture: *You think Sarto killed him?*

Blitzkreig1: *It's possible. If Sarto's responsible for the disappearances and wanted to divert suspicion, it would make sense to pin them on someone else and then get rid of that person.*

Futuresuture: *So what now?*

Blitzkreig1: *I'm not sure. Let me do some research and get back to you in the morning.*

I expect him to sign off, but a few seconds later, another message blips onto the screen.

Blitzkreig1: *How are you doing?*

My throat cramps and my fingers hesitate over the keyboard. I can't handle the idea of talking about Sarto's email yet, and I don't have the guts to apologize for how I lost it earlier.

Futuresuture: *I'm fine.*

There's a long moment of nothing. I figure he can tell I'm lying and doesn't know what to say. But then Carrier Pigeon tells me he's typing.

Blitzkreig1: *Good. Try to get some sleep. I'll be there at nine tomorrow, and we'll put together a new plan.*

When I wake up Saturday morning, the memory of the email blindsides me. I lie in the dark a few minutes, trying to dig my way out. Even though nothing's really changed about my situation, I feel like I've lost my whole life all over again.

The muffled sound of chanting doesn't help. What are those people doing out there? Don't they know the Cascadian government is falling apart? You'd think they'd have better things to gripe about.

I need a distraction, so I go online and look up the latest information about anesthetics for MB patients. Zoey has several options, even if she's *not* willing to consider the totally prime opportunity to be awake during surgery.

Just before nine, I head downstairs to pull back the big wooden platform. The trapdoor creaks open right on time and Logan steps into the basement. Alone.

"Where's Zoey?"

Uneasiness flickers over Logan's face. "Dad decided she should spend more time at home. Her nurse was complaining about her being gone so much. But don't worry," he adds. "I still plan on coming as often as I have been."

The determination in his eyes makes me want to believe him, but it can't stop a quiver of doubt from slinking through my insides. It's like nothing's sacred. What am I going to lose next?

"We'll handle it, okay?" Logan says. "You don't need to worry. Oh, and I brought you something." He shucks off his backpack, unzips it, and pulls out a stuffed animal. "Zoey thought you might need something to keep you company at night."

"Thanks." My fingers brush against his, sending a tingle across my skin as I take the fluffy purple frog. Its fur is so soft, I can't stop myself from rubbing it against my cheek. I'd like to think I'm tough enough not to need a stuffed animal, but it's not like I'd be kidding anyone.

I give Logan a smile. "Tell Zoey I appreciate it."

"I will. Let's go upstairs. I learned some interesting things last night."

A week ago, this would've been the point where he put his hand on my shoulder and turned me toward the steps. Instead, I follow him up them on my own.

We go over to my booth, where I sit down across from him, setting the frog between us. Logan rests his hands in front of him on the table—clasped, like he doesn't know what to do with them. Is he nervous being here with me by himself?

"So . . ." He clears his throat. "I looked up what I could access of your grandpa and Sarto's military records."

The statement drives all thoughts of Logan's awkwardness from my head. "Yeah?" I'm not sure I'm ready to hear this. As long as I don't, I can hold onto a tiny speck of hope.

Logan doesn't give me that option. "They were stationed together in Colombia in 2033. Their commanding officer died in an ambush from what was eventually ruled to be friendly fire—which means he was accidentally shot by his own men."

"So Grandpa was telling the truth? What if he only thought he saw Sarto taking him out? I mean, that's possible, right?" I hate the desperation in my voice. It sounds so—desperate.

"Of course it's possible. But we now know that they were together, like your Grandpa claimed, and we know this officer died in a suspicious way. It's not looking good for Sarto."

Crap. I knew this was coming. Why does it feel like such a shock? I look down, running a finger over the soft fur on the frog's head.

"Hey, what's wrong?"

I can't answer.

"Piper. Talk to me."

"I . . . I got an email . . ." The last word catches in my throat and crumbles. It would take dynamite to get anything past it, so I open my computer, launch the email program, and turn the screen in Logan's direction. Not wanting to see his reaction, I go back to smoothing the frog's fur.

He's quiet, and when he finally speaks, there's a hint of worry behind the normal calm in his voice. "Did you reply to this?"

If I try to answer, I'll start blubbering like a little kid. Isn't it obvious from the fact that there's no return arrow beside the email icon?

"Piper . . . did you answer it?"

I shake my head.

"Okay. That's good." He's quiet again, and then he sighs. "I'm sorry. I know how badly you must have wanted this to be real."

I keep petting the frog. There's no way I'm going to let myself lose it like I did yesterday. I've got a *little* pride.

Logan rubs one hand over the other. I can tell it's killing him not to reach for mine. He wants to and I want him to and he's way too honorable to do it.

He shuts the laptop and pushes it aside. "Look—I know you're worried that if I were to give you a hug it might lead someplace you don't want to go. But I think I could keep it platonic."

A smile wrestles its way through my sadness. Logan has got to be the sweetest guy I've ever met. Without looking up, I nod.

He gets to his feet, comes around to my side of the table, and wraps his arms around me. Some small part of me wants to resist, but I'm too damned tired to bother. I lean into his hug, resting my head against the sturdiness of his chest and smelling the fresh, clean scent of him. It takes every bit of toughness I can muster to keep from blubbering.

"We're going to get this worked out," he says, his strong hands reassuring on my back. "I know you were hoping it could be over, and losing that hope must be awful. But Bailey, Zoey, and

I aren't going to give up. We'll stick with you, no matter what."

The intensity of his tone tugs at something in me. If they aren't ready to bag it, I can't either. I take a deep breath and pull away. "All right," I say. "What do we do now?"

Logan's hand lingers on my shoulder. "We keep digging until we find something we can pin on Sarto. He was in the military for twenty years, and I can't get at most of those records, but when he retired and moved to Seattle in '52, there were a couple of things worth noting." He finally lets go, and I sort of wish he hadn't. "Right after he applied for the position of police chief," he says, sitting back down, "his biggest competitor's thirteen-year-old son was involved in a bizarre accident. She wound up pulling her name from the pool. His other challenger was accused of sexual harassment at exactly the same time. It turned out the story was completely fabricated, but it was enough to cast suspicion at a critical moment."

That's all he's got? It's not the most convincing evidence. "All that could be written off as coincidence," I say.

"Right. Sarto's been good at covering his tracks. But this shows a pattern, and if we can get Congress to start an investigation, that pattern might be important. I wish I could find something shady about his campaign for mayor, but it seems he actually earned the city's trust through the way he dealt with the Great Quake."

I nod. "Yeah, Grandpa mentioned that in his first journal."

"Speaking of those journals, did you learn anything else last night?"

"Just that Grandpa tried to warn Cooper about Sarto and didn't get anywhere. I haven't read past the election though." I know Logan would understand why, and still, I can't tell him.

He rests his hands on the table, palms down and fingers spread. "I don't want to butt into anything private, but there might be more information in those journals. Would you mind if I read them?"

It's weird, how conflicted I feel about the idea. Why should I care? Passing the job off to Logan will mean I won't have to delve into the dark months after the accident. "No, that's fine." I dig the stack of notebooks out of the mess on the table and push it toward him. "I'd kind of like you to do it here though. It's not that I don't trust you, but—"

"You don't want to risk losing them. I understand."

He spends the day sitting across the table from me, reading the journals as I answer emails and Connect Me comments. It's a lot easier to find the energy for that with him around. Even though we're quiet except for Logan's occasional laughter about some Grandpa-ism, the silence feels safe and full. I can almost forget Sarto's attempt to trap me and the grumble of protestors outside.

Around three o'clock, I get a Carrier Pigeon message from Zoey.

Greengirl007: *I guess my brother's over there, huh?*

Futuresuture: *Yeah.*

Greengirl007: *Did he tell you what my dad said?*

Futuresuture: *Yup.*

Greengirl007: *It sucks.*

Futuresuture: *Yeah. It does. I'm sorry.*

Greengirl007: *So . . . I've kind of been wanting to ask you something.*

Futuresuture: *Okay.*

Greengirl007: *Well, you know how you were telling me about the things they could do so I wouldn't have another bad reaction to anesthesia? Could you maybe send me some links so I can read about that?*

Futuresuture: *Sure. I'll get them to you later tonight.*

As a research junkie, Zoey could easily look all this up herself, which means she wants me to know she's thinking about that surgery—maybe so I'll tell Logan and she won't have to.

I'm doing just that when the Emergency Alert pop-up takes

over my computer screen. The image of Sarto gives me a jolt. His bruise is uglier now, and I hope it hurts.

Logan gets up just as I'm turning the laptop so he can see it.

"Citizens of Cascadia. I regret that I have yet more bad news to deliver. Further investigation has uncovered a series of emails that confirm Jefferson Cooper's involvement in the kidnappings. In addition, an unexplained influx of cash to the Cascadia Fund has been connected to these crimes. The devastating truth is that our president—a man we all loved and trusted—was financing his green energy projects by selling citizenship in our country to wealthy Americans. And he was displacing your friends and neighbors to make room for them.

"It broke my heart to read what Cooper had to say on the matter: 'The impoverished are a burden on society. Eliminating them will make Cascadia stronger, and if we can bring in wealthy Americans who will not only pay a premium for citizenship, but actively contribute to the economy once they're here, it's all the better.'"

Sarto hesitates, eyes closing and forehead creasing. He lowers his head for a few seconds before looking back up to continue. "We have apprehended one of the kidnappers. In a plea bargain, he revealed that the president gave him direct orders to round up the targeted families and deliver them to an abandoned lumber mill near Yakima. Upon investigation, the mill was found burned to the ground, and human remains were located on the premises. Those remains have yet to be identified."

The floor drops out from under me. It's a lie. It has to be. And still, I feel like I've been shoved off a cliff. The only thing keeping me from plummeting to my death is Logan's hand, which has found its way back to my shoulder.

"Our investigation will continue," Sarto says. "In the meantime, the Cascadia Fund has been frozen and all projects connected to it have been suspended. I wish we didn't have to do this, and I apologize to everyone who will be put out of work, but the funds simply aren't there.

"This must come as a great shock, especially to those who have lost family members. Please accept my deepest regrets. The coming days will be a dark time for all of us, but I have faith that we will be able to pull together as a nation and move beyond this terrible tragedy."

The video ends, leaving the Emergency Alert symbol glowing on the screen.

"It's not true," Logan says, his grip firm. "You know that, right?"

I pull my attention away from the computer to look up, focusing on his eyes. I can trust those eyes. I can count on them.

"Piper, it's only a story. He designed it specifically for its shock value."

And it's working. "He took over the government, Logan. He got rid of the president. How are we going to beat a guy like that?"

"The same way any small rebel force has taken down a tyrant throughout history. It might seem as though Sarto has all his bases covered, but I can guarantee you, he's slipped up somehow. We need to find that weakness and exploit it."

The look he gives me—hard-jawed and resolute—should be convincing, but it's not. No matter what Logan's managed to pull off so far, this is just too huge.

My worst fear leaks out in a whisper. "But what if we can't?"

"We have to." Logan's grip tightens. "This isn't just about us anymore. It's about the future of Cascadia. We're the only thing standing in Sarto's way, and we've got a moral obligation to stop him."

CHAPTER 9

Logan

I don't want to leave Piper alone after Sarto's announcement, so I spend the rest of the afternoon with her. After we've posted a message on Connect Me debunking his statement, and emailed the people who've contacted her through the website to reassure them, I offer a chess lesson as a distraction. It's only the fourth time we've played. Piper has the fundamentals down, but she's nowhere near as enthusiastic about the game as I am. And though there's something satisfying about teaching her, it's also frustrating. It's hard to hold back when I can so clearly see a path to victory.

I've come up with a compromise. I play the way I normally would, but when she makes an imprudent move, I give her a chance to change her mind. And when I execute a tactical maneuver, I explain what I've done and why it worked.

"Are you sure you want to do that?" I ask as Piper takes the pawn I've left as bait for her knight. She hesitates, studying the board.

"Oh crap. I'm totally forked," she jokes, realizing that in the next move I'd be able to capture either her queen or her knight with my rook, and there's no way she can save them both. She returns the pieces to their original positions and moves her queen instead. "I'm not sure what you see in this game. It's so complicated."

I smile. "Exactly. Once you're more comfortable with the basics, you can start setting up attacks, and that's where it gets interesting."

"Maybe you should show me some of those instead of letting me repeatedly make a fool of myself."

"You're not making a fool of yourself. You're learning. But if you'd rather, we can go over some tactics." I start with one she's already seen, rearranging the pieces to render her remaining knight useless. The rules won't allow her to move it because doing so would leave her king open to my bishop. "Okay, you should know this one already."

"Pin," Piper says.

"Good." I shift the pieces on the board, setting up another attack I've used in the past. Now her queen is in danger from my bishop, but to save it, she'll have to sacrifice her rook.

"Um . . . skewer?"

"Right. See, like I said, you're learning." I show her a few more, including some combinations that incorporate two of the more basic maneuvers.

"Okay, that's pretty cool," Piper admits. "I can see why someone who likes strategy could really get into this."

I glance up at her. "Are *you* getting into it?"

"I'm starting to."

"Good." It's been a while since I've had a chess partner. Dad only taught me the game as a means of attracting me to more intellectual pursuits than football or the military. Once I made it clear I wasn't abandoning those interests, I was on my own.

"Is that why you want to join the Army?" Piper asks. "Because you like strategy?"

I begin setting up another combination. "Partly. But it's also an opportunity to be a leader. There's something really gratifying about being in charge of a team."

Piper fakes a shudder. "Not for me. It's too much responsibility. I mean, look at what we started with the videos. All these people are coming to me for help, like they think I can do something about the disappearances, and I'm just as lost as they are." She shakes her head. "It's scary, having people relying on you."

"It can be," I say. "But consider what we've accomplished. People have hope now. Things are happening. That wouldn't have been possible without the four of us stepping up to take the lead."

"I guess," Piper says. "But on the other hand, maybe all we've done is give everyone false hope, topple the Cascadian government, and get the president killed."

By morning, all of Cascadia is talking about Jefferson Cooper's supposed betrayal. Those who never liked him have been quick with the I-told-you-so's, while his loyal fans are in mourning, devastated by Sarto's "evidence." Zoey's been crying off and on since I told her what Piper and I discovered. Fortunately, Dad thinks this is due to her being disillusioned about her hero, rather than learning of his possible demise.

Despite the political turmoil, protests continue outside the White Eagle. This isn't of much consequence to Zoey and me, but Bailey isn't happy about being driven into the tunnel. Her job watching her father's properties has always given her an excuse to be seen on the premises. Now, she's reluctant to have anyone connect her with the demolition.

It's hard on Piper, too. The chanting creates a constant drone, just loud enough to be annoying. "Why can't they go away?" she says Sunday afternoon. "Is that too much to ask?"

Bailey grunts. "Probably, considering how badly their priorities are screwed up. We just lost our president. What difference does it make if the White Eagle gets torn down?"

With the reality of that at least six months away, the protesters are more a burden than an asset. Even though they might possibly delay the demolition, the attention they're drawing keeps all of us on edge.

We're sitting around what has become our "powwow table," just behind the wall that juts out to house the kitchen. Piper's regular booth is too cluttered to allow the four of us enough elbow room. Besides, we need space for Bailey's pies. She brought them last night and wouldn't allow Piper or me to touch them without Zoey here.

We've been brainstorming for an hour now, but we're not

getting anywhere. Bailey's as red-eyed as Zoey, and both are trying not to show it. Reminders of Cooper's disappearance are all over the news, and Sarto's pressuring Congress to start impeachment hearings so he can permanently claim the role of Commander in Chief. He's also fired nearly all the Pittock staff, or "Pittock minions" as the media dubbed them early in Cooper's presidency. Apparently, when one of them brought Cooper a glass of water during a press conference, he'd joked about how he "wasn't used to having minions," and some opportunistic journalist ran with it.

"Maybe we need to find another laptop to bug," Bailey says. "That first one sure didn't get us anywhere."

"That doesn't mean it won't," I counter. But I'm losing hope as well. It's been four days, and if DeBrassie were communicating with his superiors by email, we should have seen something by now. Especially in light of recent developments.

"Isn't there anything in the journals we can use?" Zoey asks.

"Yes, but nothing that will stand up on its own. The best we could do is cast suspicion." In the later notebooks, Piper's grandpa described the fragging incident in detail, along with a few other shady occurrences regarding Sarto's military career, but it would be easy for the vice president to dismiss the accusations.

"Why wouldn't that be enough?" Zoey asks. "All we need to do is get people to start looking closer."

"Sarto would write off my grandpa in a heartbeat," Piper says. "Everyone who's met him knows he's totally into conspiracy theories. The whole reason he kept a written journal was because he thought an electromagnetic pulse was going to wipe out the computers. He probably thought he was doing future historians a big favor by keeping a record of Cascadian history."

"Exactly," I say, nodding. "It wouldn't be difficult to discredit his claims. The journals are helpful, but alone they won't build a convincing case against Sarto. He's going to be hard to take down. If there's one thing I've learned in the past few days, it's that he's expert at twisting facts and deluding people."

Piper, who's sitting to my left, slumps back in the booth. "It's hopeless."

"It's *not* hopeless," I say, even though the few ideas we've come up with seem ineffective or too difficult to pull off. "Let's go over the list again."

Zoey tucks her long hair behind her ears and peers down at her laptop. "Film another broadcast, make a spreadsheet of legislators and their political leanings, reply to Sarto's email and try to trick him, start a wave of anti-Sarto graffiti and hope it takes off, bug a different laptop."

"That's all crap," Piper says, running her hands through her hair. "None of it's going to work. None of it's going to change anything."

"We have to start somewhere." I keep my voice soft and shift my weight so my leg presses against hers. After reading the journals, I have a new understanding of her loss. The grief her grandpa experienced following the accident provided a clear reminder that his kidnapping wasn't the first time the family had been torn apart.

"The most logical approach is to convince someone in Congress to launch an investigation," I say. "We don't have the power to take Sarto down ourselves, but once the government begins looking into the situation, we can come forward with the evidence in the journals."

"So we're back to the spreadsheet," Zoey says. "How long is that going to take to put together?"

"I don't know. Hours at least. Maybe several days. There are twelve senators and thirty-three representatives. It'll take a lot of research to learn how they feel about both Sarto and Cooper."

"So what are you waiting for?" Zoey gives me a cheeky look that doesn't have its full effect with her face blotchy and her eyes swollen.

"Good point. We have three computers here. We can split this up and make it go more quickly." I borrow Zoey's laptop to copy and paste a list of names from the government website. After dividing it into three groups, I send it out. Since we're short one computer, I take the notebook Piper bought for her grandpa the day of the kidnapping and use it to work on a speech. I'm torn over whether we should hit Sarto hard and fast with a challenge to his story or let him sweat over what Piper will do. There are advantages to both, but it's probably best to start spreading doubt right away, so we can connect with Cooper's supporters and spur them into action.

The notepad takes some getting used to. I've rarely written anything using this method. But there's an appeal to the way the pen feels on the paper. I think I could enjoy it, if it weren't for all the ugly lines through my text, where I've changed my mind and don't have the convenience of a delete key.

We work in a silence that's interrupted only by the murmur of protestors outside and an occasional comment about one senator or another. At least Zoey and I have plenty of time. I've bought us a whole day by telling Dad I was taking her to an outdoor concert in Troutdale. What we'll do tomorrow, I don't know. I'm still trying to sell my sister on the idea that she'll make more headway with her nurse if she acts a little nicer.

When we've been at it several hours, Zoey startles us with a gasp.

"Bonus! I just got an email from DeBrassie. And the subject line is 'Re: The Hall Family.'"

"What?" Piper says.

But Zoey isn't listening. "Holy—President Cooper's not dead!" Her mottled face breaks into a grin, and she thrusts both fists in the air. "Yes!"

"Let me see!" Bailey, who's sitting between Zoey and the wall, abruptly swings the laptop around to get a better look.

"What does it say?" Piper asks, her voice notching up.

Bailey starts reading. "'We're obviously not getting any-where. It's time to take a more persuasive approach, but we can't risk being overheard. I'll send someone tomorrow at 2:00 to pick up Cooper.'"

"Who sent it?" I ask.

"There's no name, but it came from Brutusfidelis at Mail-stop dot com," Zoey says, her tone still triumphant. "Oh wait. Looks like *someone* doesn't delete the incoming message before he replies. This thing goes on for*ever*."

I slide out of the booth to see, but before I can get to my feet, Zoey's crowing again.

"It's instructions. Oh wow. I think this came from Sarto! Check it out: 'Piper Hall has become too much of a problem. We're going to have to step things up. I've got a plan worked out for pinning this on Cooper, and I'll need you to babysit him.'"

By this point, Piper and I are crowded around the laptop, reading over one of Zoey's shoulders while Bailey peers over the other.

"'I've secured the Presidential Suite at the Benson. You and your men will pose as contractors from Quality One, there to upgrade the security system on the eleventh floor. Your cover story is that we're preparing the building for future visits from foreign dignitaries. Go to the concierge desk and ask for a card key. They'll be assigning one of the elevators to you so you won't have to worry about unexpected visitors.'"

"Wow," Bailey says. "Did we hit the motherlode, or what?"

"He's alive!" Zoey chirps, slapping Bailey a high five. "He's alive, and he's not the kidnapper!"

I shake my head. "Amazing. I think you're right, Sparky. This has to be Sarto." While I'd hoped bugging DeBrassie's email would lead us to his boss, I never expected that boss to be the VP himself.

The text jumps up the screen as my sister suddenly scrolls

to the bottom of the email.

"Hey!" Bailey shouts. "What are you doing?"

"Starting at the beginning. It'll make more sense that way."

Together, we read the first email, which assigns DeBrassie, who is apparently Sarto's main henchman, the task of apprehending Piper's family. It provides their address, names and ages, and a few details about everyone's schedules. Next comes DeBrassie's report of how the operation went wrong, followed by a scathing response from Sarto.

"Ha!" Piper says. "Serves that bastard right. I hope he lost as much sleep over it as I did."

A few minor replies follow, going back and forth to detail the hunt. After the first broadcast, Sarto turns up the pressure. But it isn't until the last couple of exchanges that things really get interesting. Apparently, our videos did more than just threaten his racket. They also put a kink in a more sinister plot.

"Sarto was planning to have the president assassinated?" Zoey squeaks.

The email describes how the hit was to take place at an election rally in late August, perfectly timed so Sarto could step into the presidency and ride the wave of public sympathy into re-election. He'd planted men who were loyal to him among Cooper's agents to make things easier for DeBrassie, but our videos put increasing pressure on the government. That's when Sarto came up with a solution to solve both of his problems at the same time. "Cooper won't be as easy to get rid of as Daskalov was," he wrote, "but that doesn't mean it can't be done." His plan involved having Cooper's bogus agents stage an attack on him then deliver Cooper to DeBrassie, who had been reassigned from his post watching our house.

"The thing I don't understand is why Sarto's keeping Cooper alive," Piper says. "Wouldn't it make more sense to get rid of him?"

"Yes," I say. "Unless Cooper has information he needs."

"But why the Benson? It's not exactly a remote location."

"True," Bailey agrees, "but it's close to Pittock. And isn't it on the Federal Tunnel system? Maybe Sarto wants an easy way in so he can question Jefferson."

"Torture him, more like," Zoey says. "What else do you think 'a more persuasive approach' means? We need to get him out of there."

"You're kidding, right?" Piper's face is etched with disbelief.

Zoey turns on her. "I know you hate him, but his life is in danger. As soon as Sarto gets what he wants, he's bound to kill him."

"That's not our problem," Piper says.

"Of course it's our problem! Number one," Zoey holds up an index finger, "Sarto wouldn't have locked him up if it wasn't for us—"

"No, he just would've had him assassinated."

"—and number *two*," Zoey raises a second finger, glaring at Piper, "we can use him. Plenty of people aren't going to listen to you, but they *will* listen to Jefferson Cooper."

"She's right," I say. "If we can convince them of his innocence, they'll follow him anywhere. The simplest way to overthrow Sarto would be to turn the public against him. Even if that doesn't work, Cooper's inside knowledge will be invaluable to our cause."

Piper shakes her head. "It's too dangerous. If you want to save him, we should go public with what's in this email and let the cops sort it out."

"The cops are in on it," I remind her. "What happened to you proves that. Besides, there's not enough time. Sarto's sending someone for Cooper tomorrow afternoon."

"And we can get a video out in a few hours."

"True, but Sarto might have Cooper killed before anyone could confirm our claims and look into the matter."

Despite what she might think, I'm not looking forward to

this attempt. In fact, the idea of it terrifies me. But if there's any possibility we can save the president, we have to try.

Piper locks her arms across her chest, her chin tilting upward. "And just how are we supposed to rescue him?" she demands. "We don't have the manpower. We don't have weapons. We don't even have any idea of how to get him out."

She's right on every count. Every count but one, that is.

"Oh, I've got an idea," I say. "Sarto saw to that."

End of Episode 3

The story continues with Episodes 1.4-1.6
Liberation, *Requisition*, and *Desperation*
Available winter 2015
* * *

Author's note: Those of you who live in the Portland area will know that the Rose Garden has been renamed after a company I don't choose to advertise in this book. This deal happened before publication, and I could have made an adjustment, but I elected not to. Fifty years from now, it's unlikely this company will still have a contract with the Rose Garden owner's successor. I choose to believe sentimentality will prevail and the original name will be restored.

ACKNOWLEDGMENTS

One of Tom McCall's strengths was his ability to recognize other people's good ideas and transform them into reality. He was a catalyst—a person who could bring together various elements to create something greater than the sum of their parts. A similar thing happened to me when I began planning this series. As I talked to people about my idea for the Pacific Northwest to secede in response to a rush of climate refugees, they offered all kinds of great insights, plot twists, and details. I learned there was already a movement to form "Cascadia," a bioregion that would define the Pacific Northwest in its own terms. Drawing upon that history, along with Portland's culture and colorful past, I was able to put together something much more interesting than what I would have dreamt up on my own. The bottom line is, I can't take credit for everything in this story.

That said, I'd like to thank those who contributed awesome ideas and details: Laura Marshall, Marla Bowie LePley, Beth Miles, Alice Lynn, Barb Froman, Angela Carlie, Julian Blankenship, Roxie Matthews, Moma Escriva, Pat Lichen, Bob Earls, Rose Lefebvre, Magan Vernon, GP Ching, Jacqueline Carl, Helen Wand, Mark Petruska, Craig Hansen, Jessica Greif, Gretchen Sass, Steven Ganz, and Neil Bradley.

I'd also like to express my appreciation to my critique groups, Chrysalis and Wow, my copy editors, Allison Hitz and Bob Martin, and my great team of beta readers: Beth Miles, Elle Strauss, Alice Lynn, Barb Froman, Melanie Curry, Bob Martin, Angela Carlie, Stacey Wallace Benefiel, Connie Barr, Malana Ganz, Sharon White, and Cari Jermann.

A lot of research went into this book, and many people assisted with that, including Zack Barrer at the White Eagle

Saloon, who was kind enough to give me a tour of the establishment. The staff at Pittock Mansion provided fascinating information about Cascadia's "White House," and those at the concierge desk of the Benson Hotel answered myriad questions about the layout of that building. Joe Streckert of Portland Walking Tours was also helpful, educating me about Portland's sordid past and clearing up myths about the Shanghai Tunnels. The staff at the Central Branch of the Multnomah County Library (which becomes the Congress building in this series) helped me access additional information about both the tunnels and Portland history, but that should be no surprise because librarians are just cool that way.

I'm particularly grateful to Alexander Bartich for the use of his Doug flag. I had enough work to do without having to design one of my own. How fortunate that he'd already done so, and that the Timbers Army have helped to popularize it. It's always nice when you can incorporate existing cultural references into your work.

There's a strong soccer element in this series, and I know nothing about the sport, but fortunately, I have friends who do: Sean and Wendy Herrin and Kelly Garrett. Thank you for explaining the nuances, as well as how soccer compares to American football.

I've always been fascinated by medicine, but it wasn't until I set out to create a character with a medical background that I realized how much I don't know. Sharon White and Cari Jermann spent a great deal of time in person and through email educating me. In addition, Christine Fletcher, a veterinarian and talented YA author, provided a number of valuable details that I can't talk about here without creating spoilers.

Another of my interests is meteorology, and again, I didn't realize how little I knew about it until I started reading the Fox 12 Weather Blog. One day, I will find the time to study up on the subject. In the meantime, I owe a huge debt to KPTV channel 12 Chief Meteorologist Mark Nelsen for reading my manuscripts and fact-checking my climate data. He also made some suggestions about future weather forecasting technology that were very helpful.

While Zoey might be a computer genius, I am not. I am indebted to Max Bell and Neil Bradley for providing the technological information to make this series accurate. Both spent time educating me, but Neil went above and beyond, chatting with me endlessly on Facebook until he drummed some basic computer concepts through my thick skull.

Finally, I'd like to thank my husband Bob Earls who knows much more about politics, government, and history than I ever will. He's spent more hours than he probably cares to count discussing the fine details of the plot with me and talking me out of bad decisions. While it might be annoying to be blindsided by statements like, "you know, Canada would never let all its western ports go without a fight," I'd rather hear it *before* publication.

ABOUT THE AUTHOR

In addition to being a YA author, Lisa Nowak is a retired amateur stock car racer, an accomplished cat whisperer, and a professional smartass. She writes coming-of-age books about kids in hard luck situations who learn to appreciate their own value after finding mentors who love them for who they are. She enjoys dark chocolate and stout beer and constantly works toward employing *wei wu wei* in her life, all the while realizing that the struggle itself is an oxymoron.

Lisa has no spare time, but if she did she'd use it to tend to her expansive perennial garden, watch medical dramas, take long walks after dark, and teach her cats to play poker. For those of you who might be wondering, she is not, and has never been, a diaper-wearing astronaut. She lives in Milwaukie, Oregon, with her husband, four feline companions, and two giant sequoias.

Connect with Lisa online:

Facebook: http://www.facebook.com/LisaNowakAuthor
Website: http://www.lisanowak.net
Blog: http://lisanowak.wordpress.com
Newsletter: http://bit.ly/LisaNowakNewsletter (sign up to be notified of new releases)

CPSIA information can be obtained
at www.ICGtesting.com
Printed in the USA
FSOW01n2223291214
4226FS

9 781937 167295